SITTING DUCK (A PATRICK FLINT NOVEL)

PAMELA FAGAN HUTCHINS

SKIPJACK PUBLISHING

FREE PFH EBOOKS

CHAPTER ONE: HIKE

Patrick

Hiking boots broke through the thin layer of ice and into the snow melt underneath, splashing water up and onto Patrick Flint's ankles. He'd sprayed half a bottle of Scotchgard on his lower extremities—which had hurt, because the dang stuff was so expensive—but still he was soaked to the skin from the knees down. Ten-pound weights on each ankle and wrist and a seventy-pound backpack amped up the splash factor. He felt heavy. Like the Incredible Hulk-heavy. Not that Patrick kept up with the TV show, other than over the shoulders of his fourteen-year-old son Perry and the boy's girlfriend Kelsey. Someone had to make sure there was plenty of daylight between the teenagers on the couch.

Patrick cleared the frozen puddle that stretched all the way across the two-lane road. He landed on the crust beyond it, and his foot sunk into mud, the combination a result of nearly sixty-degree temperatures the day before and thirty-degrees through the night. Today would warm up, too, although it was still brisk out. *Thank goodness.* The sun was just rising—bringing with it a brilliant display of purple, orange, yellow, and red strata—and he'd been hiking with this load for two hours already. Sweat rolled down his forehead and back, and he wiped it from his face.

"Spring in the Bighorn Mountains," he muttered. "Tomorrow will probably be a blizzard."

Ferdinand shot him a look. The icy mud coating the Irish wolfhound's wiry hair made him look even more scraggly than his norm, which was pretty darn scraggly. But it wasn't unusual for Patrick to talk to himself. It was probably his tone that had surprised the dog. Patrick wasn't a whiner. One of his mottos was *no pain, no gain.* And he loved the outdoors, in most seasons. The mud and ice season, while short, was not his favorite, though.

"Cut me some slack, Ferdie. You're not even carrying any extra weight. I should strap sixty percent of your body weight on your back and then we'd see who has the bad attitude."

He hefted the pack. It was chafing his shoulders and needed an adjustment. Glancing at his watch, he made an executive decision. It was time for a short break. Then he would need to pick up the pace. This was his one full day off without being on-call for the hospital in Buffalo, and he didn't want to squander it. It was going to take him at least two hours to hike back to his truck, parked at the edge of town on Klondike Road. Despite his ambitious workout plan, he'd promised his wife Susanne he'd be back in time to meet her at the home of their best friends, Henry and Vangie Sibley, for an update from the private investigator the Sibleys and Flints had retained to track down the Sibleys' foster son Ben. Ben had been the boyfriend of the Flints' daughter Trish. He'd been more than a boyfriend to her, really. He'd given her a promise ring before leaving for college. The young man had run off a few months before—leaving her—and it had rattled Trish to her core. She'd been doing better lately. Patrick and Susanne intended to be back at their house before Trish got home from cheerleading clinic, in plenty of time to act like it was any other normal Saturday, so she wouldn't ask questions about where they'd been. They didn't want her to know about the investigator or the meeting. A reminder of Ben might trigger a backslide.

Patrick unclipped the front strap on his pack, more than ready to set the frame up in a dry spot for his break. *Bring on the trail mix and cold water. Moleskin for my feet and shoulders.*

"Teenagers. Sheesh."

This time, Ferdinand woofed. The dog was loyal to Trish and Perry. Patrick could disrespect the mountains, but he'd better leave the kids out of it.

He ruffled the furry head level with his hip. "What? It's true. I wouldn't relive those years of my own again for anything." The teenage years were nothing but angst, hormones, and life-altering decisions. He had a wife and two kids to prove it. But he did love the three of them with all of his heart and soul.

After a long drink from his canteen, Patrick poured some in a metal bowl for Ferdinand. He spotted a bald eagle perched on a wooden sign on a fence post as the dog lapped up the water. The burned-in lettering below the creature had weathered away, although it looked about the right size to warn visitors NO TRESPASSING. The bird cocked its white head, studying Patrick with intense, hunter's eyes.

"Good morning," Patrick said. He felt a surge of awe, of energy. A renewal of spirit and purpose. After a sighting of a bald eagle, he believed he could do anything.

Instead of answering, the raptor spread its wings, creating an arch of brown feathers. Patrick guessed the span to be well over seven feet. Maybe close to eight. *A big male.* But light, Patrick knew, with its hollow bones weighing only half as much as its feathers. Then, with a few mighty flaps, the bird arose, awkwardly at first, its yellow feet dipping toward the earth, then stronger and more gracefully as it gained height. Patrick tented a hand over his eyes, marveling at the lethal power above him, knowing an eagle could spot prey as small as a rabbit from a mile away, differentiate it from the flora around it with excellent depth perception, dive at it like a guided missile, and snatch it into the air with its curved, razor-sharp talons. The bird soared in a wide circle, moving faster than the effort it appeared to expend would suggest. *Riding the thermals.*

When it had disappeared from view, Patrick pulled his six-inch pocketknife from its holster, unfolded it, and admired the engraved SAWBONES on the grip for a moment. It had been a gift from his friend and co-worker, Wes Braten, and Patrick didn't feel dressed without it on his hip. Squinting at the old sign, he took aim, then hurled the knife. It hit dead center but bounced off and into the snow.

"The goal is to stick into the target," he said, his voice sardonic. *Not as good a hunter as the eagle.* Then he realized he was talking to a knife and chuckled.

Ferdinand ran as if to fetch it.

"No, dog. That's not a stick." Patrick reached it first, dug into the snow hole until he found it, refolded it, and put it away. He wasn't dissatisfied, but he was only batting about .500 on knife throwing, a skill he'd been working on lately. Practice made perfect, and he wasn't getting enough of it.

After he put up the canteen and bowl, Patrick opened his pack. It fell over and the paperback he'd been carrying with him to read on breaks fell out of the pack. *One Hundred Years of Solitude* by Gabriel Garcia Marquez. So far the spine was uncracked. He retrieved and downed his trail mix and put some moleskin on his heel and his shoulder where the strap had rubbed. Then he put everything away, crouched, and slipped his arms into the straps on his backpack. He took his time with the adjustments until it was just right. He couldn't afford any hot, raw spots that could derail his training.

When he was set, he took off at a faster clip than before with Ferdinand running circles and zig zags around him. The road graded upwards, and he climbed in silence for a while, breathing in the fresh air and enjoying the scents of ranchland. Clean air. Wood smoke. An occasional whiff of manure that wasn't completely unpleasant. Even better than the smells were the sounds. Or lack thereof. In the stillness, all he heard was the huff of his breath and the lowing of cattle, somewhere not too far away. He crested the rise, glad not to be contending with the ubiquitous Wyoming wind, and turned around, looking back into the distance. He could just make out the north fence line of the Klondike Ranch, a working cattle and guest operation that had been around since the 1880s. Most of the pastureland between here and there was brown between large patches of snow. In a month, the grass would sprout and grow tall overnight, and not too long after that, wildflowers would turn this area into a riot of color.

Beyond the ranch was Crazy Woman Canyon, one of his favorite places in the world. The last vestiges of sunrise were bringing out the pink in the face of the cliffs that overlooked the creek of the same name as the canyon. Snow still clung to the mountain face. It was almost worth the threat of blisters and chafing just to earn this view. It brought back memories of past trips up the canyon, past the granite, limestone, and shale formations. He looked forward to the road opening soon. Even in summer, the ascent of the canyon was harrowing. Huge boulders hugged the road. The behemoths had fallen centuries before, carved by the creek into overhangs, caves, and openings large enough to drive moderately sized vehicles through.

Next weekend, if the snow had melted enough, he would park his truck at the base and hike up the canyon. At least as far as the snow would allow. He smiled. If he was going to have to suffer, he might as well do it in some of the most spectacular God-given beauty around.

He began to sing *Glory Hallelujah*. It seemed fitting. Ferdinand fell in to step and howled along. Patrick smiled as they continued their duet.

A vehicle engine revved behind him. He stopped singing.

"Come on, Ferdie." He caught the dog's collar in his hand and moved to the snowy roadside. His feet squished and sunk. The snow had only been a mirage, a cover. It was mostly mud below, without any spring growth to firm it up.

WHOOP WHOOP.

The loud squawk startled him, and he turned so quickly that he bumped into Ferdinand, then tumbled onto his behind, wrist deep in cold mud. He just thought he'd been wet before. Icy water soaked his underwear. Everything below his waist contracted. Not a good feeling, and he uttered a few choice expletives, words he only used because there was no one around to hear.

He looked up. A Johnson County sheriff's department truck.

It stopped while Patrick was still flopping around. *Like a pig in a ring, just before the wrestlers come out.* Not like a respected physician. A door slammed, and footsteps approached. Patrick crawled onto all fours—not an easy feat with the heavy backpack shifting from side to side—and heard a familiar voice. One that matched a familiar face.

"We got a call about a vagrant casing ranch houses out this way. Seen anyone matching that description?" The mirth in Deputy Veronica Harcourt's voice was as unmistakable as her signature coronet of blonde braids.

Patrick staggered to his feet. "Very funny, Ronnie."

The Amazonian deputy crossed her arms. "I'm serious. And I'll need to see some identification."

"How about you let me go based on my past good works and stellar behavior?"

She laughed. "I know better. Should we give Susanne a call?" The Flints had lived next door to Ronnie and her husband Jeff when they first moved to Wyoming.

"Whatever you need to do to clear me so I don't get shot, do it. Because I'm not carrying my wallet."

"What in hell's half acre were you doing out here before dawn anyway?"

"I'm training to climb Mount Rainier."

"Mount where?"

"Mount Rainier. In Washington. It's one of the tallest mountains in the continental U.S. After that I'd like to do the seven summits."

She lifted a brow in her sun-kissed face. Even in the winter, she had a tan. Not for the first time, Patrick questioned his career choice. Doctors worked inside. His first career choice had been to work outside as a wildlife biologist. But they didn't make much money, and he had a wife and two small children at the time. He'd picked medical school instead of a master's in biology.

"What, pray tell, is the seven summits?" she said.

"The seven summits are the highest mountains of each of the seven traditional continents."

"Mt. Rainier is one of those?"

"No. It's a warm-up. The seven summits are Mount McKinley in Alaska for North America, Aconcagua for South America, Kilimanjaro for Africa, Elbrus for Europe, Vinson for Antarctica, Kosciusko for Australia, and Everest for Asia."

Patrick held back any further detail, even though he couldn't list the seven summits he intended to climb without itching to dive into the deep end of what he found to be a fascinating discussion. According to Susanne, it was anything but fascinating. Yet, in actuality, the peaks qualifying as the seven summits are not a settled issue. Far from it, and Patrick had researched the matter thoroughly. The bragging rights hinge on the definition used for a continent. In particular, the location of the border of a continent. There were two major points of variation, from what Patrick had read. The first was Mont Blanc versus Mount Elbrus for Europe. It was contingent on whether the crest of the Greater Caucasus Mountains is taken to define the Greater Caucasus watershed, which marked the continental boundary between Asia and Europe for the region between the Black and Caspian Seas. This classification placed Mount Elbrus in Asia instead of Europe. Patrick disagreed with it and counted Mont Elbrus for Europe. The second contended summit was Puncak Jaya versus Mount Kosciusko for the continent of Australia. It pivoted on whether the Sahul Shelf or only the mainland Australia was defined as the continent. Patrick ascribed to the view that classified Kosciusko as Australia's tallest peak. He had his heart set on climbing Elbrus and Kosciusko. And he would have loved to talk about it. But Ronnie didn't look like she needed her head to explode this early in the morning.

She said, "I've heard of a few of them. When's your Rainier climb?"

"August."

"Why aren't you climbing up there?" She pointed at the mountains.

"I'm building muscle and mileage right now. Altitude training will start soon. After some snow melt."

"Better you than me. I don't suppose you want a ride home?"

Part of Patrick wanted to say yes. That would be the part that felt the miles he'd already logged that morning. The other part—the part that was determined to get his body into peak condition for the upcoming challenge—welcomed the exertion. "I'll be good. Thanks, though."

Off the road, Ferdinand boomed out a WOOF, then unleashed a rolling, ferocious growl. Patrick's mind went straight to predators. Coyote? Mountain lion? Bear?

"Ferdie," he called. He unlatched and dropped his backpack beside the road. "Ferdie! Come back here. Come!" When the dog didn't appear, he trotted toward the sounds, the moderate speed the best he could do in wet jeans and footwear.

"I'm going with you." Ronnie's voice was right behind him.

"I've got my .357 Magnum. I'll be all right." Patrick knew better than to hike in a remote area unarmed, and the pocketknife didn't count.

"Ferdie was my neighbor. If he's in trouble, I want to be there, too."

Patrick pushed down the bottom strand of a five-wire fence with his heavy boot, lifting the strand above it to create an opening. Ronnie scrambled through, then returned the favor for him. Ferdinand grew more frantic, now interspersing barks with growls. Patrick's heartbeat accelerated. That dog was more than a pet. He was family. A faithful companion, loyal protector, and best friend. Patrick couldn't let anything happen to him. He wanted to move faster, but the going was too rough. It was hard enough to stay upright at a trot on the slick, uneven mix of grass hummocks, rocks, mud, snow, and ice on the ground.

"What in the heck is he into?" Patrick said, panting as he hopped over increasingly larger rocks. Ahead of him, he saw the ground fall away. A drop off.

"I hate to imagine."

Patrick noticed that Ronnie wasn't panting, but she hadn't just walked eight miles with one-hundred-and-ten extra pounds either.

CHA-CHUNK.

The unmistakable sound of the pump action of a shotgun brought Patrick to a sharp halt. He would have stopped anyway, since he'd reached the edge of a steep, twisting ravine, but the gun made his stop a lot faster. He threw his hands in the air. Beside him, Ronnie did the same.

"Stop right there." It was a man's voice. Gruff. Terse. Cold.

"We're stopped," Ronnie said. "I'm Johnson County Deputy Veronica Harcourt. May I show you my badge, sir?"

"I don't care if you're God, the Father, and the Holy Ghost. This is my land, and you're trespassing."

"Our apologies," Patrick said, wincing. "I was walking my dog along the road, and he took off after something. That's him raising Cain in the ravine. We came to get him."

The man's voice grew louder. Harsher. "You need to control your animal. This is a working ranch. I've got newborn calves out here. If I find your mutt ran one of them down, I'll shoot the blasted thing."

"I understand. I couldn't be sorrier. But I'll pay for any damage. I promise. Just please let me fetch my dog."

"Go, then. Get him out of here."

Patrick snuck a glance at the angry rancher. The shotgun he was pointing at Patrick and Ronnie seemed nearly as tall and wide around as the spare man, whose body was encased in nothing but a baggy red suit of long underwear and a pair of high-heeled cowboy boots. But his size and attire weren't his most striking traits. That honor went to the black patch covering one of his eyes. *Pirate of the High Plains.* A matching black felt bowler was crammed low on his forehead. It was quite the look, but, since the rancher was the one with the gun out, Patrick kept his amusement to himself.

Ronnie extended her hands, lowering them slowly. "Put the safety on that shotgun and point it at the ground. We're no threat to you."

"That dog's a threat to my livelihood."

"And I'm on my way to get him," Patrick said, although he was still frozen in place. Something about the gun pointed at the sweet spot between his shoulder blades made it hard to get moving.

As if offended by the rancher, Ferdinand whipped his barking and growling back into a frenzy. The rancher gave his gun an emphatic shake in response.

Ronnie frowned. "What's your name, sir?"

"Wilfred Mitchell."

"Mr. Mitchell, sir, I'm telling you to put the safety on and point the gun at the ground. Now."

Patrick decided not to stick around to see how the standoff between deputy and rancher played out. He wanted to get Ferdinand the heck out of there before the angry man shot his dog. He slipped and slid down the side of the ravine, somehow managing to stay upright all the way to the bottom. Climbing back up wasn't going to be a picnic. He glanced around and up. Dark clouds were moving in from the north. The sight made him realize that the temperature had dropped, too. There had been no mention of a storm on the news the night before, but, clearly the weatherman's prediction of sunny weather had been wrong.

Ferdinand resumed his barking and growling.

Patrick's ears told him the dog was near—probably just around the first bend. "I'm coming, Ferdie. It's okay, boy. It's okay."

The gulch floor was narrow and flat and splotched with cow

manure. *Something fragrant to add to the mud on my boots.* In the excitement of the rancher's appearance, Patrick had forgotten his worry that Ferdinand might be in a standoff with a predator. Patrick pulled out his pistol and pointed the barrel at the ground. He drew a deep breath and rounded the corner, ready for anything.

Or he thought he was ready for anything. A big animal. His dog caught in a trap. An out-of-season rattler. But what he found his dog guarding was something no one could ever truly be ready for.

A person. Beaten to a pulp. Unrecognizable. The blood, fresh. Possibly dead. *No. No, no, no.* But wishing it were different didn't make it so.

"Good boy, Ferdie. I've got it now."

The dog whined, sniffing at the person.

Patrick's medical training kicked in, and he sprang into action.

"Ronnie, I need you down here," he shouted. He was already crouched beside the person. The hair was short, and the coat disguised the gender of the body. He pushed up the sleeve of the padded flannel jacket and searched for a pulse at the wrist. Patrick wanted to search for injuries, but that would have to wait. He watched for breath signs. He saw none.

Wilfred's voice was more of a snarl than Ferdinand's had been. "She's not coming down there. I ain't letting the two of you out of my sight together."

Ronnie's voice was exasperated. "Enough, Mr. Mitchell. We're not cattle rustlers. What is it, Patrick?"

"It's a person, Ronnie. Ferdie's guarding a very injured person."

"The hell you say!" Wilfred shouted. "How'd he get past me?"

Patrick heard footsteps and looked up. Ronnie stood on the lip of the gulch, Wilfred beside her. The man lifted his gun again, pointing it at Patrick. Ronnie put her hand on the barrel and pushed it back down. "A person?"

Patrick said, "Yes. Call for an ambulance."

"Do you have a pulse?"

"No. I'm starting compressions. Whoever it is hasn't been gone long. I might be able to bring 'em back."

Patrick put the heel of his hand in the center of the person's chest and stacked his other hand on top. He didn't feel the edges of a brassiere, and the breasts themselves were so small that again gender wasn't clear. He started firm two-inch-deep compressions, his elbows locked and arms straight, counting upwards toward thirty. He cut a glance over his shoulder. Ronnie had fended off Wilfred and disappeared. Patrick hoped she was running. He didn't like being left alone with the armed and half-crazy rancher, especially when his own guard was down and his back literally turned. It wasn't just Wilfred that made him nervous, though. The dead person under his hands was so warm that whatever or whoever did this couldn't be far away. The attack was recent. Extremely recent. So recent that . . . he looked for Wilfred as he reached thirty compressions. *That Wilfred could be the culprit.* But the rancher was gone.

Patrick swept a finger into the person's mouth and upper throat to check for obstructions. Finding none, he pinched the nose shut and gave two quick life breaths. He resumed compressions, but his eyes searched for Wilfred.

Behind him, he heard rocks tumble down the slope, then a heavy thud. "Wilfred? Mr. Mitchell?"

A louder thud, then a shotgun blast, so close to Patrick that the retort was like hot shrapnel to his ear drums. He had the sensation of something passing far too close to the side of his head. He dropped his body to cover his patient, freezing there for a few beats, waiting for a second shot that didn't come. Staying low, he scanned his body for injuries. He didn't think he'd been hit. But adrenaline could mask pain, so he patted himself down anyway.

Why did Wilfred shoot at me?

When he was satisfied that he was all right, he returned his attention to his patient. Blood flow stopped when the heart quit beating, so the patient wouldn't bleed if shot, but pressurized blood could still leak from the body for up to an hour. He probed for signs of a leaking wound, ready to apply pressure to save the blood volume—but found none.

Hackles rose on Patrick's neck. Was the rancher readying himself to take another shot at them? And how had he missed? The rattling rocks that announced his arrival had been only a few feet behind Patrick, the very definition of point-blank range.

He called, "Mr. Mitchell?"

But all he heard of his own voice was a ringing, echoey buzz inside his head. The shotgun had stunned his hearing. He searched for the rancher at the bottom of the ravine. All he saw was the shotgun laying on the ground. He swiveled in the other direction.

And there he was. Wilfred. The man was hunched over with both hands on his knees, his back heaving. A portion of Patrick's hearing returned. He heard retching, although the sound was still muffled, like he had cotton in his ears.

Obviously, Wilfred was no threat in his current state and without his gun. Patrick resumed compressions but kept one eye on the rancher.

"Leslie Anne," Wilfred said, his voice a croak. He lurched over and stumbled down on his knees beside Patrick. "My Leslie Anne."

"You know her?" Patrick said.

But Wilfred's only answer was his grief. Pushing up against Patrick, the man curled into a ball with his head pressed on the woman's—presumably Leslie Anne's—hip.

CHAPTER TWO: FREEZE

BUFFALO, WYOMING
SATURDAY, MARCH 18, 1978, 7:30 A.M.

Perry

PERRY FLINT FLOPPED onto a nubby couch in the great room of his house, in front of the cold fireplace with the empty spot above the mantel his dad was saving for a big horn sheep trophy mount someday. He was completely wiped out from an early spring football practice. Five a.m.! What were the coaches trying to do to them? He was too tired to even shower in the locker room back at school. *Okay, that isn't completely true.* He probably would have showered if the upper classmen hadn't been using the facilities at the same time. As an incoming freshman, aka an eighth grader, Perry was a head shorter and a few dozen pounds lighter than most of them. They had hair growing in places Perry only had smooth, Pillsbury Doughboy skin. Their voices were deep and didn't crack like his. And they liked to initiate the younger boys into the high school football fraternity with affectionate gestures like wedgies, towel whips, and noogies to the head. *No thanks.*

Perry had to get moving, though. He'd promised his girlfriend that he'd spend the day with her. Their plan was for Kelsey to come over as soon as his dad got home, which he hoped was soon but probably wouldn't be, knowing his dad and all things related to whatever he was currently obsessed with. He sniffed under his arms. *Pee-uuu. Not good.* He needed to shower and change pronto, even though his stomach was growling. Usually, his mom had a second breakfast ready for him after weekend practices. Eggs, pancakes with butter and maple syrup, bacon, and a tall glass of orange juice. He wished she hadn't had to go to her college in Sheridan today. And not just because of the missing second breakfast. If she were here, Kelsey could come now.

He groaned, stood, and stretched, which made him see spots. *Whoa, light-headed.* The house was quiet and empty. Not even Ferdinand was home—he was with his dad. He shivered. Partly because it was spooky to be home alone. Partly because it was cold in here. The temperature had dropped suddenly at the end of practice. The clouds had been dark and heavy, and a storm was definitely coming. That shouldn't mean their house would get this cold, should it? True, his dad liked to keep the thermostat super low. *Because he's the cheapest man in the history of the world.* But it was always set to the same temperature, and it never felt this cold.

Just as he reached the bottom of the stairs, the phone rang. He walked over and picked the receiver up from the wall phone in the kitchen. "Flint residence, Perry speaking."

The feminine giggle brought heat to his cheeks. "You sound so polite."

"Hey, Kelse. Yeah, you know my parents. They make me say it." He twirled the phone cord around his finger. Just talking to Kelsey on the phone gave him a funny feeling in his stomach. The good kind of funny. She'd only been his girlfriend for a few weeks, but he'd liked her for a long time. Even when she was his friend John's girl. But he wouldn't think about John. Couldn't think about him. Remembering John's death was like getting all the air crushed out of him over and over again. It was hard enough going to practice every day, thinking it should have been the two of them playing together out there, on the road to a state championship their senior year. John the quarterback, Perry his star wide receiver. It didn't matter that everyone else thought Perry was too short for the position. John had believed in Perry's hands and the great chemistry that almost made it like they could read each other's minds. Perry, about where John wanted him on the field. John, about where to put the ball so that only Perry could catch it.

"I think it's cute," Kelsey said.

Short guys hated being called cute. Or so Perry had always thought. Coming from Kelsey's lips, he decided cute wasn't that bad. Anything she said or did would be okay with him, as long as she liked him. Because he couldn't for the life of him figure out why she did. She could have any guy in school if she wanted. She was that sweet and pretty. What guy could resist her long, dark hair or her big, brown eyes? Or that smile, especially when she smiled at him.

He grinned. "Maybe."

"How was practice?"

"Hard. The coaches almost ran us to death. It's like they think it's track instead of football, you know?" Perry stretched the curly phone cord to walk to the thermostat on the other side of the dining area. It seemed to be set at sixty-six, the temperature his dad enforced as the max setting in the winter. Well, maybe he just felt cold because he'd been sweating.

"I'll bet you were amazing," Kelsey said.

"I don't know about that." Perry took the phone to the picture window. It looked out over the deck and yard and creek. Right now it was mud mixed with a little snow, but in the spring and summer it was green and pretty. Clear Creek was mostly thawed and running past the rows of cottonwoods on its banks. It was an awesome backyard with lots of birds and deer and the occasional raccoon and badger. A great place to throw a football with his dad.

"I do. Wyatt Evans said the coaches have been talking about you."

Wyatt Evans? Wyatt was a junior. He was going to start at tight end next year on varsity. And he was one of the guys who had been hazing Perry. But why would Kelsey be talking to him? He was Trish's age. Three years older than Perry and Kelsey. He couldn't ask her that, though. She would think he was possessive. Jealous. Insecure. *Guilty as charged.* "What did they say?"

"Well, I don't know this for a fact, but I heard they're going to let you practice with varsity."

Perry's heart slammed inside his ribs so hard it was almost painful. *Varsity? As a freshman? As a* shrimp *freshman?* "No way. That can't be true."

"That's what he said."

"What else did he say?"

She paused. "Uhhh, that you're gonna get pounded. But that you're all grit, no quit."

"He said that? All grit, no quit?"

"In those exact words."

"Whoa." Perry sunk into a chair at the kitchen table. For a moment, he didn't care why Wyatt was talking to Kelsey, he was just glad Kelsey could tell him this. Then the moment was over, and he wished he was big enough to whup Wyatt good for talking to his girl.

Kelsey's voice was light and sing song. "My boyfriend is going to be the only freshman on the varsity football team."

"We'll see."

"Yes, we will. And I think I'm right." Her words lifted his spirits. Maybe Wyatt wasn't a threat. "So, when is my boyfriend going to see me today? My mom needs to go to the grocery store. She wants to drop me off at your place on the way."

"I'm not sure. My dad's not home yet."

"From his crazy hiking workout? You know, people are talking about seeing him outside town with weights strapped all over him and a giant backpack, when it's not even light out?"

Geez, Dad. Why couldn't he just go to the track and run laps? He was so extreme. It was humiliating. "Yeah, um, that."

"What about your mom?"

"She's at a thing in Sheridan." Life had been completely different since his mother re-started college forty-five minutes away. Trish was his ride to most places. That was okay, other than she had been a big downer ever since her boyfriend Ben had left town. Perry couldn't wait to get his own license. But that would be two more years. Basically, forever.

"Where's Trish?"

"Cheerleading clinic."

"Oh, yeah. I forgot about that. She's totally going to get it."

"You think?" Perry thought his sister was a geek. Brainy and shy. A little on the skinny side, especially after a year of running cross country and long-distance races.

"It's her breakout year."

Perry laughed. "You mean breakup. Ben dumped her."

"Well, that means she isn't going with anybody. It doesn't hurt that she's available. Boys vote, too. And she's sooo pretty."

"You're prettier."

"Ah, thanks, Per-Bear."

Perry frowned. Cute was okay. But he'd been wrong when he thought anything she said or did was okay. Per-Bear was . . . embarrassing. He hoped she never said it in front of anyone else. "Per-Bear?"

"*My* Per-Bear."

The frown turned upside down. "Let's keep that one between us."

"Okay, *Per-Bear.* Hey, my mom really wants to leave. Is it okay if she drops me? We could wait for your dad outside on the deck or something?" She dropped her voice to a whisper. "I won't tell her he isn't home yet. She would *freak out.*"

So would his parents. But how uncool would he be if he told Kelsey not to come? Sitting on the deck was a good compromise to the "no girls in the house when parents aren't home rule." He couldn't lie to his parents, but if they assumed that he hadn't known Kelsey's mom was going to drop her off without them here, he wouldn't correct them. "I guess."

"Cool. I'll, like, be there in fifteen minutes."

They said their goodbyes, and Perry sprinted to the shower, thinking about the back deck and how no one could see them out there if Kelsey decided to let him kiss her.

CHAPTER THREE: INTERVIEW

BUFFALO, WYOMING
SATURDAY, MARCH 18, 1978, 8:00 A.M.

Ronnie

RONNIE HARCOURT WIPED snow from her sunglasses. The sun had disappeared as the front edge of the storm hit, and she was only wearing the sunglasses to keep the darn stuff out of her eyes. She glanced at her watch. Breakfast time had come and gone hours ago. What had started as a simple callout for a report of a possible vagrant casing homes had gone completely sideways. She had worked the previous night shift and been due to punch out right after the call. Now she was facing hours of investigation and the coordination of body removal from the crime scene.

First up, an interview with the property owner, Wilfred Mitchell. *Oh, joy.* The rancher was standing beside her in shell shock, still wearing only his boots, long johns, and hat. And his eyepatch of course. Wilfred was such a character that she couldn't believe she didn't already know him, living in the area all her life as she did. But she had already pegged him as antisocial, and she wouldn't be surprised if he was something of a recluse as well. Certainly, his body odor wouldn't be welcome in polite society. The man's stench could fell a rhinoceros at twenty paces, and Ronnie had always been sensitive to smells. She wished she had some of the Mentholatum she rubbed under her nose at autopsies, but it was back at the sheriff's offices.

She gathered her thoughts, thinking back over the events of the morning as she formulated her questions for Wilfred. Thank goodness the vagrant call had turned out to be about Patrick Flint. He was a good sort to have around when finding an almost dead or recently deceased body. As was Ferdinand, who might make a decent Search & Rescue dog. She shuddered. Or cadaver dog. But weren't the fast hounds—like the Irish wolfhounds—considered sight hounds, not scent hounds? She'd always heard their skill was spotting movement from a long distance and chasing after it. It made her think of how events had started at the Mitchell ranch. She wondered what Ferdinand had seen, if anything, that had attracted him out to the victim in the ravine.

Speaking of movement, she caught sight of some of her own. Man and dog were headed her way, and it looked like Patrick intended to come talk to her. When he'd been unable to revive the woman, he'd waited with the body for the arrival of the EMTs. She pointed him to her truck. She needed to have this conversation with Mr. Mitchell first. Patrick nodded and moved out of the snow and wind, leaning against the truck as a wind block. Within earshot of her interview, but she didn't mind. The dog ran in concentric circles, joyfully unconcerned about the gruesome find now that he'd passed responsibility on to the humans.

Then more movement. A truck sped up to within feet of Mr. Mitchell, then slid to a stop on the gravel. Mr. Mitchell didn't react at all. A man who had to be nearing his eighties climbed out and limped over to Mr. Mitchell. His pants were held up by suspenders or they would have hit the ground. Ronnie decided to let whatever was about to happen play out in the interest of gathering information.

"What did you do this time, Wilfred?" he shouted.

Mr. Mitchell barely glanced up. "Leave me alone, Tristan. Leslie Anne's dead."

The old guy glared at him. Then he took a step back, nearly falling. "Well, I'm sorry to hear that."

Now Mr. Mitchell raised his eyes. "Where's your fancy cane?"

"Somebody took it. Wouldn't happen to be you, would it?"

"I don't want anything of yours. Now leave me alone. This here deputy's waiting to talk to me."

"This isn't over."

"It never is."

The angry old man limped back to his truck. He sprayed gravel as he accelerated toward town.

Ronnie said, "Who was that? He seemed upset."

Mr. Mitchell shrugged. "Tristan Babcock. He's a nasty piece of work. He's always upset."

"Are the two of you feuding?"

Mr. Mitchell cut his eyes back to the ground. "No more than him and anyone else."

She nodded, then pulled out her notepad and pencil. "Mr. Mitchell, tell me your relationship to the victim."

The man's face was splotchy in the same color as his long johns, and his eye patch was damp from tears. At the mention of the deceased, he stared off into the distance, east toward Gillette away from the mountains, not appearing to hear her.

She licked her lips and tried again. "Mr. Mitchell?" She raised her voice. "Wilfred!"

He shook himself and met her gaze. The man had been through a trauma—heck, he'd accidentally fired his gun as he'd fallen to the ground when he'd seen Leslie Anne and could've blown Patrick's head off in the process.

She softened her tone. "Tell me about your relationship to the victim. Please."

"Victim." His voice trembled, so unlike his strident tone earlier. "Her name was Leslie Anne Compton. And she was my, uh, my, uh, my w-w-w-woman."

Having only known the man for an hour, Ronnie was still surprised to hear this. So, she sought clarity. "Did she work for you?"

He scowled at her. "She pulled her own weight, but she wasn't no hand, if that's what you're asking."

"So, she was your girlfriend?"

Annoyance seemed to be tempering his gentler emotions. "Ain't that what I said?"

"Just confirming."

"She ain't the only woman who wants me neither. And I ain't the only man who wanted her. She had fellers pestering her all time."

Ronnie kept a straight face. "I'm sure. How long had you and Miss Compton been in a relationship?"

"Purt near two months now."

"Is she from Buffalo?"

"No."

"Does she have family here?"

"None 'cept me."

"How'd you come to know each other?"

He growled, then said, "Are you going to go find who did this to her or make me jaw about our love life all day?"

Ronnie nodded. Interviews were often fishing expeditions. The victim was an unknown person. Wilfred might be the only good source of information about her, and, once he figured out that the boyfriend or husband is usually the first person the cops look to in the murder of women, that source might dry up. "Bear with me, Mr. Mitchell. I promise it's important that you tell me how she came to town, where she's from, and how you know each other. Can you do that?"

His lips moved silently for several seconds, then he nodded.

"She's from Moorcroft or thereabouts. I, uh, I gave her a ride one day, and we hit it off. Been together ever since."

"Gave her a ride?"

"Picked her up. When she was hitching."

"When was the last time you saw Miss Compton?"

"She made me breakfast, then I went out to check on some fence." *In that get up?* Wilfred broke eye contact. He looked up at the sky, then quickly down, blinking away snowflakes. "It took me an hour or so. Some of my cows had wandered off to the west side of my place. One of 'em had calved. The other had gotten her damn self tangled in some wire. After I got her straightened out, I headed back. I saw you and that doctor feller and, well, you know the rest."

Ronnie wrote *no alibi* on her notepad. "Did you see or hear anyone else, anything suspicious?"

He looked back up at Ronnie. "Not this morning. But last night we gave a traveler some supper. I didn't let him in the house. Leslie Anne wrapped the food up in some newspaper and took it out to him. He asked to sleep in our barn, but the weather was good, and I told him to be on his way."

"And he left?"

"Yes."

"Did either of you know him?"

"I didn't. I don't reckon Leslie Anne did or she woulda said so."

"Did he act strangely or threatening in any way?"

He shook his head. "He was polite, if a little odd." *A case of the pot and the kettle.* "Didn't say much. But I didn't like the way he was looking at Leslie Anne when I came up on 'em. She said he had just knocked on our door and asked for work, water, food, and a place to stay. I would have turned him down, but Leslie has—had," his voice broke, "a soft heart."

"Do you get many people like that wandering through?"

"Every so often. Not many."

"What did he look like?"

He nodded at Patrick. "Like him, but dirtier. And with clothes on their last threads."

"Tall or short?"

"Medium."

"Heavy or thin?"

"A little meat on his bones, but normal size."

"Hair color?"

"Greasy but not too dark."

"Eyes?"

"What would I be doing staring into another feller's eyes?"

Again, Ronnie pressed her lips together. She scribbled down the description. A rattling noise on the road signaled the approach of a vehicle. She looked up. Dilapidated was a kind description of the dark blue El Camino that pulled to a stop. A wall-eyed woman whose long gray braid suggested she was sixty-plus climbed out. A stiff wind would have blown her south to Kaycee, nearly fifty miles away. She brushed dust off her creased blue jeans and approached.

"Wilfred? What's happened?" she said.

Ronnie held up a hand. "Ma'am, you need to move along."

Feisty rose up in her posture and expression. "Do you need my help, Wilfred?"

"No," he said, his voice a mutter, his eyes not lifting to the woman's. "You heard the deputy. Move along, Wanda."

"Is it Leslie Anne? Did something happen to her?"

Ronnie was suddenly interested. "What's your name, ma'am?"

"Wanda Carmichael."

"Why do you ask about Leslie Anne?"

She backed away. "Because Wilfred looks like he's upset, and I don't see her anywhere."

"Have you seen Leslie Anne?"

"Today? No. But I saw her at our little country church with Wilfred last weekend. And Wednesday night."

"Do you live near here?"

"Not really. I live closer to town."

"What brought you out this direction?"

Her eyes darted to Wilfred, then back to Ronnie. "I dropped eggs off at an elderly friend's house. Then I was just coming by to check on Wilfred, like normal."

"You don't gotta check up on me, Wanda. Leslie Anne takes . . ." Wilfred stopped. His throat bulged.

Wanda glanced at Ronnie.

"What's the name and address of the friend you took the eggs to, Ms. Carmichael?"

Wanda recited the information, and Ronnie took it down, then took Wanda's phone number as well. "Did you see anyone near Wilfred's ranch on your way out to your friend's?"

"I saw a hobo."

"Is that the man you saw?" Ronnie pointed at Patrick.

The woman gasped. "It just might be."

"I'll be in touch if I have any more questions, Ms. Carmichael."

"Missus. Rich is passed on now, but I was a wife for forty years."

"Yes, ma'am. Missus it is."

Wanda made slow work of leaving, casting long, suspicious looks at Patrick as she went.

Ronnie returned to Wilfred. "Did you see anyone else in the last twenty-four hours, especially this morning?"

"Our hand didn't show up for work. He's only part-time."

"What's his name?"

"Dabbo Kern. He's been helping me out for a few months now."

"Do he and Miss Compton get along?"

"Yeah. He liked her. Too much. Would blush when she walked in a room. Made advances at her once, before he knew she was my woman. Leslie Anne said he was a harmless ole duffer, but might be he didn't like her telling him no. You think he did it?" Wilfred frowned. "By God, I'll bet he did. You've gotta go pick him up. He's a suspect. A durn possible killer!"

"We'll sure talk to him." Ronnie made a note of his name. "Does he live in town?"

"I s'pose."

"Do you know anyone who had ill feelings toward Ms. Compton?"

"Besides Dabbo?"

"Yes."

"Not ill enough to beat her face in and kill her. There's no call for that, no call at all."

Ronnie couldn't have agreed with him more. But he hadn't really answered her question. "Any enemies?"

"I don't rightly know."

"Anyone Ms. Compton didn't like, or who was upset with or didn't like her?"

"Her daddy and her brother, or so she said."

"Do they have names?"

"The Comptons. In Moorcroft."

"Or thereabouts," Ronnie muttered. "What was the nature of her problems with them?"

"They didn't approve of her. Felt like unmarried women belonged to their families. She finally ran away. Which is when I found her."

Whoa. Ronnie put two stars by *Comptons in Moorcroft.* "Had they made threats against her?"

"Not to kill her, far as I know. But plenty of other kinds. I told her not to tell 'em where she'd landed, but I believe she'd been in touch with her mama. Plus, there's her old beau."

"What's his name?"

"Bull Folske. And, before you ask, he lived near Moorcroft, too."

"Did that relationship end badly?"

"I 'spect she broke his heart. But her daddy demanded a settlement from Bull for deflowering her and depriving the family of her labor. Leslie Anne said Bull refused, and she was afraid they'd come after the two of them. That's when she left and found me."

One of Ronnie's colleagues approached her, a man ten years her junior who went by the nickname Radish because of his bright red hair and glaringly white skin. "Ronnie, I found something."

Ronnie held up a finger. "Anything else you can think of to tell me that would help us find Miss Compton's killer?"

The rancher pursed his lips and shifted his eyes to his feet. His eyes were shiny as tears welled up again. "No."

"Please call me if something occurs to you. Can I call anyone to be with you now?"

A tear spilled. "No, ma'am. Leslie Anne was the only people I got. Now I ain't got no one."

"My condolences for your loss, Mr. Mitchell."

He nodded and started walking back toward his house.

Ronnie turned to Radish. "What did you find?"

Radish's bright eyes were excited. "A wallet. It was just up the gulch from the victim."

"Whose is it?"

"A man. I didn't recognize the name and, um, I guess I got a little excited and now I can't remember it, but his address is listed as the next ranch over. It's covered in blood and . . . stuff. I left it there."

Ronnie grunted. That sounded promising. "Good job, Radish. Give me a second to finish my interview and we'll go see it together."

Wilfred shifted from one foot to the other and turned toward his ranch.

Patrick rose and walked over. "You need me for anything else, Ronnie? It's a long walk back, and I've gotta meet Susanne out at Piney Bottoms."

"Not now. But let's debrief later. I need to make sure I capture all the good stuff rattling around in your brain."

"Whatever good is in there, it's all yours." He saluted her, said goodbye to Radish and Wilfred, then whistled for Ferdinand and headed down the road toward Buffalo.

Ronnie grabbed gloves and evidence bags from the toolbox in the bed of her truck. A yawn threatened. A thought niggled her brain. Something she hadn't asked Wilfred? She couldn't dredge it up. As with Patrick, she could always circle back with Wilfred later. After she'd slept. Or had a pot of coffee. Or both. But they'd have to wait. A woman was dead, and it was her job to give her justice. "Mr. Mitchell, thank you. Please call me if you think of anything else, and I'll do the same."

He nodded.

She turned to her co-worker. "Now, lead the way, Radish."

CHAPTER FOUR: CHEER

Trish

"Hey, Encyclopedia Flint. What are you going to say in your valedictorian speech next year?" Jillian Tupelo punctuated her words with a perfect Herkie jump. Her red pigtails bounced in the air. Red heads were supposed to be freckled-faced and picked-on. Jillian wasn't either thing. She was popular and outgoing and had perfect skin. She had also been a cheerleader for years. In junior high, and now in her sophomore and junior years in high school. Everyone expected her to be captain of the squad next year. "You'll be the smartest cheerleader ever." She winked broadly for the other girls in the gym. "April Fool's! You'll never make the squad."

Except it's still the middle of March. Joke's on you, Jillian. But since they were supposed to be practicing jumps, Trish didn't answer Jillian.

She tried her own Herkie. One leg forward, one leg bent at the knee. She felt ridiculous. Uncoordinated. Like a loser. Why did it have to be uncool to be intelligent? Jillian's words smarted because she meant them unkindly, not because Trish wanted to be dumb. *Like her.* Being called Encyclopedia Flint should be a compliment. Except that she knew no one else but her thought so.

Marcy leaned toward her, her signature brown braids swinging forward, and whispered, "Ignore her. She's just trying to mess with your head. She's jealous of you."

She did a split jump. It was perfect. Marcy had taken tumbling classes when she was in elementary school. She was short, too, like most of this year's squad. A guard on the basketball team with a crazy high vertical jump. Trish felt like a giraffe in this crowd. Marcy was also the one who had corralled Trish into trying out for cheerleader with her. Something Trish might never forgive her for.

"Jealous? Hardly," Trish said.

"Worried, then."

"Marcy, I'm too tall. I can't jump an inch off the ground. I'm no threat to her."

"You're good enough to pass the clinic. Then it's a popular vote."

"People at school barely even know who I am, other than as the victim of a creepy kidnapping." A memory Trish wished would fade, from when her boyfriend—ex?—Ben was forced to help his dad and uncle kidnap her as part of their revenge on her dad. "And the ones that do know who I am think like Jillian. 'Encyclopedia Flint.' The brainy girl. Not the cheerleader type. Please let me just quit."

"Noooo. I want to do this together." Marcy's voice was a wail. She grabbed Trish by her arms, and her perfume nearly knocked Trish over. Love's Baby Soft, Trish knew, because she'd given it to Marcy for her birthday. "And this is good for you. Track is over. You need something. You know—to keep your mind off things."

Which only served to put Trish's mind right back on that thing. Ben. Tall, dark, and handsome Ben. Sweet, gentle, adventurous Ben. She put her hand to her chest, where her promise ring hung from a chain under her shirt. Gone, split, out-of-here Ben. Who she hadn't heard from since he'd left a note on her door telling her that he was never going to be good enough for her. Telling her goodbye. She gritted her teeth and tried her jump again, throwing all her emotion into it.

"Hey, that was pretty good," Marcy said. "Much better."

The cheerleading coach blew a whistle. "All right, girls. Move in where you can hear me, please." The frowzy woman smoothed her hair. With her pockmarked skin and complete lack of muscle tone, Trish couldn't picture Mrs. Griffin as a cheerleader. But maybe experience wasn't a prerequisite for coaching it.

Twenty or so girls crowded around Mrs. Griffin. The excitement and nerves were palpable in the air, even in the smell of sudden, spontaneous perspiration around the gym. Today had been the last day of clinic. It was time for each girl to perform for the judges. The winners would advance to a student body vote. Trish wanted to crawl under the bleachers rather than run down the gym mat, a la a "grand entrance into a pep rally or football stadium." She'd rather parade naked through the halls of the school than do the pom-pom dance routine in formation with the rest of the aspiring cheerleaders.

"First up will be Jillian," Mrs. Griffin said. Most of the girls cheered. Trish clapped without enthusiasm. It was hard to fake liking someone as mean as Jillian. "This is a great chance for the rest of you to show your spirit. I'm always watching, as are the rest of the judges helping me make this momentous decision." She waved to a line of women who looked like they were just out of college. "All former cheerleaders. Now, remember to smile and show your Bison spirit, everyone! Take it away, Jillian!"

Coach's pet.

Jillian stood straight, threw her shoulders back and chin up, and flashed a brilliant smile at the judges and Mrs. Griffin. Then she ran down the mat and executed a perfect round-off, back handspring, and back flip. She pumped her arms in the air in a circular motion, then leaped up and up and up, touching both toes.

"Go Bison!" she screamed.

All the girls cheered wildly.

"Yay," Trish said, clapping. "Yay." Her voice sounded insincere, but she pasted a smile on her face.

Mrs. Griffin said, "Great job, Jillian. Girls, she's set the bar high. It's up to each of you to strive to achieve her level of excellence."

Trish wanted to vomit. She could pretend to be sick, run for the locker room, and never come back. She tensed, ready to flee. *It isn't too late. Just go!*

"Next up, Trish Flint," Mrs. Griffin said.

Yes, it is.

The applause from the other girls sounded lackluster to Trish's ears. She moved to the head of the mat. Held herself up to her five feet seven inches in height. *No pain, no gain,* she heard in her head. Her dad's voice. But what did his mantra have to do with cheerleading tryouts? This wasn't a physical test. But it was a mental and emotional one. And those made it incredibly painful. *Okay, I hear you, Dad.* Her parents had taught her and her little brother Perry to always do their best, at whatever they did. She had planned to run to the end of the mat, yell, "Go Bison," and do a Herkie. It was her best jump, even if it wasn't as good as Jillian's toe touch. Then she remembered something she could do better. Mrs. Griffin had even complimented her on it more than once. Her splits.

"Such long beautiful legs. Such an elegant split," Mrs. Griffin had said.

Trish had seen Jillian give her a side-eye glare at Mrs. Griffin's words. The girl had bulkier thighs and shorter legs than Trish. Her split was two inches above the ground, which made her legs look even squattier.

"Trish? Are you ready?" Mrs. Griffin's voice was chirpy.

Trish nodded. She had a passable round-off. Instead of bouncing into a back handspring like Jillian, she could bounce into the splits, then leap up and finish as she'd planned.

Okay, then. I'll give it my best at what I'm best at.

She nodded at the judges like an Olympic gymnast, then raced down the mat. It was another thing she excelled at. Running with grace. So, she made the most of it. When she was right in front of the judges, she launched her hands at the mat, threw her body in the air, whipped her legs up and twisted them around, landing with them both on the mat together, facing the way she'd come. Her momentum and performance adrenaline sent her into a jump, higher than she'd expected. For a split second, she panicked. But there was no backing out now. A plain round off was lame compared to Jillian. Trish threw her arms straight into the air and kicked her right leg forward, left behind her, and landed in a split on the mat.

The WHACK of the impact of her legs and core drew a loud gasp from everyone watching. There was dead silence as Trish leapt to her feet.

"Go Bison," she shouted, feeling like the world's biggest dork but smiling as wide as she could. Ben's face flashed into her mind. *Eat your heart out, Ben Jones. This is me, trying out for cheerleader. You should never have left me.* She put everything she had into her jump, her right leg stretched in front of her, her left leg bent and hiked slightly behind her, her arms out and fingers touching her right toe.

As suddenly as it had begun, it was over.

For a moment she froze on the mat, uncertain what to do with herself in the deafening quiet. Then the gym erupted in cheers. Louder than for Jillian. Crazy loud. Trish felt like a deer staring into the headlights of a steamroller.

What just happened?

She rushed into the mass of girls, wanting to hide. Everyone was hugging her and slapping her on the back at once. Snippets of their words penetrated her short-circuited brain. "Where did you learn to do that?" and "Did it hurt?" and "Oh, my gosh, I'd never be brave enough to try that!" She looked up and caught a venomous stare from Jillian.

Marcy pulled her into a ferocious hug, tears in her eyes. "I knew you could do it. A star is born."

CHAPTER FIVE: OFFER

Susanne

"Thanks for coming in today, Susanne." Professor Todd Renwick pushed away sandy blond hair that hit the top of his wire-rimmed glasses in front and hung to his collar in back.

The man had to be at least Susanne's age—thirty-six—but the young women in her study group were all atwitter about him. She supposed he was handsome in a tweedy, academic way, but she was immune to the appeal of men other than her husband. What she liked about her professor was that he was an engaging teacher who made geopolitics and international relations easier for her, which was important with the limited time she had to prepare and study. She was enjoying his class a lot more than she'd expected.

Unlike this visit to his office on a Saturday morning. The walls seemed to crowd into her. The scent of cigarettes was cloying. An open pack of Winston Lights. An overflowing ashtray. No windows.

No ventilation. There wasn't room for anything in the tight space other than stuffed bookshelves, the scarred desk the professor sat behind, and the wooden chair in front of it.

Susanne perched on its edge. "Of course. You said it was important." She was giving up half a day for this meeting, counting the drive time each way. Those were precious hours on Patrick's day off, especially since he was spending so much time training for mountain climbing. She grimaced, remembering Patrick's silhouette that morning as he walked to his truck by porchlight, but she wiped away her expression quickly, not wanting to give the professor the impression she resented being here. Even if she did, a little. "Is it my last paper? I know I'm not the best—"

"No, no, you're doing very well." His voice held a trace of an accent. Minnesota or Wisconsin, she thought. She glanced at the diplomas on the wall. A degree from the University of Iowa. A Ph.D. from—yep—the University of Minnesota. A midwesterner. He twirled a fountain pen through his fingers. Susanne found herself staring as it wove its way pinky to pointer, pointer to pinky. "So well in fact that I wanted to invite you to work for me."

Susanne wasn't sure she heard him correctly. "Work for you?"

"Yes. You have a great work ethic. You're smart. You have your head on straight—not like most of the twenty-somethings in the class." He waggled his eyebrows. "I need someone to help me with research over these next few months. Say, from now through the start of the fall semester."

She was flattered, but her first thought was the one that flew out of her mouth. "My life is already bursting at the seams."

He held up a hand. "I only need a few hours a week. And I can offer you course credit for independent study. Up to four hours."

She frowned, weighing the opportunity. She had planned to take one course over the summer. Independent study hours could replace that. In the long run, though, political science wasn't her interest. If she were going to devote extra time to a subject area, shouldn't it be something relevant to teaching kids? It's not like she was going on to get her own Ph.D. in political anything.

As if he read her mind, he said, "I looked up your records. I know you're pursuing an elementary education degree. My field of research would enhance teaching social studies or history. And if you wanted to go on to teach college students, it would be a feather in your cap."

Her, a college professor? She'd never even considered it. The idea sparked inside her. "Wouldn't I have to earn an advanced degree to teach college?"

He twirled the pen again. *So strangely mesmerizing.* "It helps, but it's not required at most community colleges."

She chewed the inside of her lip. "I'll need to think about it." And to talk to her husband, since this would have an impact on their whole family. "It's a change of direction and a big commitment for me. When do you need an answer?"

"How about a conditional yes for now, and a final answer at the end of next week?"

Susanne stood. "That's okay, I guess."

Professor Renwick laughed. "You seem like you're in a hurry. I thought I'd buy you a cup of coffee to celebrate our new working relationship." He pulled a cigarette from the pack and a lighter from his desk drawer.

"But I didn't say yes." To the job or the coffee. But should she? She'd been working hard on learning to say no. Raised in Texas by her mama to be a Southern lady, no didn't come easily to her lips. And when an authority figure asked something of her, the difficulty increased exponentially.

"It was conditional, but you did. I'm optimistic. And confident." He put the cigarette between his lips and flicked the lighter. Held it to the tip of the cigarette. When it caught, he sucked on it like an oxygen mask and put the lighter away.

Yuck. She checked her watch. If she left now and ran her errands, she'd barely make it to Story and Piney Bottoms Ranch on time to meet Patrick for their meeting with the Sibleys and their private investigator. Holding up the schedule wasn't an option, nor was running errands later. She had to be home for her daughter. Trish was probably going to be cut in cheerleading clinic today, and she'd need consoling.

"I'm sorry. I have to be back in Buffalo. But I appreciate the offer."

"I live in Buffalo, too. Any chance you can give me a ride back?"

"Um, I'm not going right now. I have a meeting in Story first. I'm sorry."

"That's all right. It's just that some crazy dude and his floozy girl-friend t-boned my car yesterday. Then they blamed me for it. I thought they were going to take me out to the back forty and shoot me." He laughed at his own joke. Susanne smiled. "But I can catch a ride home in a few hours from the same person who brought me to Sheridan. No problem."

"All right. I'll be on my way then." She picked up the denim shoulder bag with crisscross stitching that she'd made herself and took the one short step to the door.

The professor beat her to it. He paused with one hand holding his cigarette and the other on the doorknob, holding it closed instead of open, his body pressed toward hers by the tight confines of the office. The irritating cigarette smell was worse the closer it got to her. "Not only smart and beautiful, but conscientious. I'm going to enjoy the heck out of working with you, Susanne."

"Um, thank you." For some reason, his compliment made her suck in her stomach and pull her arms closer to her body to avoid any accidental contact, with him or the burning cigarette. "See you in class." She couldn't open the door with his hand on it, so she broke eye contact and stared at it.

"Of course." He opened the door and stepped back but still held the door, his arm at about her eye level. "Ladies first."

She ducked under and scurried out, heart pounding. *What are you afraid of?* Maybe she spent too much time at home. She wasn't used to men outside of her family, wasn't accustomed to the idea of working for one. It's not like she'd been out burning bras with her generation. She'd gotten married. Raised two kids. Put her education and career on hold. *What would Gloria Steinem do?* she wondered. It nearly made her laugh—Gloria wasn't her style. She forced herself to turn back to him with a smile. "Thanks again."

He looked up and met her eyes, then nodded and leaned against the door frame to his office. Took a drag on his cigarette, pursed his lips, and blew the smoke upward.

Was he checking out my behind? She walked faster. She was a mature woman. A wife. A mom. The halls of Sheridan College were filled with women younger, prettier, and far more available than her. There was no way he was attracted to her. To think so was pure vanity. Besides, Professor Renwick was the first person at the college to single her out for her intellect and drive. He was offering her a way to break out of the pack. She needed to take it or not on its merits, not on figments of her imagination.

She opened the door to exit to the parking lot, and a bone-chilling wind buffeted her backwards. She'd expected the unforecasted storm to pass while she was cocooned inside with Professor Renwick, but instead it had gotten worse. Icy snowflakes were falling from the sky, hard and fast. This would slow the driving to a crawl. She had planned to grocery shop in Sheridan before driving to the Sibleys—the prices and selection were better in the larger town than in Buffalo—and she'd have to hurry if she was going to fit it in.

She accelerated carefully out of the parking lot. Concentrating on the road in the deteriorating conditions might take her mind off her conundrum: whether to accept Professor Renwick's intriguing job offer. And his unsettling behavior.

CHAPTER SIX: MEET UP

Story, Wyoming
Saturday, March 18, 1978, Noon

Susanne

"Sorry I'm late," Patrick said.

Susanne watched her husband as Vangie escorted him into the dining area to join Henry and Susanne at the Sibleys' big farm table, one that she knew saw heavy usage three times a day by the Sibleys and their ranch employees. The kitchen and dining room was one of Susanne's favorite places. In the kitchen, it always smelled like something sweet had just come out of the oven. This time, if her nose didn't deceive her, it was chocolate chip cookies. The dining area was homey, ranchy, and filled with mementos of a working life, with farm and ranch implements preserved as art on the walls along with pictures of award-winning livestock and produce.

But the décor did nothing to soothe her today. Her husband might be handsome, fit, and—as her grandmother loved to remind her —a "good provider," but lately he was never available. In his zeal for the seven summits, he seemed to have forgotten he'd committed to help more with the kids and household so she could complete her degree. And here he was, late again. The plan had been to talk about the search for Ben before the investigator arrived. Now they were running out of time. She'd been hoping Patrick would even arrive a little early, since she was dying to tell him about her job offer. But it would have to wait. Her stuff usually did. Good thing Susanne's migraines hadn't been as bad lately.

"Wicked weather out there," he added. He was still clad in the blue jeans and sweatshirt he'd worn for his hike that morning. Susanne checked his feet. And his hiking boots.

"Isn't it though?" Vangie took a seat beside her husband and baby. She pushed her dark pixie cut hair behind one ear. She sounded perky and inviting. Susanne might be from Texas, but, hailing from Tennessee, Vangie was truly southern. From her voice to her manners and her impeccable attire. She made blue jeans look like theater wear.

Susanne gave Patrick the stink eye. "How's Perry?" Her voice sounded a little tight. *Good. He needs to know inconveniencing other people is not okay.*

"Didn't he have a ride home from practice?" Patrick's brows furrowed.

"Yes. To meet Kelsey. You were their chaperone."

A flash of recognition crossed his face. His blue eyes softened. "I forgot."

"And Trish—have you heard anything about the cheerleading clinic yet?"

"I, uh, I didn't make it home. I've been stuck at a death scene with Ronnie. Ferdie is waiting in the cab of the truck."

After hearing his answer, Susanne felt shrewish. The excuse was a good one. But honestly—he always had one, between his job and his outdoor adventures.

Henry was bouncing baby Hank on his knee. A pint-sized cowboy hat slid over his face, and the boy laughed and tipped it up, just like Susanne had seen Hank do dozens of times. The daddy's boy was starting to walk. He'd probably be riding a pony behind his dad soon. His dad looked like he'd been tending cattle. He was dressed in a work shirt and chaps splattered with things Susanne didn't like to contemplate. There was a hat line across his forehead and a crease in his hair. His face and ears were wind-reddened, and his lips chapped.

"Not anyone we know, I hope?" Henry said.

Patrick shot him a grateful look. "You know Wilfred Mitchell out south of Buffalo?"

"Crotchety old bastard. No great loss."

"Henry!" Vangie held out her arms for Hank, who buried his face in Henry's shoulder, then relented and leaned toward his mother with a mischievous grin. She swooped him onto her lap.

"Well, it's true," Henry said.

Patrick nodded. "I agree, but he's still alive and kicking. It was on his place, but it was Leslie Anne. His girlfriend."

"Girlfriend? Hard to believe any woman would hitch her wagon to Wilfred's. So, how'd she die? Did she kill herself to get away from him?"

Vangie shot him a glare over Hank's fuzzy head.

"Nope. Murdered. Beaten to death."

Susanne put a hand to her chest, her fingers gripping the V-neck collar of her sweater. "Oh, my goodness." She hated to hear this, but she wasn't surprised by it. Trouble and Patrick were synonymous terms. Ever since they'd moved to Wyoming, though, trouble seemed to arrive in the form of violent crime. Kidnappings, assaults, murders. Was it him? Was it them? Was it the town or the state? Maybe they were just on a run of bad luck. *Dear God, let our luck change soon.*

But Patrick wasn't on the schedule or on call. "Why did Ronnie call you in? *How* did she call you in?"

"She didn't. She was checking out a report of a vagrant, which turned out to be about me. I guess I do look a little strange out there with my pack and weights." Susanne snorted. Patrick gave her a toothy smile. "But then Ferdinand ran off. He was going nuts, so I chased after him. Ronnie came as my backup. Mitchell saw us and tried to roust us with a shotgun."

"That's the Wilfred I know and love," Henry said.

Patrick nodded. "When I heard the action, I may have wet myself." Henry laughed. "After we convinced him to let me go get Ferdie, I found the dog standing guard over a very recently deceased person. Leslie Anne. Wilfred was so grief-stricken that he accidentally discharged his gun and nearly took me out."

"He shot at you?" Susanne's voice came out a little screechy.

"Not on purpose."

"Leslie Anne who?" Vangie said.

"Compton. From around Moorcroft. You know her?"

Vangie shook her head. Henry did likewise. Susanne hadn't heard of her either.

"Does Ronnie have a suspect?" Susanne asked.

A knock sounded at the front door before Patrick could answer.

CHAPTER SEVEN: REPORT OUT

Patrick

Patrick broke off answering Susanne as everyone looked toward the sound of the knocking, the atmosphere suddenly tense. Patrick wanted to hear what the investigator had to say. But he was afraid of bad news. He suspected they all were.

"That'll be him." Henry stood. Over his shoulder, he added, "Your life is more exciting than mine, Flint. By far."

"That's not a good thing," Susanne called after Henry.

Patrick laughed. *Is Susanne upset with me?* Her comment had sounded a little barbed. He put his hand on her knee, but she didn't acknowledge it.

Vangie walked into the kitchen with her toddler on her hip, where she turned up the heat under her stovetop percolator. "Time to put Hank down for an N-A-P. Say bye-bye, Hank." Vangie turned him toward Susanne and Patrick.

The little boy waved in a jerky motion, smiling so big he showed all of his very few teeth. Then a split second later he was bucking and thrashing, trying to force his mother to put him down. Vangie whisked him away without giving in. His ensuing screams were loud enough to spook the cattle in the back pastures.

Patrick heard Henry and another male voice exchanging greetings. While he and Susanne had been active participants and investors in the search for Ben, they'd never met the investigator in person. The Sibleys and Flints had pooled their resources. Private investigations didn't come cheap.

He hoped the man had made progress.

Patrick scooted closer to Susanne on the side bench. He leaned toward her, taking her limp hand. "I really am sorry I didn't make it home. Finding Leslie Anne and dealing with law enforcement really set me back."

"I understand. But you could have at least stopped in someone's house and borrowed a phone. Or dropped by on your way here. I would have understood if you left a message with Henry about running late or not being able to come. You could have even brought Perry and Kelsey with you."

"I didn't think of it. I was so focused on getting here close to on time." The smell of freshly brewed coffee started to hit Patrick's olfactory sensors. *Coffee. Oh, how I need coffee after this morning.*

"Well then, don't blame me if you're a grandpa in nine months."

"He's a good boy. She's probably not even there. He knows the rules."

She arched her brows. "Really? And you weren't a good boy when we were his age and first dating?"

Patrick frowned. "Point taken."

"I know you're busy, but so am I, and we need to be able to count on each other. I need to be able to count on *you*. And you do realize that it's always something, don't you? This time it's a good reason. Next time it will be a good reason. And the time after that. But you have to figure out how to work things out to meet your commitments. Like other people do. Like I do."

His mouth tightened. "I hear you."

"I'm not sure hearing me is the same thing as agreeing and planning to make changes. And I have news that I need to share with you. An offer I need us to evaluate together."

Ouch. Can't she see I'm doing the best I can? That I love her and the kids? And that compared to most of the couples we know, we do better? That I do better?

Henry re-entered the room with the investigator, just as Vangie rejoined them from putting Hank down for his nap. Just when things might have turned heated between him and Susanne. Patrick was thankful for the interruption. He sized up the person beside Hank. The slight man with a wispy goatee didn't match his mental image of a private detective. He'd expected someone taller. Thicker. More imposing.

"Patrick and Susanne, this is Forest Lamb. Forest, this is Dr. and Mrs. Flint, and this is my wife, Vangie," Henry said.

"Nice to meet you all." Forest walked over and shook both their hands before moving on to Henry's wife.

Good that he acknowledged us both. Susanne hated it when men ignored the women in a conversation. Forest had avoided a serious loss of brownie points with her.

Vangie said, "Have a seat on the bench across from the Flints, Mr. Lamb."

"Forest, please." He sat on the bench and set a briefcase on the table, which he opened. He pulled out a stack of folders.

"Forest it is then."

Henry returned to the head of the table.

Vangie grabbed a tray from the kitchen, whisked a towel off of it, and started chocolate chip cookies circulating, along with a stack of plates and napkins Patrick hadn't noticed. She returned with a tray holding the coffee pot, five cups, a bowl of sugar cubes, and a small cow-shaped cream pitcher. She set it in the middle of the table. "Help yourself, everyone." Then she took the other end, her elfin features now resolute and serious.

Patrick was first to grab a cup. He poured a cup, black, and passed it to his wife. She nodded at him. He made one for himself, also black. "Forest?"

"Light and sweet," the man said.

"While you're pouring, how about matching that order for Vangie and me?" Henry grinned. "And I can get you an apron if you'd like."

"Don't be a sexist, Henry," Vangie said, without rancor.

"I just think Patrick would look good in pink ruffles, honey."

She rolled her eyes at her husband. Patrick finished handing out cups and added four cookies to his plate, since he'd missed lunch. He bit into the first one and nearly groaned. Vangie baked like Betty Crocker. The woman could run a successful bakery if she wanted. He chased it with coffee and felt a jolt of energy, like his entire being was clamoring for the kick.

"I wish I had better news for you folks," Forest announced in a high, grating voice.

To Patrick's ear, it lacked gravitas. Or maybe Patrick was judging him by the content of his opening statement. It hadn't been what any of them wanted to hear. He reached for another cookie. Somehow, without realizing it, he'd already wolfed down two. His stomach rumbled.

Henry sipped his coffee, then tented his hands. The investigator hadn't taken any cookies. "We don't expect miracles. We just want our son back. We've paid you a lot of money to find him."

My thoughts exactly.

The Sibleys had taken Ben in as a teen out of juvenile detention and made him their own in only half a year. In that same time, Ben had stolen Trish's heart. Or maybe it was the other way around. All Patrick knew was that the young man with the troubled past had turned out to be a good soul who they all missed as if he'd been with them forever. Originally he and Susanne had disliked Ben, albeit with good reason. He had participated, however unwillingly, in his father and uncle's kidnapping of Trish and been sentenced to juvenile detention for it.

But we were wrong about him. A throbbing started behind his brow. Had it only been three months since Ben had vanished in the wake of a bogus arrest on his first night as a college student at the University of Wyoming in Laramie? It felt much longer. It also felt incredibly unfair that Ben had left town thinking he was in serious legal trouble when his name had been cleared only a few days later. Would he have stayed if he'd known?

"Yes. I can appreciate that, Mr. Sibley," Forest replied.

Henry held up his coffee. "Call me Henry. Let's all dispense with the formalities."

Forest nodded.

"Have you learned *anything* about Ben's whereabouts?" Patrick asked.

"A bit. Mostly where he's not." Forest pulled some papers from one of the folders.

"We already know where he's not. He's not here." Vangie's voice cracked, tugging at something in Patrick's chest. Her cookie and coffee sat untouched in front of her.

How much worse would he feel in her shoes? What if Trish or Perry left with no word? Just the thought brought chest-crushing grief. He swallowed down a lump in his throat.

"Let me clarify my statement." Forest cleared his throat and rattled the sheaf of papers in his hands. He studied them for a moment. "He definitely stopped for a few days in Cody, Wyoming, where he stayed with an old friend of his from high school. A fellow named Grady Hemphill. Mr. Hemphill helped Ben round up supplies and funds for what Ben told him was a move to Alaska, without specifying exactly where. He promised to write to Mr. Hemphill, but Hemphill claims not to have heard from him since he left."

"Grady Hemphill." Henry wrote the name down.

"It will be in my report, including Mr. Hemphill's phone number and address."

Henry kept making notes.

"While I was in Cody, I also interviewed some family members, old teachers, and other friends of Ben's. None of them had heard from Ben or admitted knowing where he would be going, but I've included their contact information as well." He paused for questions but continued when there were none. "From there, he didn't leave me much of a trail. I knew he said he was going to Alaska, but that's a long drive and a big state. I didn't know if he was telling his friend the truth. I didn't know if he had the money to get there. And I wasn't sure what obstacles might delay or derail him along the way, so I made no assumptions. First—and every few days thereafter—I called directory assistance in Alaska to see if he'd established a phone number. So far I've had no luck. Thanks to your retainer, I was able to map to Prince George, British Columbia and start making long distance calls to gas stations along the way."

"Why Prince George?" Susanne asked. Her cookie was on her plate, but she'd nibbled a corner off, and a crumb stuck to her lip.

A surge of tenderness coursed through Patrick. *Ah, this woman he loved. Even when they butted heads.* He reached under the table and took her hand again. This time, her return grip was firm.

"No matter what route Ben might take or where in Alaska he might be headed, the last town of any size in Canada before Alaska is Prince George. I imagined he would drive north through Montana and Alberta. It's the most direct route. But he's a young man. What if he decided to veer west and explore California, Oregon, or Washington? See a little of the Pacific Coast? He'd still drive north through Prince George from there. But, again, I don't know if he has or will ever make it that far. So, I got out the Yellow Pages at the library in Billings and worked the most obvious routes first, looking for anyone remembering his truck or a young man of his description."

"The possibilities seem endless." Vangie pressed a palm to her forehead, rubbing in circles.

"It can be a bit tedious, but that's my job. And it bore fruit, ma'am. I found people who believed they saw him in Bozeman and in Kalispell."

Susanne dropped Patrick's hand and leaned forward, knocking into her coffee cup and catching it before it tumped over. "You found him."

"I found traces of him. But only after he'd moved on. We were just lucky I was looking so soon after he passed through. I was only two days behind him in Kalispell. An old man there even said he let Ben park his truck behind his station overnight while he slept."

Everyone was leaning toward Forest now.

"In his truck? At that time of year? It's a wonder if he didn't freeze to death." Vangie looked stricken.

"Well, ma'am, I can't imagine he has the money for hotels, based on his financial situation. And Mr. Hemphill, his Cody friend, said Ben had barely scraped up the money for gas."

"That'd be what I would expect," Henry said.

Forest nodded. "The route narrowed down to one thanks to the Kalispell sighting. It seemed like he would be driving half a day between stops and camping at night, if his first day on the road was an indicator. But when I made calls along that path, I couldn't find anyone who saw him. Not in any of the little towns or in Banff or Jasper. Nothing. And it's a good thirteen-hour drive between Kalispell and Prince George. I didn't think he'd make that all in one stretch."

"He's a tough kid." Henry's voice was gruff.

"I'm sure he is. But I didn't find him in Prince George either."

Patrick used his forefinger to drum the table, stopping just short of pointing it at Forest. The surface of the coffee in his cup rippled. "Did you double back? Try to catch different workers at some of these potential stops?" He wanted the man to feel pressure.

But Forest shook his head. "I didn't have to. I caught up with him in Hazeltown."

"Where is that?" Vangie said. Her eyes were bright.

"Nearly to Alaska."

"How long ago?" Susanne asked.

"Well, there's the rub. I just got word of it last week. But it was over a month ago."

"No!" Vangie clapped her hand over her mouth.

"And from Hazelton, he had choices. He could have headed north toward Anchorage. Or west toward Ketchikan."

"Trish, my daughter, believes he'll try to get a job on a fishing boat," Patrick said.

Forest sighed and spread a map of Alaska out on the table, pushing and smoothing at the folds. He traced the coastline from the south in a curve to the northwest. "Lotta towns. Lotta islands. Lotta fishing boats."

Patrick's stomach dropped like a bag of rocks. He was glad he'd finished his coffee and cookies, because suddenly he had no appetite. He'd known Alaska had miles and miles of fishable coastline. But now, studying it on the map, there was far more than he'd expected. "If he's short on money, chances are he was heading for the nearest port."

Forest nodded. "Yes, but here's the deal, folks. Like you said earlier, Mr. Sibley, you've paid me a lot of money. By my figuring, we've burned through about half of it. Unless you have the appetite to double down, we need to agree on the most likely area for me to focus on."

"West," Henry said.

"Agree," Vangie echoed.

"Dr. and Mrs. Flint?" Forest said.

Susanne and Patrick said, "Agree," at the same time.

"All right. We're in agreement that we're closing off the northern route. I'll be looking for his trail west to Ketchikan. It's only reachable by ferry. And the other islands up that section of the coast, same thing. He's basically marooned there if he runs out of money and doesn't find work."

"Understood." Henry and Vangie nodded at each other.

"I'll get back to it, then." Forest stood and folded his map. He laid it in his briefcase, then returned papers to folders and folders to his case.

"What if you find someone who's seen him?" Susanne asked.

"Then it may be time to continue this hunt in person. But that could get expensive if you want me to do it. It might be that one of you wants to give it a go instead."

"We can cross that bridge when we come to it." Whether it was the caffeine, the sugar, or the decision on search strategy, Patrick felt a growing sense of optimism. Ben was a capable kid. He'd find work, a place to live, food to eat. And they'd find him.

They all stood, thanked Forest, and said their goodbyes. Susanne and Patrick walked outside together. Patrick grabbed an ice scraper and cleared Susanne's windshields and windows first. He was lost in thoughts about the investigation when he started on his truck. When he'd finished, he was surprised. Susanne had already started her engine and was revving it a bit.

Patrick opened her door and leaned close. "Why don't you drive ahead of me? That way if you have trouble, I'll be right behind you to help." He puckered and Susanne kissed him. Her lips were cold but soft.

"And if you have trouble?" she said.

"I've got my shovel. But it wouldn't hurt to keep an eye on me in your mirror."

She nodded.

Patrick shut her door and got in his cold truck. Ferdie uncurled his body, stood, and wagged his tail. "Good boy. Sorry I had to leave you out here. Looks like you had a good nap."

Ferdie curled back up. The dog didn't seem to notice how much the temperature had dropped in the car.

Patrick turned on the ignition, then the defrost on full blast. He stared into the snow falling on the glass, waiting for Susanne to lead off. The snow was covering it fast, but it was fluffy rather than icy. That was good. He turned on the windshield wipers, thinking about the possibility that he'd need to chip in more money for the investigation. He was doing fine as a small-town general practitioner, but he wasn't getting rich. He and Susanne were going to have to discuss a cap on spending before they squandered Trish and Perry's college funds. They had signed on to this primarily because of Trish, although they'd kept the investigation a secret from her so as not to get her hopes up. Who was to say, though, whether at this point Trish would even want them to keep looking? She and Ben might be done for good. The boy had left her with a fresh promise ring on her finger. There had been no word from him to their daughter since.

Susanne pulled away from her parking spot. Patrick made a U-turn, heading out the long drive to Little Piney Road in nearly half a foot of snow behind his wife. He hoped she'd drive carefully on the way home. This wasn't the time to end up in a ditch. Somehow, though, despite the fact that his mind wasn't completely clear, he'd arrived at a critical thought without consciously realizing it. They couldn't put a price on Ben's safety. And the boy deserved to know his name had been cleared and his future was untainted by the nonsense in Laramie.

It's what he'd want for his own kids. It's what they had to give to Ben.

CHAPTER EIGHT: KISS

Perry

PERRY SCOOTED CLOSER to Kelsey on the bench seat out on the deck. Everything was covered in snow, including Kelsey's red wool hat, which now looked white. It made everything seem quiet and like they were a million miles from anyone. He had never had so much fun that didn't involve sports. They'd made a snowman earlier by the creek. He'd fetched a carrot for its nose, a cowboy hat for its head, and a fishing pole. It looked pretty good, if he did say so himself. Then they'd taken turns sledding down the sloped yard for a while, which reminded him of when he'd built a snow ramp off the deck a few months before and ended up rocketing off the embankment and into the semi-frozen creek. After he'd put the sled in the garage, they'd taken a walk, visited the horses, and made snow angels in the front yard. When they'd run out of things to do and his parents still weren't home, they'd sat down here.

"Are you cold?" he asked her.

She wrapped her arms around herself. "A little."

Even though they'd been going steady for a month, Perry had never kissed her. He'd held her hand at a movie once. He'd imagined kissing her. Could now be the time? But he couldn't just go for it. This was a multi-step process. He screwed up his courage and slid his arm around her shoulders. "Is that okay?"

"Much better." She smiled at him, her face so close to his that he could see the different colors of brown in her eyes and smell the sweet, pink strawberry goo she'd plastered on her lips.

He tried to think of something else to say, but his mind had gone totally blank. His mouth was so dry he probably couldn't have gotten any words out anyway. He looked down at his feet. She was going to think he was a goober.

Then the weight of her head pressed into his shoulder. The snow from the fuzzy ball on her cap was cold and wet against his cheek, but he didn't mind. He wanted to cheer. Shout. Jump up and down. Afterwards. Right now, he wanted to hold completely still and enjoy this. *Wyatt ain't got nothing on me.*

"Do you mind my head being on your shoulder?" she asked.

He cleared his throat. "Not at all. I, um, I like it." He reached across his lap and put his gloved hand on her red mittened one.

She flipped hers over, so that they were sort of holding hands. Her leg was touching his. Hand, arm, leg, shoulder. She was touching him in four places at once. *Holy cow. Holy cow. Holy cow.* "Perry?"

"Yes?"

"Have you ever kissed a girl before?"

He closed his eyes. There was no cool way to answer this question. He tried to be funny. "Uh, do my mom and grandmother count?"

She lifted her head from his shoulder. Their eyes met. "Not really." She smiled, then it disappeared. "I haven't kissed a boy either."

"But what about John?" he blurted, then regretted it. Too late to bite his tongue.

She shook her head.

"Oh." *Way to bowl her over with your great conversational skills, dummy.*

She tilted her head. "It would be fine with me if I was your first kiss, and you were mine. What do you think?"

What did he think? He thought his head was going to explode. But he couldn't figure out what to do next. What to say. How to act.

"Perry?"

"Yeah. I mean, I think so. Yes. Good idea."

Her smile this time was almost a laugh. "So, are you going to kiss me, or not?"

"Sure." He cocked his head, leaned in, leaned further in, aimed for her lips . . . and bumped noses with her. *Geez, way to go, Casanova.*

She giggled. "This isn't as easy as I thought it would be."

He couldn't have her thinking that. *Just do this, Flint.* He dove in and planted his lips on hers. His first thought was how warm they were. His next thought was that he had no idea what to do now that he'd made contact with them. And his third thought was *who the heck is the big man in the backpack standing ten feet away from us?*

He jumped back from Kelsey. "Hey!" he shouted.

"What's the matter?" Kelsey sounded like he'd hurt her feelings.

The giant grunted.

"What are you doing here?" Perry didn't like the man in their yard. Especially not with Kelsey here, between them. He whispered in her ear. "Go in the house."

She turned and saw the man. Her eyes went wide. "Okay," she whispered back. She jumped up and ran inside.

"Lock the door," Perry shouted. He doubted she'd heard him. He put his arms across his chest, hoping his jacket made him look less like a pipsqueak. That and the two inches he'd grown this school year. "This is private property. You need to leave. Not wander around in people's backyards."

"Do not lust in your heart after her beauty or let her captivate you with her eyes," the man said, his voice monotone. He stared at Perry.

There was something weird about how the guy looked. *Yeah, and about what he just said, too. Really weird. Is that about me kissing Kelsey? Did he see us?* Perry's dad would say it was like the lights were on, but nobody was home. The man's eyes were vacant. It made Perry nervous, but he didn't want to show it.

"Did you hear me?" His voice cracked. "Go."

The man didn't nod or say anything else, but he turned and walked to the creek heading downstream toward town. That was good enough for Perry. He got up, trying to look nonchalant and tough, Clint Eastwood tough, on his way to the back door. Kelsey opened it and let him in.

"Is he gone?" she said.

"Yeah. He split."

She grabbed his jacket on either side of his chest and pulled him to her. "My hero."

Perry put his arms around her and kept his eyes trained on the backyard, his heart pounding hard against his chest, but not from a kiss this time.

CHAPTER NINE: CELEBRATE

Trish

Trish let the phone ring ten times, but no one picked up at her house. Where the heck was everybody? Well, she'd done her best to let her parents know where she was, celebrating passing the cheerleading clinic at an impromptu party at Jillian's house. Just the thought made her snort. Two things together that made no sense. Passing the clinic. And being at a party at Jillian's. *Jillian's.* Who would have thought it?

Trish hung up the phone, feeling nauseous. Cheerleading tryouts. In front of the whole high school. The judges had cut the clinic down to the final twelve. Only six girls would ultimately be selected by the student body. Marcy had made the cut, too, and they'd come to the party together. *Thank goodness.* Trish wasn't sure Jillian would have let her in if she hadn't shown up with Marcy, but she'd stood aside for them at the door. Not far enough to keep from bumping Trish with her shoulder though. *Totally on purpose.*

She rejoined Marcy at the top of two short stairs. The other girls were dancing to "Stayin' Alive" in the sunken living room. It felt weird to have the lights off and music playing loud in the middle of the day.

Marcy grabbed Trish's arm. "I love the Bee Gees." Her voice was a shrill squeal, and Trish winced.

"Dance to them then. I have to find the bathroom," Trish shouted.

"Are you sure?"

"Yes. I'll see you in a minute."

Marcy bounded down the steps and joined the two lines of girls. They were all doing the same dance moves at the same time, like a drill team. Trish figured it must be something from the movie her parents wouldn't let her go see because it was rated R. *Saturday Night Fever.* Not that she cared. She'd been pretty apathetic since Ben left. Honestly, nothing sounded fun anymore.

She wandered down a hallway until she found a restroom. Sitting on the closed toilet lid, she perused her surroundings. It was a half bath with needlepoint homilies on the wall and lace edged hand towels hanging from a rack. Trish didn't need to *go,* she just needed a moment to catch her breath. She'd gone from a fall spent running with the cross-country team and happily being part of the Ben-and-Trish duo, to a winter of isolation and heartbreak, to whatever-this-was that was happening to her now. Passing cheerleader clinic. Attending a party at Jillian's house. She smoothed the sweatpants she'd put on over her shorts, tugged at the neck of the sweatshirt layered over her t-shirt. She pushed stray wisps of hair off her face with both hands, stretching the skin on her cheekbones and around her eyes. She didn't feel like herself. Nothing about her did. This was what most girls dreamed of. Girls like Marcy.

Why didn't it make Trish happy?

Ben's face flashed in her mind. *Yeah, that's why.* Because she'd trade this in a second to have Ben back in her life.

"Ben," she whispered. What was he doing now? Where was he? Was he thinking of her, too? Her mood plummeted as her mind started down the familiar rabbit hole. She'd prayed so many times for him to call. To write. To come back. She'd given up praying that he'd return to her. She'd be happy just knowing where he was and that he was all right. Sometimes she prayed that her parents would at least act like they cared about what happened to Ben. But what had she gotten for those prayers? Nothing. God had answered by not answering.

"No," she said, her voice startling her, loud in the silent bathroom. She was so tired of feeling sad. "No. This stops now."

She stood up and looked at herself in the mirror. Big blue eyes stared back at her. A center part, her blonde hair pulled back into a high ponytail. A pimple by her left eyebrow. Traces of lip gloss on one of her front teeth. She wiped it away, disgusted with herself. Why would Ben be thinking about her? He'd left. He hadn't called or written to her. He had a new life. Maybe even a new girlfriend. Someone older who didn't have zits and knew how to wear makeup.

It was time for Trish to get a life, even if it wasn't a better one. That could start with dancing to the Bee Gees.

Why not? It had to start somewhere.

She exited the bathroom just as the front doorbell rang. Trish had a view straight out to the entrance. Jillian must have been expecting someone because she was standing with her hand on the doorknob. She threw open the door.

"Hi, boys," she said, stepping back to let in a stream of guys. More guys than there were girls, in fact. Then her voice changed to something infinitely more coquettish. And squealy. "Dabbo. You came!"

A much older looking boy—man, really—shot Jillian a smile. He had more muscles than any of the guys on the football team and wore a mustache and felt cowboy hat. He reminded Trish of something. An ad. She frowned. Marlboro cigarettes. He was that kind of cowboy. He walked straight up to Jillian, planted his lips on hers and swooped her over backwards.

She giggled.

His voice was gravelly. "Don't make me hang around a bunch of high school kids for nothing, beautiful."

She batted her eyes at him.

After Trish quit staring, she realized what a mess she was in. She wasn't allowed to go to boy-girl parties without any adults home, and Jillian's parents had gone to Chico Hot Springs for the weekend, in Montana. She whirled, ready to grab Marcy and get the heck out of Dodge. She didn't want to be grounded for the next month, just when she had finally decided she was ready to live again.

"Hey, Trish," a deep voice said. "Congratulations."

Wary, she turned back. It was Wyatt, a curly-haired boy from her class. Was it her imagination, or had he grown a foot and put on fifty pounds since she'd last seen him? Or last noticed him, at least. He looked more like a man than a boy, with dark hairs on his upper lip and teeth free of the braces he'd worn for years.

"Hey. Thanks, I guess," she said.

Someone had turned the music down, and ten more girls had crowded around the boys. Trish heard a pop top, then smelled something spicy and almost grassy. She recognized that smell from somewhere. Behind Wyatt, she saw a boy passing out cans of beer and another hoisting a huge bottle of some kind of alcohol. Beer. She'd smelled beer, like her dad sometimes drank at dinner. *Uh uh.* This would result in triple death penalty grounding.

"Marcy," she shouted. The music swallowed her voice. She dashed into the throng of girls and boys and pulled on her friends' arm. "Marcy. I have to go home."

"What?" Marcy said, still grooving even though she was no longer in the makeshift dance pit. It was another Bee Gees song. *Night Fever.*

"No parents. Boys. Alcohol. I can't be here."

Marcy rolled her eyes. "Oh, come on, Trish. We just got here. Don't be so, you know, *square*."

"I mean it."

Marcy whispered in her ear, her voice sharp. "This is our chance. All the cute guys are here. The popular guys."

Trish shook her head violently.

A big hand landed on her shoulder. Trish jumped, wheeling. It was Wyatt.

"Are you okay?" he said, leaning down so she could hear him.

"I, uh, I just need to convince Marcy to give me a ride home."

"You're leaving already?"

"Yeah. I've, uh, I've got to be somewhere."

"I can give you a ride."

She took a step back, bumping into one of the other girls. Whoever it was gave her a little shove, and she was catapulted in the other direction. Wyatt caught her and kept her from falling on her face. Trish wrestled out of his grasp.

"Thanks," she said.

"Great. I'll just run get my truck."

"No, I meant thanks for catching me."

But it was too late. Wyatt was jogging to the front door, keys in hand.

CHAPTER TEN: VISIT

Patrick

Patrick drove along Clear Creek, pulled into his driveway, and parked in front of their two-story home beside Susanne's Suburban, Trish's truck, and another pickup he didn't recognize. It always made him smile that they'd left a house in a warm weather state that had a two-car garage only to have none at either place they'd lived in Wyoming. He would have thought every house here would have a place to protect vehicles and keep them warm, but he saw very few of them. Nights like this when the weather was especially bad did make him remember them fondly from Texas.

But even the lack of a garage couldn't dim his love for this place. The Flints had bought it when Susanne relinquished her objections to Wyoming and committed to a life in Buffalo for their family. She called it her dream home, and he had to agree. It was spacious and beautiful, with a view of the mountains, a creek in the backyard, and facilities for their horses. Of course, she'd started redecorating as soon as they'd moved in, but he could live with that. *Happy wife, happy life.*

And she'd announced her plan to finish her college degree not too long after, even though it went against the bargain they'd struck when Trish was born. Susanne had wanted to stay home to raise their kids. He'd liked the idea and agreed to be the breadwinner. She'd dropped out of college and the rest was history. For her to pull a changeup was surprising. And for it to be this early? He thought she'd finish her degree, if at all, after Perry graduated from high school and pursue a career later.

Still, he loved her and believed in her. He wanted to get behind her dreams. He'd promised he would. It was just that execution was so much harder than he'd expected. Even as teenagers, the kids required a significant amount of time and oversight. His work as a physician was demanding, and he had dreams outside the four walls of a hospital, too.

They'd have to talk, as much as he dreaded it. She said she had an offer for them to discuss. She was unhappy with how things were going. He loved her. He owed it to her to figure this out.

At the entry, Susanne was just shutting the front door behind her, having beaten him home by half a minute or so. Ferdinand whined, then barked, then pawed at the window on the passenger side of the truck. Patrick followed the dog's line of sight. Through the fast-falling spring snow he saw something moving on the side of the house.

"You've got eyes like an eagle, dog." He squinted. The form took shape. "Son of a buzzard bait." It was a man, walking toward the road across their yard. At first he thought the man was NBA-tall, then realized he was wearing a backpack on a tall frame. Like the one covered in snow in Patrick's truck bed. *What is someone doing backpacking in this weather? In town? In my yard?*

"Stay," he said to Ferdie. He threw the door open, closing it quickly behind him in the face of his unhappy friend.

He shouted, "Hello, there, Backpacker."

The man didn't turn toward him. Didn't stop. But he didn't speed up either. Maybe he hadn't heard him.

Patrick jogged in his direction, glad for the weight of the .357 Magnum still on his hip. "You there. Guy in my yard. Stop."

This time the backpacker broke into a run. He scrambled across the road. With the snowfall, Patrick lost sight of him as he entered the woods. He hadn't gotten a good look at him. Not at hair color, face, or even skin color.

The front door to the house flew open.

Susanne peered out. "Patrick?"

Patrick's pursuit had taken him nearly out to the road. "Over here." He trotted back to his truck. The snow was deep and heavy. His breath came out in frosty puffs and back through his nose like frozen sandpaper.

"What's going on?"

He decided not to worry her. "I thought I saw something and went to check it out. It was nothing." He opened the door, letting Ferdinand out and grabbing his keys.

The dog took off, baying, in the direction the man had gone. Even in the accumulated snow, Ferdinand was fast. Not as fast as a greyhound, but a close relation. Patrick should have anticipated it and grabbed his collar. He hollered at the animal, but it didn't do any good. He'd be back after making sure his home grounds were clear of intruders. Sighing, he reached for the white lump in the truck bed that was his backpack. He hefted it, showering his face with more snow. He headed for the house, head down, and was surprised when he reached the porch to find Susanne still standing in the doorway. Without a coat.

"What's the matter?"

She pulled the door partially closed. "You want a list? It starts with 'I told you so'."

"What is it?"

"Our kids need us more than ever at this age. They're old enough to make independent decisions, but not old enough to make good ones."

"Susanne, tell me what's going on. Are Trish and Perry okay?"

"See for yourself." She threw the door open and gestured him ahead of her.

CHAPTER ELEVEN: REVEAL

Susanne

Perry, Kelsey, Trish, and the boy Susanne didn't know were sitting at the dining table, as they'd been ordered to do before she'd gone to see what the holdup was with Patrick and Ferdinand. There was a bowl of buttery popcorn in front of them and mugs of sweet-smelling hot apple cider. Apparently, they'd been having quite the party. Susanne seethed. Partly because the kids had broken the rule not to have opposite sex friends over without their parents at home and partly because this had happened on Patrick's watch. He hadn't even checked in on the kids all day.

She had to be able to count on his word. *Have to. Especially if I'm going to take this job. Am I going to take this job, though?*

Patrick stopped at the head of the table facing the young people, arms crossed, lips moving and no sound coming out. *Good. At least he realizes the gravity of the situation.* Ferdinand—who had returned five minutes after chasing off the backpacker, telling no tales—ran up to Kelsey and the boy, checking out the newcomers.

Susanne nudged him. "There'd better be a life-or-death reason for this," she said to the kids.

Trish crossed her arms, a mirror of her father. "I haven't done anything wrong. You should be congratulating me, not jumping my case."

"Excuse me?" Susanne said.

Ferdinand slunk to the hall then to the laundry room and plopped down on his bed. The dog didn't like conflict.

"Wyatt just gave me a ride home from a party and walked me in to make sure I was okay when we saw your cars weren't here. A party I left because the parents weren't home, boys came, and they brought alcohol."

"What?" Susanne shouted. "Why were you even at a party in the middle of a Saturday? Without permission?"

Trish's voice rose to match her mother's. "I called. No one answered. Jillian invited all the girls who passed the cheerleading clinic over to her house. I didn't even want to go to the dumb party. Marcy was my ride. I had to go because she did." She paused, then plowed onward. "Thanks for the congratulations, by the way."

Susanne and Patrick exchanged a glance. Susanne winced. It was what they'd been afraid of. That Trish would be cut and Marcy wouldn't, forcing their daughter into bad situations to keep up with her friend. Trish didn't have any business trying out for the squad. As awkward as she was. What had she been thinking? What had *they* been thinking?

The boy cleared his throat. "I'm, uh, I'm Wyatt. Trish is telling the truth. She couldn't get Marcy to bring her home, so I offered. I heard she was, like, really awesome at the clinic."

"I'm glad you did good, honey," Patrick said, his voice soothing, like he was talking to a frantic parent in the hospital.

"That's all you can do, is your best," Susanne added.

"What is wrong with you guys? I made the cut!" Trish said.

"Oh!" Susanne stared at her daughter. *Maybe she's confused?*

Trish rolled her eyes. "Whatever."

"I think what your mother meant to say was congratulations." Patrick grinned. "We're proud of you. But you should never have brought a boy in the house without us here."

"Oh, my! Wow!" Susanne said.

Trish shook her head.

"I was on my way out, Dr. and Mrs. Flint. I didn't even take off my coat." The young man was zipped into a puffy winter jacket. "You can check my engine. It's probably still warm."

Patrick shook his head. "That's fine."

"I should get going. Unless you want me to stay, Trish?" He turned puppy dog eyes on their daughter.

"No, I'm good. Thanks for the ride."

His face fell. "All right. See you at school. You, too, Perry. Kelsey. Nice to meet you, Dr. and Mrs. Flint."

"Let me walk you out," Patrick said.

It's not like he's a small child or a girl.

"That's okay, Dr. Flint."

"Well, uh, be careful."

"I will." He stood, offering his hand to Patrick. They shook, and the boy marched to the front door and out into the storm.

Patrick walked to the side light window and watched him.

Susanne raised her eyebrows at Trish.

Her daughter shook her head. "He gave me a ride. That's all." She rubbed her arms. "It's freezing in here. Did someone turn off the heat?"

Susanne had been so angry that she hadn't noticed until Trish mentioned it, but once she did, she realized it was as cold as a meat locker. She checked the thermostat. It was set to sixty-six, as per normal in the winter. But the temperature reading was sixty-one. "Patrick, our heater isn't running."

Her husband turned, nodding. "I'll check it in a minute. First, it's time we heard from Perry. You've been awfully quiet, son. I think you've got some explaining to do."

Perry jumped to his feet. "I'm sorry, Dad. Kelsey's mom dropped her off—"

"We didn't know you weren't here, Dr. Flint." Kelsey batted big brown eyes.

Susanne frowned. *Is that on purpose?*

Perry nodded. "I told her we had to wait outside. And we did. For the whole morning."

"Then this giant, scary man snuck up on us. Perry made me go in the house, then he yelled at the guy until he left." Kelsey beamed at Perry.

"After that, we were scared to go outside. Kelsey called home to see if her mom could pick her up, but no one was answering."

Susanne narrowed her eyes. The convenience of an intruder just when they wanted a reason to come inside? Yeah, right.

"How long ago was he here?" Patrick asked, then turned back to watch out the window.

He's buying that story?

"Maybe like an hour ago?" Perry said. "I dunno."

The look on her husband's face when he turned back to face them made Susanne's throat tighten. "Patrick?"

"There was a big guy wearing a backpack in our yard when I got home."

"What?" Perry and Susanne said the word at the same time.

"There really was an intruder?" Susanne said.

"You didn't believe us?" Perry's face reddened. "Nice, Mom."

"Perry, watch it." Patrick's voice was hard. Then he turned to his wife. "I can't be positive it was the same guy, but it's a pretty big coincidence to have two big guys in our yard in one day. Especially in this weather."

At our house. And we just let Wyatt go out there. No wonder Patrick's keeping an eye on him. "Do you have any idea who it is or why he would come here?"

He gave her a significant look. "No. But I don't like it."

She felt queasy. The doorbell rang again.

"That's probably my mom." Kelsey got up and headed toward the door.

Susanne pictured the man lurking outside. "I think Patrick should be the one who answers it."

Patrick nodded. He'd already been looking out the window. "It's Wyatt."

The phone rang. Susanne picked it up, one ear listening through the phone, the other trained on her husband and the teenage boy at the door.

"Hello?" she said.

"Sorry, Dr. Flint, but I have two flat tires," Wyatt was saying.

In her ear, a woman said, "This is Marilynn Jones. Kelsey's mother."

"Hello, Marilynn. This is Susanne Flint. I'm Perry's mother. I think we've met at football games or some other school events." She watched as Patrick stepped outside with Wyatt.

Trish walked to the entryway, then leaned against the wall with her head back and eyes closed.

Perry and Kelsey ignored the Wyatt issue. They were focused like lasers on Susanne's phone call.

Marilynn said, "I was on my way to pick up Kelsey, but I've had a fender bender. Just slid right down the hill on Main. It was icier than it looked."

"I'm so sorry to hear that. I hope you're okay."

"I'm uninjured, but I can't say the same for my car. I'm waiting on a tow truck. I'd ask my husband to pick Kelsey up, but he works for the railroad, and he's out of town this weekend. I'm afraid it may be several hours before I can get her, after I get the car to a mechanic, and rent something to drive until my car is fixed."

Susanne decided it would be cruel to pile on to the woman's bad afternoon by telling her that Perry and Kelsey had been alone at their house all day. "That's no problem. Kelsey is welcome to eat dinner with us."

"Thank you so much. I'll be there as soon as I can."

"See you then."

Susanne hung up. She smiled at Kelsey. "You're eating dinner with us. Your mom is fine, but she banged up her car."

Kelsey squealed. "Yay!"

Not much empathy for her mom.

Perry grinned.

"But can I borrow a sweater? I don't want to wear my big coat in the house."

From the entryway, Trish spoke without moving or opening her eyes. "Give her my gray Disneyland sweatshirt. It's in my top drawer."

Perry sprinted up the stairs. Susanne's son was a boy with a new lease on life.

She joined her daughter. "Have you seen what the problem is?"

Trish groaned. "The problem is that I'm not interested in Wyatt, and I want him to leave."

"No, I mean outside."

"I haven't looked."

Susanne tried the sidelight window, but it had frosted over. She scraped the frost away with her fingers. Pressing her cheek against the glass, she was able to see through with one eye. She gasped, stepping back, and pressing her fist to her lips. Patrick and Wyatt were nowhere to be seen, but a strange man was staring in the window at her.

CHAPTER TWELVE: SUSPECT

Patrick

PATRICK AND WYATT trudged back from the barn. He felt a tickle on his neck. Snow accumulated on his head and slid down the collar of his coat. *I should have worn a hat and scarf.* He brushed some off with his hand. The trip to the barn had been a bust. Patrick's last truck had been the same make and model as Wyatt's, and he'd thought he'd kept some of the old tires, but no such luck. What was more troubling than the lack of spares was the condition of Wyatt's driver's side front and back tires. They weren't just flat, per se. They'd been slashed. It was time to call the sheriff's department.

"My parents are going to be, like, pissed. Uh, I mean mad." Wyatt said. "How could this even happen?"

"Maybe you drove against something sharp. The point of a stick. A jutting piece of concrete." But Patrick suspected it had been done with a knife. "Unless you made someone really mad?"

"You mean enough that they'd do this on purpose?" Wyatt stopped short, slipping.

Patrick caught him by one arm and kept him upright. "Yes. That's exactly what I mean."

Wyatt shook his head and started walking toward the house again. "I don't think so. Wait—does Trish have a boyfriend that would be upset about me driving her home?"

Would Ben be upset? Patrick was beginning to doubt the depth of the boy's feelings for his daughter. What kind of man would walk away and break Trish's heart like Ben had done? But Ben was in Alaska. Whether he would be upset or not wasn't germane to Wyatt's tires. "I don't think so."

"I guess I'll have to ask Trish to give me a ride home."

They neared the front steps. Before Patrick answered, he noticed a man at their front door. He frowned. Not a man wearing a backpack, which was good, but who would be out in this storm? It had snowed a foot so far today. Another inch just since he and Susanne had returned from Story. *Fat chance I'm letting my daughter drive in these conditions.*

"Hold up," he whispered to Wyatt, grabbing his arm again. The two of them froze, side by side. Patrick put his hand on his holstered gun. Louder, he called, "May I help you?"

The man turned. It was Wilfred Mitchell, still wearing the eye patch, bowler, and cowboy boots, but thankfully now clad in what looked like oil skin coveralls under a similar, heavy jacket. Even in that get-up, he looked ready to blow away in a medium-stiff wind. "Dr. Flint. I think I know who killed my Leslie Anne."

Patrick released Wyatt. Why would Wilfred come here and not the sheriff's office? "All right, Mr. Mitchell. Let's get inside out of the cold and talk."

Wilfred nodded, silent now. Patrick opened the door with Wyatt behind him. He motioned Wilfred in first. The three men walked in single file. A dark shadow lunged for them, tail wagging. *Ferdinand.*

Susanne screamed. "I have a gun. And my husband is right

behind you." Behind her, on the wall leading from the entry past the great room and into the dining area, their new painting of a bald eagle provided the perfect backdrop for her. The bird's feet were extended into the water of a lake, talons snatching up a fish. Not to be mistaken for anything but fierce despite its beautiful feathers. Wild, confident, and free.

Wilfred threw his hands in the air. "Don't shoot."

Ferdinand sniffed the man's shoes and pants legs.

Patrick closed the door and rushed past him, Wyatt shadowing him. Susanne was standing in front of the couch holding a fireplace poker over her head, pushing Trish behind her with the other arm. Perry and Kelsey hunkered by the fireplace. Susanne's eyes were ferocious. *Mama tiger. And a Grade A faker. There was no gun in sight.* "Susanne, it's okay. This is Wilfred Mitchell. I met him this morning at his ranch south of town. His girlfriend passed away today."

Her mouth fell open. Her eyes drilled into the man, then back to Patrick. The poker fell to her side. "Mr. Mitchell. When I saw you looking in our house, I misunderstood. My apologies. And my condolences on your loss. May I get you something to drink? A hot chocolate or some coffee?"

Patrick thought she'd never looked more beautiful, and it was hard to keep from grinning, despite the circumstances and their tense interactions earlier. From warrior to hostess in two point five seconds.

"I'm all right, ma'am. I won't be sticking around long."

"Knock, knock?" Ronnie's voice said.

Ferdinand rushed to greet his old friend. Ronnie petted him like they'd been separated for months instead of hours.

Patrick hadn't heard her drive up. Or the door re-open. He was just glad she was here. "Come on in, Ronnie. Susanne, I wouldn't mind some coffee. And it looks like we have a houseful."

"Hi, Ronnie. And no problem. I need some, too." Susanne headed for the kitchen.

"Deputy Harcourt." Wilfred sounded rattled. "What are you doing here?'

"I was on my way home and wanted a few words with the doc. Why are you here?"

Wilfred shook his head, slowly at first, then almost violently. "I ain't no more. I'm leaving." He all but sprinted out the door.

Patrick frowned. He almost went after the man but decided not to. Wilfred was an odd bird. Patrick didn't like having a man who acted that erratically in his home with his wife and kids. If Wilfred wanted to talk, he could use the telephone.

"Did that man just leave?" Susanne called from the kitchen.

Patrick heard running water. "He did."

"Could he be the one you guys saw by the house earlier?"

"Nope," Perry said.

"Wasn't him." Patrick rubbed his forehead.

"Wait—have you guys had a problem?" Ronnie asked.

"We had someone hanging around earlier, but he's gone. I'll call you if he shows up again."

"All right." Ronnie unzipped her coat and took off her hat and gloves. "Wilfred didn't seem to like me questioning him this morning. And the rest of the day didn't go much better between us."

"He said he thinks he knows who killed Leslie Anne."

"Nice of him to tell me." She zipped her coat back up. "I'll make this quick, mainly because your house is freezing. But also, because now I have to go after Wilfred."

Shoot. I need to check on the heating system. Maybe call for a repair. But at Saturday "after hours" prices? "Perry, make a fire, please."

"Yes, sir." Perry and Kelsey started building a kindling teepee. Ferdinand supervised.

He heard Trish mutter to Wyatt, "Did you air up your tires?"

Wyatt answered in the same volume. "They're slashed. I'm going to need a ride."

Patrick kept his attention on Ronnie. "What've you got for me?"

She rubbed her hands together briskly, then blew on them. "While I was out at Wilfred's place today, he had visitors. Leslie Anne's father and brother."

Patrick hadn't tried to eavesdrop on her interview of Wilfred, but he did have excellent hearing. "It sounded earlier like Wilfred isn't fond of them."

"That's an understatement. I had the joy of witnessing their first meeting."

"Ugly?"

"Very. They blamed Wilfred for Leslie Anne's death. Although what they seemed most rattled by was that Wilfred hadn't paid them a settlement for his 'use' of her." Ronnie made air quotes on either side of her head. "They said the last man to court her without a settlement didn't get to keep her and he was no different. Wilfred accused them of treating her like chattel and killing her."

"Whoa. So, he blamed the Comptons as well as Mr. Dabbo Kern."

"Whoa and woe. Both kinds. Yeah, he's spreading the accusations around. We kept the three of them from adding to the body count. Just barely. Oh, and we—Radish, rather—found a blood-covered wallet out near the crime scene. It belonged to the neighbor. A guy named Tristan Babcock."

"Did you talk to him?"

"Couldn't find him. I surely want to. He could have dropped it because he killed her or was a witness. Or it could have been stolen. Who knows. But none of that's why I came by." She frowned. "Do you have windows open or the air conditioner on? Seriously. It's like a deep freeze in here."

Patrick shrugged, then, with a wry voice, he said, "Go on." The scent of coffee brewing started permeating the room. The anticipation was almost as powerful as the caffeine.

"I'm wondering what you thought about the cause of death."

"I'm not a forensic pathologist. I recommend you get one to take a look at her."

"I know. We will. Just a gut reaction to what you saw would help me, though."

"The obvious injuries are pretty persuasive, don't you think?"

"Humor me."

"Okay. Let's talk this through." Patrick nodded slowly, letting his thoughts percolate before he spoke again. "I can't rule out a heart attack, stroke, or some underlying condition. But in general, she looked to be a healthy, well-nourished woman. I saw no evidence of an allergic reaction, but I can't rule out poisoning. There were no marks on her neck or petechiae in her facial skin or eyes, so she didn't appear to have been strangled, suffocated, or choked. Her neck wasn't at the kind of unnatural angle that would have suggested it had been snapped. There were no cuts. No gunshot wounds. The bleeding, the short time frame, and the nature of the injuries are consistent with sudden traumatic injury from blows to the face and head. From my observation, the most vicious blows were to her face, especially across her orbital bones. The ones around her eyes. I didn't see evidence of cranial fracture or what you might call a head stove in. My guess is that one or more of the blows to her face caused a traumatic brain bleed. And that whatever was used was extremely hard. Probably metal. Based on the indentations, I'd also guess it did not have a smooth surface."

"Oh my gosh," Kelsey whispered, but loud enough that Patrick heard her.

Patrick looked over to the seating area. Fire lit, Perry and Kelsey had moved to the couch, where they were too close together and staring at him. Trish was sitting cross legged in an armchair looking disinterested. Wyatt was leaning in to catch every word from his seat on the hearth. Ferdinand was curled up in front of the fire, enjoying the warmth.

He winced. "Sorry, kids. Ronnie, let's move into the dining area." The two of them moved to the far side of the slab table, closest to the window and farthest from the young people.

Susanne came from the kitchen seeming flustered, bearing two cups of coffee, which she handed to Patrick and Ronnie on her way to the great room. "Everyone under the age of eighteen, uh, go play outside until Ronnie leaves."

"Um, strange dude out there and snowstorm, Mom?" Perry said.

"It's not like it's any colder out there than in here," Trish said. "But, yeah, are you serious, Mom??"

"Fine. Find a program to watch on TV. Quickly. And turn it up loud." Susanne stood, tapping her toe, but also cocking her ear toward the dining area.

Perry and Kelsey didn't look thrilled to tear any of their attention away from Patrick and Ronnie. Sighing, Perry turned on the TV and began flipping channels. Susanne returned to the kitchen. Perry stopped on a show playing orchestral music, but he dialed the volume down to barely audible and Patrick couldn't hear it anymore.

"Was that the kind of gut reaction you were looking for?" Patrick asked Ronnie, his voice low.

Ronnie matched his. "Exactly what I needed. Thanks."

"I'll bite. Why do you need it?"

"Just a theory I'm working on."

"Which is?"

"That whoever struck Leslie Anne wanted to blind her. To stop her from looking at something or seeing something, or maybe even because she saw something. Possibly they didn't even mean to kill her."

Patrick felt his lips move as he thought her words through. Then he spoke aloud. "Or maybe it means that she was facing her attacker and fighting back."

"Maybe. But even then, wouldn't the blows be to the top or side of the head? It's hard to hit someone in the front of the face from head on unless you're pushing."

She may be right. Patrick didn't like visualizing it. "If you're right, does that tell you who the killer is?"

She sighed. "Not yet. But I have a feeling it will lead me in the right direction."

CHAPTER THIRTEEN: RETURN

Buffalo, Wyoming
Saturday, March 18, 1978, 4:00 p.m.

Ben

BEN JONES PARKED his truck on the road outside the Flint house, electing not to pull into the crowded driveway. The way the snow was coming down, there was no way he could turn around or back out. *Figures that I drive all the way from Alaska on good roads and get to Buffalo in time for the storm of the century.* This drive had been easier than the one up to Alaska in January, though. Then, he'd slept in his truck, freezing his hind end off, covering himself in all of the clothing he'd brought. No sleeping bag. No blankets. He'd barely had enough money for gas, much less a hotel, or even food. He'd pushed the mileage every day to minimize the number of meals he had to eat on the road, or skip, before he got to Alaska and found work. The whole way, he prayed—out loud a lot of the time—that he didn't flat a tire or blow a rod in his engine or wreck his truck, because if he did, he'd be stuck wherever it happened. Stuck and unable to run from the law if it showed up at his door, looking to hold him accountable for a crime he'd been framed for back in Laramie. What had been an old, high-mileage truck before now boasted nearly 4000 more miles. He'd learned to take care of the little problems himself. It was running better than when he'd arrived in Alaska.

For the drive south, he'd had a wallet full of cash from three months crewing in frigid conditions on a fishing boat, earning a premium because he worked no matter the weather. Captain Harley loved his strength and attitude. Ben loved being part of a fraternity of toughness and making his own way. He'd grown to appreciate the sting of the icy water on his face, reminding him he was alive and free. He never ceased to marvel at the bounty of the sea, even in the dead of winter, for those hardy enough to go after it. The mountains, the town, the ocean, the islands—they were rugged and beautiful. Life in Alaska was good. Really good. Cap had set him up in a boarding house. It wasn't fancy, but it had everything he needed, and the people left him alone, mostly. He wasn't Ben Jones, co-conspirator and nephew of convicted murderer Billy Kemecke and son of kidnapper Chester Jones. Ben Jones from juvie. Ben Jones who was dating the girl he'd helped kidnap. He was just Ben, a guy you could rely on aboard the *Fishy Business*.

He kept every cent he didn't spend on room, board, and essentials. Because of the money, the trip back to Buffalo was easier. He had good food in his belly. Slept in hotel rooms with real beds and heaters. Could pay for gas outright, instead of bartering for odd jobs for willing station owners. But still, he'd driven long hours and slept short ones. Not because he had to, but because he wanted to. He was coming home to make things right.

He looked toward the lights shining from the house, only one hundred feet or so away. Trish's truck was outside. Was she home? In this storm, he imagined all the Flints would be around the fire. It wasn't time for dinner yet, but maybe there'd be chili or stew on the stove. It would be warm, it would smell good, and, best of all, Trish would be there.

He swallowed hard. More than anything in the world, he wanted to knock on the door. He wanted to pull Trish into his arms and beg her forgiveness. All of their forgiveness. Ask for their help with his legal problems in Laramie, which he had probably made a lot worse by leaving. Tell Trish about his Alaskan adventures. Fold back into her life and draw her into his.

Convince her to make things work long distance and follow him to Alaska when she finished college. Because Ben didn't want to come back. He wanted Trish. He loved Trish. But he wanted to make a life with her up north. Had to make a life there.

Rotating his neck and popping his knuckles, he summoned his courage. He had come this far. It was time to be a man and follow through, no matter how hard it was to get the words out or whether Trish and her family kicked him out on his rear. He zipped his jacket, jammed a wool cap over his ears, slid his fingers into his gloves, turned off the engine. In the stillness, his ears rang. His nose tingled from a mixture of the cold and the smell of exhaust blowing back in the strong wind from his tailpipe. He forced all the air from his lungs in a few powerful exhales, opened the door, and got out.

He could do this. He would do this. He *had to* do this.

CHAPTER FOURTEEN: SPIRAL

Buffalo, Wyoming
Saturday, March 18, 1978, 4:30 p.m.

Trish

Ever since Ronnie had been gone, Trish's dad had been working on the heating. After an hour or so, it didn't seem like he'd made any progress. The house was getting colder. Trish fiddled with the fringe on a pillow. She had wanted to ask her dad to take Wyatt home. With him obsessed with the heaters, that wasn't going to happen. She was stuck with Wyatt here. *Why couldn't he take a hint? "Not interested" was radiating from every cell in her body, practically flashing like a neon sign on her forehead.* He was a nice enough guy. He was popular. Athletic. Not completely dumb like most of the jocks. Fairly good looking. Marcy would probably smack her upside the head later when she told her friend about this. But Trish felt nothing. Not even flattered he was interested. Just numb.

"The temperature in here is down to fifty degrees," her dad said, emerging from the basement—an unfinished, cold space and home to the utility closet where the furnace, air conditioner, and water heater were—and stomping his way to the thermostat. He glowered like he wanted to pound it with a hammer. Ferdinand's toenails clicked on the stairs, and he appeared beside her dad. "Even with the fire." His lips kept moving, but no sound came out.

"I don't think the heater is working at all," her mom said. *Duh.* "The stove is working, though. Beef stew will be ready in forty-five minutes."

Her dad shook his head. "I forgot to tell Ronnie about Wyatt's tires being slashed."

Wyatt's tires were slashed, and no one had told the cops?

Her mom's response was pretty much identical to Trish's. "His tires were *slashed*? Let's call her back out here."

He nodded.

"And do you want me to call a repair place? Not that I don't think you'll be able to fix it. But just in case."

Her dad had already disappeared down the stairs, Ferdinand right behind him. "Fine." His voice was muffled.

"I'll make those calls just as soon as I get dinner under control. Don't burn the stew, Susanne," her dad said.

A few seconds later, Trish heard loud clangs and clanks. She winced. *Dad is gonna kill that thing.*

Wyatt grinned. "The stew smells great, Mrs. Flint. Yum." He leaned closer to Trish.

She leaned away. The stew did smell good. Chunks of beef, carrots, onions, potatoes, celery, and a rich, thickened broth. Trish's mouth watered. Her mom wasn't a great cook. She wasn't even a very good one. She liked to tell people that she kept her family alive and the rest was gravy. But she made three things well. Fried chicken, beef stew, and chili. She *thought* she made chicken spaghetti well, too, but that was impossible as chicken spaghetti was awful no matter who made it. Trish didn't want Wyatt staying for dinner if she could prevent it.

"Your parents are probably worried about you. How are you going to get home?" she asked him.

"Maybe you can take me."

"I can't drive in this weather." She had, once before. When she'd chased after Ben. She'd ended up stuck in a drift. Ronnie had given her a ride, and her dad had dug her truck out. "My mom is cooking dinner and my dad is working on the heat. Why don't you call your parents? Or a friend?"

His grin faded. "I mean, it's, like, just as bad for anyone else trying to drive as it is for you. So, I guess that means I'd better not ask." *Great.* She hadn't thought of that. "Maybe the snow will stop soon."

Perry and Kelsey were on the couch. He leaned into her and whispered in her ear. The girl giggled. If their parents had been in the room, they'd have told him to leave room for Jesus between them.

Perry said, "Who wants to play Monopoly?"

"Me!" Kelsey said.

"Trish?" Wyatt asked.

The last thing Trish wanted to do was sit around on a Saturday night playing board games with Wyatt, Perry, and Kelsey like they were on some double date. The thing she wanted most was to go up to her room and burrow under the covers. Her mother would never permit it while she had a guest, though, even an unwanted one. Sitting here beside Wyatt was excruciating. Maybe Monopoly would make it less so.

"Okay," she said.

"Cool!" Perry said.

He ran to the dining table and set up the board while the stew bubbled, and their mom consulted the Yellow Pages. She dialed a number and put the receiver to her ear as Trish, Kelsey, and Wyatt settled into their chairs.

"Oh, dear. That much to come right now?" her mom said. She put her hand over the mouthpiece and shouted a price to their dad.

His response from the basement was a string of mild curses. Trish could count on one hand the number of times she'd heard him use bad words. Clearly ringing out at the end, though, was "I'll pay that over my dead body."

Perry and Trish looked at each other. Perry burst out laughing. Trish put a hand over a smile. It fell away quickly. As cold as it was getting in here, it might be over all their frozen stiff dead bodies.

Her mom raised her eyebrows. She moved her hand and spoke in a sweet voice. "I'll call you back to schedule on Monday if we aren't able to fix it ourselves. Thank you." She hung up the phone, then consulted the Yellow Pages again.

"I'll be the banker," Perry said.

Wyatt folded his arms over his chest. "No way. I'm the varsity player. I have seniority. I'll be the banker."

"Perry is going to practice with the varsity." Kelsey beamed.

Wyatt rolled his eyes. "I'll believe that when I see it." He pulled the play money across the table.

Anger flared in Trish. "I have the highest GPA. I'm the banker." She snatched the money away from Wyatt and started passing it out.

Her mom picked up the phone, dialed, put it to her ear, then smiled and said, "Hello, this is Susanne Flint. I wonder if you have anyone available to come look at our heater, and before you answer that, you'd better give me your best price, or this phone call is a waste of your time and mine."

Trish wondered what had happened to calling Ronnie. *Maybe she just hadn't heard her mom make that call.*

CHAPTER FIFTEEN: SHOCK

Buffalo, Wyoming
Saturday, March 18, 1978, 4:40 p.m.

Ben

Snow covered Ben's work boots and the hem of his jeans as he placed his feet carefully on the incline to the Flints' driveway, only sliding a little. As he got closer to the vehicles, he identified Trish's mom's Suburban, her dad's truck, and Trish's truck, but he didn't know who the third truck belonged to. It looked familiar, though. One of Trish's friends, maybe? He didn't remember any of the girls in her class driving one like it. That didn't mean that no one had gotten a new one since he left. It had been a couple of months. A knot swelled in his throat. *I can't believe I've been gone this long without talking to Trish.* Or it could even belong to grown-ups, friends of the Flints that he'd seen around.

He approached the front door and swallowed down the lump, which felt and tasted like a ball of sawdust packed with soap. His nerves buzzed. He paused on the steps and practiced one last time the words he planned to say. "Trish, I'm sorry. I shouldn't have left without talking to you. I shouldn't have been gone this long without writing or calling. I've missed you. I love you. Please forgive me." Of course, if someone else opened the door, he would have to start with something else. Like, "Please don't close the door. I need to talk to Trish." But he'd deal with that if it happened.

He snuck a peek through the frosty side light window before knocking. He saw her. He saw her long blonde hair, her back to him. She was sitting at the table. His heart felt like it was going to explode. So close. He was so close.

He lifted his hand to knock, then froze with it in mid-air. He looked back through the window. Who was that sitting with her at the table? It was a guy. A big guy. And across from the two of them sat Perry—that was fine—and that girl he was always drooling over. Chelsea or something like that. Also fine. But the guy beside Trish was not. The guy stood up, took off his jacket, and put it over Trish's shoulders. Then he sat back down and scooted his chair closer to hers. All the way close. Like, pressed up against hers. Ben glanced back at the truck, then at the guy, comparing the two of them. And then it hit him. Wyatt Evans. The boy was a year behind him, so he hadn't paid much attention to him. He'd known he was a jock. Some football stud, or so he heard. Ben hadn't paid attention to Wyatt Evans or football. He hadn't paid attention to anything but Trish Flint.

Now, Wyatt was here with Trish on a Saturday night.

Ben folded over, bracing his hands on his knees. He couldn't draw a breath. His chest ached. His brain whirled. *I am not going to pass out. I refuse to pass out.* But he felt like he was going to.

Because clearly Trish had moved on without him. She had found someone new. There was nothing to say to her now. No reason to be here. He took two steps away from the landing and vomited up the candy bar and chips he'd bought at the gas station in Sheridan, leaving a blight on the virgin snow.

Then he ran for his truck.

CHAPTER SIXTEEN: DEFEAT

Patrick

PATRICK STARED at the mess he'd made of their heater in the cramped utility space. Ferdinand's tail wagged, thumping on the floor. Patrick couldn't fix this thing, no matter how confident man's best friend beside him seemed. He wasn't even sure he could put it back together correctly. He had to face facts. The heater was out of commission. It was a Saturday night. A storm was raging. The temperature was near zero outside and falling into the forties soon inside. They needed help, no matter the cost, or this entire house would freeze sometime soon. Busted pipes and appliances would be a lot more expensive than an after-hours callout. He'd have to get Susanne to call one of the service companies back and get them out here as quickly as possible.

"Stew's ready," Susanne called, her voice faint from upstairs.

"And I made a pot of rice. It's a little early to eat, but hot food will help us stay warm."

None of the kids answered her, but he heard shouts and laughter from the dining table.

Patrick tore himself away from the disaster area and tromped up the stairs. Ferdinand, never one to miss a call to chow, darted in front of him.

The first thing his eyes lit on when he returned to the ground floor was his wife's face. Her nose and cheeks were pink, and she was bundled up into her ski parka. "I don't know where we'll be eating it since there's a Monopoly game taking up our entire table."

Patrick stepped into the dining room, rubbing his hands on the thighs of his jeans. The only thing he'd succeeded at was getting dirty. He turned on the kitchen tap to hot. The water heater still worked, at least.

As he scrubbed his hands, Susanne was dishing up bowls of stew. Ferdinand was supervising her work. "How did it go?"

"Don't ask."

She gave him a sad face, then nodded at the bowls on the countertop. They each took two and set them by the kids, where someone had already put down a pile of spoons and the pot of rice with a stick of butter melting on top. Wyatt grabbed a bowl and a spoon, added rice, and started wolfing it down. Ferdinand walked once around the table, then selected a spot beside Wyatt as most likely to result in dog snacks. He sat tall, on high alert.

With a full mouth, Wyatt said, "This is really good, Mrs. Flint." He wiped his mouth with the back of his hand.

"Thanks, Mom," Trish said.

"We can eat while we finish our game." Perry moved his roadster past Go and stuck out his hand. Trish put two hundred dollars in it. But he'd landed on Connecticut Avenue, which Kelsey owned.

"Fork it over, Per-bear," Kelsey said.

"Per-bear?" Trish hooted. "Are you going to let her call you that?"

Susanne smiled at Patrick and handed him a bowl. Then she

picked up her own and two spoons from the table. "Maybe you and I can sit by the fire?"

He tried to smile back, but the look on her face told him he hadn't been convincing. "I think we need to call the after-hours repair guys back. I'll pay their price. Whatever it is."

The phone rang.

Susanne shrugged and answered the phone. "Hello?" Patrick spooned up a bite of stew. It smelled just the slightest bit burned, like it had stuck to the bottom of the pan over a too-hot burner. He blew on it, then stayed still and silent. He could hear a female voice on the other end of the call. The woman sounded agitated. Susanne made soothing noises and sounds of agreement, but she didn't say much for the first few minutes. "Let me ask Patrick. Just a moment."

"What is it?" he said.

"Kelsey's mom couldn't get a rental car. The tow truck driver took her home. She planned to bring their old ranch truck to get Kelsey, but the battery is dead." Dead batteries were a common malady for vehicles in the harsh winters, especially those that weren't driven often. Dead as in *never to return to life*, not *will work after a jump*.

Patrick said, "I can either try to take her home, or she can spend the night here." Susanne's eyebrows shot to her hairline. "In Trish's room. With a lot of adult supervision."

"I don't think so."

"Fine. I've done all I can with the heater. Maybe you can find us a repairman while I drive them home?"

She nodded. Into the receiver she said, "My husband Patrick will bring her home. You're welcome. Bye." She hung up the phone.

Patrick stepped over to the table. "Kids, I hate to interrupt, but it's time to hit the road. I'll be giving Wyatt and Kelsey rides home."

"Can't Kelsey eat some stew first?" Perry said.

Both Kelsey and Wyatt looked crestfallen.

Patrick nodded. "Eat fast. I've got to warm up the truck."

"I win, then," Trish said. "I have twice as much money as any of you."

"Somehow the banker always wins, especially when it's you," Perry said.

Trish stuck out her tongue. "Sore loser."

Susanne said, "I'll call the repair shops right now."

"Thanks. And Susanne," he lowered his voice, "keep the doors locked until someone from the sheriff's department gets here."

"Always." Then her face fell. "Oh, my gosh. I forgot to call Ronnie."

"It's been a few hours. I think he's gone. But I think you should still call."

"I will."

He nodded. He could trust her to be careful and take good care of the kids, always. He shoveled in three huge bites of stew, chewing rapidly.

Susanne was already dialing by the time he swallowed. He left the kitchen and went for his warmest clothing and outwear—with extra gear for Kelsey and Wyatt—and his winter "go" bag of supplies. Getting stuck in a storm was no joke, and they'd need to be prepared. Earlier today, he'd thought the worst part of his day was Ferdinand finding a dead body, but it was ever clearer that he'd been wrong.

CHAPTER SEVENTEEN: RETREAT

Buffalo, Wyoming
Saturday, March 18, 1978, 5:00 p.m.

Ben

BEN LIFTED his head from the steering wheel where it had been resting on his knuckles. Now his knuckles were wet. *I came back to Wyoming for nothing.* Nothing was left for him here. Leaving Wyoming had been the biggest mistake of his life. Leaving Alaska had been the second biggest. He just prayed he wouldn't get arrested for the Laramie fiasco before he could get out of the state, which would be as fast as he possibly could.

But what now? He hadn't planned for a spring blizzard or Trish having a new boyfriend.

It was dark out. The snow was coming down in a fury. He'd have to find a place to stay. Maybe in Sheridan. Somewhere past Buffalo and Story and all the memories. *But can I really come all this way and not stop at Piney Bottoms? I owe them an explanation and an apology, too.*

It would have to wait for another time. Or a phone call. Or a letter. He was emotionally beaten, and he just wanted to escape from the pain of seeing Trish with Wyatt.

A knock sounded on his window. Ben jumped, hitting his head on the ceiling. It was a hazard of his height.

Did Trish see me? Maybe it's her. He didn't want to talk to her. She couldn't explain her way out of what he'd witnessed with his own eyes. But when he looked out the window and into the dusk, it wasn't Trish, and his disappointment was nearly as crushing as his sadness. The person outside his window was a man. A man covered in snow. He seemed enormous until Ben realized he was wearing a backpack with a tall frame.

Ben rolled down the window. Wind and snow swirled into the cab with him. And something else. An odor. Close to the smell of a dead animal, but not quite that bad. "Yes?"

"I need a ride."

Ben had moved all of his earthly possessions into the seat beside him when the weather turned. They were piled to the roof, from his side to the door. He considered throwing some of them in the back. Then he took a closer look at the guy. His eyes were weird. Freaky flat and expressionless in the dusk. "Sorry, but I don't have any room." He felt guilty, but hitchhikers killed men, too. It was the smart decision. It just felt wrong.

The man stared at him without a muscle moving in his face, silent.

"Okay. Sorry, again. Have a nice night." Ben raised the window.

He put the truck in gear and accelerated, torn between needing to be careful because of the conditions and wanting to get the heck out of there, away from the strange man and from Trish's betrayal.

CHAPTER EIGHTEEN: FLIRT

Vangie

"I can't believe this storm." Vangie tucked Hank's favorite blanket around him in his crib. He would toss it off immediately, which is why he was dressed in fleece footed pajamas. "Night, night, sweet boy." She stroked his dark hair off his forehead.

"Good night, son." Henry said from the doorway.

"Nigh, nigh." Hank waved a hand that was less chubby every day.

She couldn't believe he was starting to talk, even if his first word had been Daddy and his second word No, with Mama only making it into third place. And he was motoring around, cruising from hand-hold to hand hold and walking—barreling—in short determined bursts that often left him with a goose egg on his forehead. The little monkey had started climbing out of the crib in the mornings too. It was time to put him in a real bed. She'd find him riding his rocking horse or wrestling with their beagle, Flash, most days. Once he'd managed to slide her step stool to the refrigerator, climb onto it, and pull the door open, where he'd helped himself to the cherry pie filling salad she'd made the night before. He loved to pick out the pineapple, then dunk it into the concoction of Cool Whip, sweetened condensed milk, pecans, and pie filling. He'd lick off the mixture and dip it again. Lick, dunk, lick. Over and over. She didn't have the heart, usually, to stop him, even if it was unhygienic. Unfortunately, that night the bowl had been too heavy, and he'd dropped it. She'd heard the crash and come running to the kitchen, where Flash and Hank crouched side by side, one dunking and licking, the other just licking, right off the floor. She was just relieved it had been in a Tupperware and didn't break, leaving Hank in a minefield of glass shards. And that Hank hadn't figured out how to let himself outside yet. One morning before too long she was sure she'd find him in a horse stall or out in the bull pasture.

Vangie whispered, "Should we feel guilty we're putting him to bed this early?"

"No," Hank whispered back. "It's getting dark because of the storm. And we'll need to be up extra early to check on livestock."

"Okay."

Henry turned off the light, and they walked back to the kitchen together. "I think this blizzard snuck up on the weatherman. As I recall, he forecasted clear skies and thirty-degree-weather for the weekend."

Vangie had grown up in Tennessee where thirty-five and rain was already considered an extreme winter event. "All the animals and hands are good?" As cold as it was in their own house, where they had central heating, it had to be rough sledding for the hands, who lived in a bunkhouse with only a wood-burning stove to warm the place. And the livestock had to endure the snow, cold, and wind in their pastures, absent a pressing reason that warranted stabling. Foaling and calving qualified. Henry had assured her many times that the herds did well with any two out of three. Snow and wind, cold and wind, or cold and snow. But with all three, the equation fell out of balance, and the animals suffered.

Henry had been out to check on everyone and everything after dinner. "Bunkhouse is stocked and locked. The guys were hanging an extra layer of blankets over the windows and stuffing rolled towels at the base of the doors. We herded all the mamas and babies into the big barns earlier today. The other horses are smart enough to seek shelter in the trees. And the rest of the cattle will hunch together and ride it out. The cattle may have some frostbitten faces by morning, but they've endured worse."

Vangie thanked her lucky stars she wasn't a cow. It wasn't the first time. "I hope the investigator made it back to Billings all right."

"I offered to put him up for the night, but he swore he'd be fine."

"Well, I made coffee and apple strudel while you were out." It was the least she could do. Ranch wives worked hard, no doubt, often right alongside their husband and hands, but whenever he could, Henry spared her the roughest of it. "Can't let Wyoming scare you back to Tennessee," he'd say, winking at her. As if she'd ever go anywhere Henry wasn't. This man and their little family were her heart. She wanted nothing more than to be together, have Ben return, and add more babies, although so far that hadn't been in the stars for them. She'd had another miscarriage a few months before, in addition to the ones she'd had before Hank was born. *All things in your time, God. But I would really love it if that time came soon.*

"I smelled it when I walked in. My mouth has been watering ever since."

There really was no scent her boys—all three of them—liked better than apples and cinnamon baking with any kind of buttery pastry. She slipped on a mitt and opened the oven. Steamy heat blasted her face. *Heavenly.* "It looks done. Do you want a slice now?"

"Now and at breakfast in the morning. You know it's my favorite."

"Can you pour us some coffee?" She pulled two of Henry's grandmother's china dessert plates from the cupboard, pausing to admire the tiny lilacs in the pattern. Only a few were left, and she handled them with care. She sliced two pieces and set them on the plates with forks. "Ice cream on top?"

"Not in this weather. Do you have any powdered sugar?" He poured coffee from their percolator into two cups, tossing in four sugar cubes for her and one for him, then adding heavy cream to both.

"Always." She retrieved it and sprinkled it atop Henry's piece. She preferred hers without a topping.

Henry returned the cream to the refrigerator. Vangie covered the strudel with a clean cloth and tucked the edges under the cookie sheet before leaving it on the stove top. Protected, but breathable.

"Want to sit by the fire?" she asked, holding the plates aloft.

"I'd rather keep you warm another way, if you don't mind a few crumbs in the sheets."

She batted her eyes at him. "Why Henry Sibley, are you suggesting what it sounds like?"

The smile he gave her took her breath away. "It is Saturday night, after all."

And if they were very lucky, maybe it was time to make another baby. Vangie laughed and led him down the hall.

CHAPTER NINETEEN: REJECT

BUFFALO, WYOMING
SATURDAY, MARCH 18, 1978, 5:30 P.M.

Patrick

FIFTEEN MINUTES of heating time later, the inside of the truck wasn't much warmer than when it had started. But they were on their way, with Kelsey in between Patrick and Wyatt, and the foul smell of wet wool hovering in the air like they'd packed along a sheep. The snow was deep and in places drifted to several feet with no sign of plowing. Getting out of their driveway and to Highway 16 had been harrowing. It seemed like the plows had been through on the highway earlier, but that another four inches had piled up since then in the path swathed down the lanes. There were no tire tracks through the new snow. Patrick drove slowly, carefully. This was not a night to get stuck.

"Could one of you turn on the radio?" he said.

"What station?" Wyatt asked, his hand reaching for the power and volume knob.

"Any. I want to be listening for emergency broadcasts."

The young man turned the dial. "Hotel California" came on through a burst of static. Patrick loved the Eagles.

Wyatt rotated the tuning dial further, stopping on "We Will Rock You."

"I love that one!" Kelsey said.

Patrick bit the inside of his cheek. They weren't going to care what the old fart preferred. He'd listen to whatever he wanted after he dropped them at their houses.

Wyatt started singing. The kid had a passable voice. Higher than Patrick would have expected, almost tenor. At first, Kelsey just giggled, but within a minute, they were shouting the lyrics of the chorus together. Patrick preferred country music, but he'd heard this one a few times. The tune had a catchy beat. Soon, his head was bobbing along as he scanned from left to right for obstacles, ice, and drifts.

They made it to town without incident. The traffic light at Main was flashing red. Patrick took it to mean "slow down a little, be careful, and don't stop for anything," which he did. A new song started. Patrick hadn't heard it before, but "Cold As Ice" seemed fitting for the occasion.

"You just ran a red light." Kelsey sounded smug.

"Flashing red. Not the same thing. Especially in a storm with no traffic."

The kids sang some more, with Wyatt strumming air guitar. The song ended. *Thank goodness.*

Kelsey said, "It's a good thing Wyatt and I live near each other, huh, Dr. Flint?"

Near each other, out by Lake DeSmet, but nowhere near the Flints. By his estimate, this round trip was going to take at least an hour. If Trish hadn't been so eager for Wyatt to leave and Susanne so desperate to send Kelsey home, Patrick would have been fine with a sleepover. It seemed like an unnecessary risk to him, driving in conditions like these. As frigid as the house was, they were all going to be gathered around the fire all night anyway.

A loud beeping tone interrupted for an emergency broadcast before Patrick answered Kelsey. He nodded at her, then turned up the volume, which was mostly static at first. When the static cleared, a nasally male voice said, "Interstate 90 and 25 are closed to non-emergency vehicles in Sheridan, Johnson, Natrona and Campbell counties until at least noon tomorrow. Motorists are advised to take an alternate route or stay home due to hazardous winter storm conditions."

Patrick hit his palm on the steering wheel.

Kelsey's forehead bunched. "What does that mean, Dr. Flint?"

Wyatt gave her a soft jab with his elbow. "It means we're making s'mores in the fireplace at the Flints' house tonight."

"Yay!" Kelsey said.

Patrick swung wide for a U-turn at Hart Street. He sighed. "That's exactly what it means." It also meant people stranded in need of medical care, and he was on shift in the morning. He hoped the doc on shift was able to make it in to the hospital tonight.

CHAPTER TWENTY: CHANGE-UP

STORY, WYOMING
SATURDAY, MARCH 18, 1978, 5:45 P.M.

Ben

BEN CRAWLED along at ten miles per hour with his hazard flashers on, headed north. Something large passed him heading south on the other side of the interstate. A plow? Visibility was too bad to be sure. Frost crept up his side and back windows. He was running the defrost on full speed, highest heat to keep the front windshield clear, and even at that he'd had to stop once to scrape. It had to be below zero or thereabouts and not a lot warmer in the truck. His breath was coming out in clouds. Steering was difficult, both because of the snow depth and the wind. The wind was howling. Wyoming was known for its wind, but this wind was like a monster, and it was pointed straight at him. It kept pushing his truck out of the snow tracks, not that the tracks were all that great. But at least they were something to follow. He hoped whoever left them hadn't driven off the road, into the drifts, where Ben would pile on top of a crashed vehicle and be covered in white in no time. Because the sideways snowfall just wouldn't stop.

When he drove out of Buffalo in January, the weather had been bad. This was worse. Maybe it was a sign that he should never have returned. That this place was inhospitable to him. Or maybe it was a sign that he should never have left—that the weather was trying to stop him. But if so, it was too late now. His place with Trish was taken. He didn't know where he was heading or how long it would take him to get there. Just that he needed to get as far away from what he'd just seen in Trish's dining room as he could.

He shivered. His cotton gloves were great for finger flexibility while driving, but they weren't enough. He needed his fishing gloves. When he'd first arrived in Ketchikan and been hired conditionally to fish with Captain Harley, the first thing Cap had done was take him to buy gear at a secondhand store. "Consider this an advance," he'd said around his pipe in his raspy voice. "And don't be buying any of that dark stuff. Bright orange. I want to be able to see you in the water to fish you out, if I have to."

Ben had tried to resist. He needed money, not clothes. He was living in his truck. He didn't even have a place to put more stuff if he bought it. But once he'd gotten out on the water on the fishing boat, with the waves, snow, and the wind buffeting them, with water splashing onto the deck and onto him, he'd seen Cap's wisdom. Ben could have died out there. Instead, he'd merely suffered, but without having to open his trap about it. They'd given him all the grunt work. Preparing and repairing. Cleaning and recleaning. Cooking for the other men. And when they'd gotten back to land, Cap had offered him a job through the rest of the winter season.

He wished he was back there now. He'd been lonely, but he'd believed Trish was his to win back. He wanted to believe that again.

His duffel bag was on the seat beside him. Stopping to layer up would be smart. To be dressed for the worst in case he had a wreck and couldn't get to his warmer gear. Unless if he stopped in this desolate area and he bogged down in the snow and then couldn't get going again. That sounded like a more likely outcome than the wreck. He kept going.

Flashing lights appeared ahead of him out of nowhere. Close by. He let off the gas then started pumping the brakes, testing for ice, not finding any.

"What the heck?" he said aloud.

Sawhorses with reflectors were strung out across the interstate. Beyond them was a sheriff's vehicle, the source of the lights. As he approached, slowing to a stop, someone got out of the sheriff's vehicle, head tucked against the wind, and walked toward him. He put his truck in park and rolled down his window. Painfully cold air rushed in. *Yeah, I'm putting on the good gloves.* When he'd worried about getting arrested before he could leave Wyoming, he hadn't envisioned a blockade. The thought almost made him smile. He knew what this was about. It was the weather, not a fugitive. Still, he put on a baseball cap from his glovebox and positioned it low on his forehead.

"Terrible night to be driving," the officer said, face obscured by a balaclava, head covered by a wool cap, voice sucked away by the wind. "And now we're having to close down the interstate except to emergency vehicles. Where are you headed?"

Ben squinted past the lights. The next exit was to Little Piney. His stomach knotted. The Piney Bottoms Ranch and the Sibleys were off this exit. His former home. "I can't continue to Sheridan?"

"Not on the interstate. And I don't recommend 87 North. I can turn you around back to Buffalo if you'd like."

"My, uh, my family ranch is nearby."

"Which one is that?"

"Piney Bottoms."

The officer peered closer at his face. "Ben?"

His blood curdled. Being recognized by a cop was not a good thing in his shoes. "Yes, sir?"

The officer laughed and leaned in to pat his hand. He caught a faint whiff of something flowery and feminine. "Yes, ma'am. It's Ronnie Harcourt, Ben."

Of all the people to stop him. Ronnie was practically best friends with the Sibleys. And the Flints. There was no way Trish wouldn't hear that he'd been in town now. "Uh, hello, Deputy Harcourt."

"Good to see you back. Everyone has missed you. Will you be around for a while?"

"No, ma'am. Just a short visit." He remembered her baby boy. Younger even than Hank. *Hank.* Thinking of his foster brother made his heart ache. If there was one person other than Trish that he'd missed like crazy, it was Hank. But that wasn't entirely true. He'd missed Vangie and Henry, too. He'd missed everything and everyone. He missed them now. It hurt. He tried to push the pain away. "How's your little boy?"

"Will is adorable. And he's probably forgotten what I look like. I haven't been home since yesterday except for a short nap. Have you been to see Trish?"

"Uh, yes."

"Great. I'm sure she was very excited."

He didn't respond. What was there to say?

"Well, I can either let you exit here to head home, or I can send you back to Buffalo. But I was at the Flints' earlier. Their heater is broken. You might be better off at home."

"Yes, ma'am."

"So, if I let you through, you'll pull straight off the exit?"

"I will."

"The plow truck just covered 87 from Story half an hour ago. I'd recommend you take it and then the road through town to your place, although I can't promise Wagon Box is in good shape."

Ben nodded. "All right. Thank you."

"Good to see you home, Ben. Take care."

"You, too."

While Ronnie walked back to the sawhorses, he put on a wool

cap, a heavy coat, and his fishing gloves. For a moment, he wondered if he could survive the night camping in his truck. *Stupid idea.* Then he eased through the opening she'd created and toward the exit ramp.

He was going home, whether he wanted to or not.

CHAPTER TWENTY-ONE: DEFEND

Perry

Perry's nose had started to run, and he swiped at it with the back of his hand. Was it his imagination or did it feel a little icy at the tip? He and Trish were watching Mutual of Omaha's Wild Kingdom. It wasn't his favorite show, but his parents and Trish loved it. He wondered if he would feel better if he got up and jogged in place.

"Trish, could you get more gear and the blankets from yours and Perry's bedrooms?" His mother was adding the last of the logs to the fire. They'd already gathered the spare blankets from the linen closet outside their parents' bedroom. "It's down to minus five degrees outside. And forty-five in here. Perry, bring us in some logs. A lot of them."

Perry leapt to his feet. The room smelled smoky. Like when the damper was closed too far. "Yes, ma'am." He hustled to the coat closet and started donning gear. The lean-to where they kept their split wood was on the side of the house. Minus five meant his heavy coat, a scarf, a hat, and his ski mittens.

"Isn't the repair man coming?" Trish hadn't gotten up from the couch. "I just went out and fed the horses. And Ferdie is comfortable." The dog was laying on her feet.

His mother closed the chain screens to the fireplace. "No. They've gotten all booked up since I called them earlier. We have to make do."

"So, what—we're camping in the living room tonight?" Trish said.

"I've been calling around, trying to find us a hotel room. But we can't go anywhere until your dad gets home. Now, move it."

Sighing, Trish stood. Ferdinand grumbled and resettled. "Fine." She headed up the stairs.

Perry was almost to the front door when a loud CRACK startled him. Glass shattered and sprayed his body. A heavy object fell to the ground at his feet. Ferdinand jumped to his feet, running in circles and barking frantically.

"Perry! Get back!" his mom screamed. "What happened?"

Perry stared at the glass on the floor, confused and unmoving. What was that thing—a brick? But how? Why? They didn't just fall from the sky. Which is when it finally hit him. Someone had just thrown a brick through the window by the front door of their house. In the dark. During a storm. With his dad gone. *Is the front door even locked?* His dad had walked through it half an hour ago with Kelsey and Wyatt. *No. It won't be locked.*

"Stay back, Mom!" He pitched his voice deep, trying to sound brave and confident when what he felt was scared and unsure of himself. He wished his dad were here.

"What is it?" She ignored him and ran over from the hearth. Her mouth made an O when she saw the glass. Ferdinand, *the big chicken*, whined behind her. She put her hand to her mouth when she caught sight of the brick. "Oh, my gosh. Who did that?"

Despite the cold, made worse by the new gaping hole, sweat ran down Perry's neck. *You are the man of the house. You must protect your mom and sister.*

Trish was frozen on the stairs. "Perry?"

"Someone is outside. They threw a brick. Stay away from the windows." He needed to lock the front door, and he needed to be armed. The shotgun and his dad's rifles were in the coat closet. To reach it, he had to cross the window on the other side of the front door. The window was narrow, but it was tall. He imagined whoever-it-was outside, looking in. It was mostly dark out there other than the porch light his dad had left on and the glow from the lights on the inside.

That meant the person could see inside the house—see Perry, Trish, and his mom—as plain as day. "Turn off all the lights."

His mom said, "Good idea." She switched off the kitchen and dining room lights. "I'll call 911."

Trish flipped off the light on the stairs.

Perry turned off the living room lights. Darkness descended, except for the flames in the fireplace, but there was nothing he could do about them. He'd lock the house first. He darted to the front door, toward the cold from the broken window. Felt an odd suction coming from it. Turned the dead bolt. It hadn't been locked. Checked the hand lock. That one had been set. *Good.* Then he ran to the coat closet, crossing the narrow window, feeling as if another brick was about to fly through and connect with his head, but nothing happened. A nose bumped his thigh. Ferdinand. *Now he wants to help.*

In the coat closet, he rummaged for the long barrels of the guns. He might only be fourteen, but he'd been shooting for half his life. He knew the difference between a shotgun and a rifle, and he wanted the shotgun. His fingers found a rifle first, and he pushed it to the back. Grabbed the shotgun. Checked the chamber. His dad didn't believe in keeping loaded weapons in a house. Too many chances for accidents. So, Perry wasn't surprised when he found it empty. He reached up on the shelf. He was surprised to find it lower than he remembered. *I have grown.* Found the box of shotgun shells, pulled it down. Set it on the floor, crouched beside it. Smelled the oily gunpowder scent as he loaded the shotgun with Ferdinand pressed against his side.

He drew in a deep breath and exhaled it. *Okay. I'm ready.* But was he? His heart was pounding in his ears. His scalp was burning hot, like it was going to erupt into flames. His breathing was fast and shallow. "I've got the gun, Mom."

"Good. Because our phone lines are dead. I can't call 911."

Every scary movie Perry had been forbidden to watch but had watched anyway played back on top of one another in his brain. The scary bad guy always cut the phone lines. That, and he snuck up on women in the shower. He'd have to make sure neither Trish nor his mom took a shower. *Has someone cut the lines?*

"So, you can't call and get us a hotel?" Trish said.

"Is that all you can think about?" Perry's voice came out snarly and had the deep tone he'd tried and failed at a minute before. "Someone just broke our window."

"Yeah, and I want to get out of here to someplace with windows and heat that's safe."

She had a point.

His mom sounded on the verge of tears. "I didn't want to upset you earlier. I've already tried every hotel in town. They're all booked up from stranded travelers."

"Maybe we can go to somebody's house? Anyplace but here," Trish said. "Maybe a deputy can give us a ride when they come."

"I . . . I hadn't called them yet. I was trying to get us help with the heat and a place to stay. And it had been a long time since that man was here."

Trish wailed. Perry wanted to join her, but he couldn't. He had to protect his family.

Through the gaping hole, Perry heard the sound of an engine. Kelsey lived halfway to Story. It had only been half an hour. It should have taken his dad a whole lot longer to drive her and Wyatt home. Fear pulsed through him. Who was here now?

"Get down," he whispered. He crouched behind the couch, shotgun barrel trained on the door.

Ferdinand stalked to the door.

"No, Ferdie!"

The dog ignored him.

Trish pounded down the stairs.

"What are you doing? You're safer up there."

"I don't want to be alone," she said, pressing in close to him. "And I'm the best shot in the family. We all know it. Give me the gun."

"I've got it," Perry said. She was kind of right. But this was his responsibility.

"Fine. Don't blame me if we all die because you miss."

"Hush, Trish." His mom squatted down on the other side of him. "I don't want to be alone either. I wish you were both upstairs. But if you're not, then I'd rather we were together. Now, Perry, give me the gun. And Ferdie, come here, now."

The dog obeyed her no-nonsense voice and joined them behind the couch.

Perry heard an engine shut off. Two car doors slammed. He closed his eyes. Not his dad. His dad would be alone. No time to pass the gun to his mom. He took the safety off the shotgun.

CHAPTER TWENTY-TWO: IDENTIFY

BUFFALO, WYOMING
SATURDAY, MARCH 18, 1978, 6:15 P.M.

Susanne

CHA-CHUNK. Perry pumped the action on the shotgun.

The sound made Susanne wince. "Wait. Let's see if we can hear anything."

"I won't fire unless a stranger opens the door, Mom." Perry's voice trembled.

That tremble isn't confidence boosting. The rank odor of fear emanated from her son. She put a gentle hand on his arm. "Just listen." Brushing hair away from her ear, she strained to catch sound over the noise of the wind. A male voice. Then a laugh. Female. Young.

Ferdinand stood and wagged his tail.

"Kelsey!" Perry lowered the barrel and switched the shotgun back into safety mode.

"And that was Wyatt." Trish didn't sound enthused, but she stood up. "Dad's home."

"But someone threw a rock through that window. They could still be out there." Perry shouted, "Dad. Hurry up. Get inside."

The handle to the front door rattled. Ferdinand trotted to it with his tail high.

Perry locked it. Which I was supposed to do when Patrick left and didn't. Susanne ran around the couch. "Patrick, is that you?"

Her husband's voice answered. *Thank you, God.* "Yes. What the —why is the front window broken?" A note of irritation crept in. "How are we going to keep this place warm now?"

Susanne unlocked the door and motioned the three of them in. "Come on. Hurry."

"Why are all the lights out?" Kelsey said, reaching for the switch.

Susanne stuck her arm out, blocking Kelsey before she could turn it on. "Shhh. Everyone in. Don't turn anything on. Stay away from the windows, too."

Patrick closed the door behind them. "What's going on, Susanne?"

She pointed at the broken glass and brick on the floor. "We've had an unwelcome visitor."

Patrick's face turned stormy. "Everyone into the hallway." He scanned the room, his eyes lighting on the armoire a few feet away. He stepped over to it and pushed it slowly in front of the broken window, blocking most of the opening.

Trish, Perry, Susanne, and Ferdinand moved out quickly, Perry still carrying the shotgun. Kelsey and Wyatt were slow to react. Susanne looked back. Their expressions were pure confusion.

Patrick put a hand on each of their backs and gave them a slight push. "Everything will be okay. Let's go." When they had gathered in a tight cluster between the great room and the master bedroom, Patrick put a finger to his mouth. To Susanne he said, "Did you see anyone?"

"Nothing. It came out of nowhere."

"How long ago?"

"Five minutes or so."

Patrick turned to his son. "Is the safety on?"

Perry checked his gun, then nodded. "Yes, sir."

Kelsey wrapped her arms around herself. Her face was puckered, looking on the verge of tears. "I don't understand."

Wyatt put a hand on her shoulder. "Someone chunked a brick through the front window."

She addressed her follow-up question to him. "But who would do that?"

Wyatt shrugged. "Probably the same person who slashed my tires."

"Is the repair company on the way?" Patrick asked.

"I'm sorry." Susanne hated piling up bad news. "They're booked up now and can't come today."

"Who else have you called?" his voice sounded frustrated. *Join the club.*

"Everyone else. We won't be getting help tonight."

"We'll go to a motel then. The temperature in here is falling fast."

"I already thought of that, and I've called every motel in town. They're all full. Stranded travelers. And Patrick?"

He scowled without answering.

"Patrick?"

"Yes?"

"Our phone lines died before I could call for a deputy."

"When did they go dead?"

"About the same time as the brick."

He wheeled and paced up and down the hall. Ferdinand cocked his head, eyes on his master. Patrick's lips were moving frantically. He turned to face her. "We need to be armed."

"Got it." Perry hefted the shotgun.

"More armed. And we need to cover the window with plywood."

"I can help, Dr. Flint," Wyatt said.

"Thank you. Then we need to get out of here."

"Where do you *suggest* we go?" Susanne didn't want to cause a scene, but she wanted to make this decision together, as two capable adults. Patrick had gone into solo commander mode, and it amped up her feelings from earlier. He hadn't even asked about her news today. Not once. *Fine. If he wants to be solo commander about this, I can be solo commander about my own life. I'm taking that job. He can just deal with it.* She kept her tone treacly sweet. "The Sibleys and Harcourts are too far away. The house next door has been boarded up with the power off since Judge Renkin went to prison." Their only neighbor had pleaded guilty to accessory-after-the-fact in the murder of his wife. It was nice to have him locked up, but an abandoned house in foreclosure next door wasn't.

"Let me think about it." Patrick rubbed his forehead, leaving a red mark. "Perry, Wyatt, follow me. We've got a window to board up."

CHAPTER TWENTY-THREE: EAT

Hank

HANK HAD BEEN PLAYING in his crib for a very long time. Mostly with his stuffed bull. It was his favorite. He heard his mama laughing in his parents' bedroom. He smelled good smells. Apples. He loved apples.

Hank stood up in his crib, holding the side rail. He listened. His daddy's voice. His mama laughing again. He leaned on the railing, throwing first one leg over it, then the other. He stepped on the bottom rung, then dropped to the ground, landing on his bottom.

The good apple thing. His stomach growled. He wobbled to the door. Put his hand on the wall in the hall. Walked to the kitchen with his footie pajamas making crinkly noises with every step. Flash ran out from the mudroom where his bed was. He gave Hank a big doggy kiss on the nose.

Where was the good smell coming from? Hank sniffed the air,

following his nose and touching the cabinets as he surfed along them. He reached the oven, where his mama made good things. It was hot. He pulled his hands away. He thought for a minute. Standing on his tippy toes, he grabbed the handle and yanked the door open. It was dark inside. No redness. No fire. And the good smell wasn't coming from in there. Holding the edge of the counter, he tried to shut the oven door. It was hard. It took him three tries, straining, using all the muscles his daddy had told him were coming from the spinach he ate, and then it only closed partway.

Flash whined and wagged his tail. Hank patted him on the head.

Hank's mama kept a stool in the kitchen so she could reach the cabinets up high. His daddy said she was pint sized, which must mean pretty. She was really pretty. Hank liked the stool. It helped him see on top of the counter. If the good apple thing wasn't in the oven, then maybe it was on the counter.

He dragged the stool to the side of the oven closest to the refrigerator, only falling down a few times on the way. He didn't think it would be in the refrigerator. His mama didn't put good apple things in there. When the stool was just where he wanted it, he stepped on it. It rocked over, and he fell on his bottom. It surprised him, but it didn't hurt because of his diaper. He set the stool on its legs and tried again, this time holding the pull to the drawer. The drawer slid out partway, but he made it up, then pushed the drawer shut. With his fingers wrapped around the edge of the counter, he peeked over the edge. It wasn't on the counter. He looked on top of the stove, where the round things are that he isn't supposed to touch. They weren't red and hot so his mama wouldn't be mad at him. There was something on the stove wrapped in a towel.

And it smelled really, really yummy.

The open oven door was in his way. And the good thing was on the far side of the door. He knelt on his stool then climbed off. Moved it to the other side of the stove. Used a drawer pull for balance. Stepped up. Grabbed the counter.

Saw the good thing, closer to him.

He touched it. Not hot. He grasped it and pulled it toward himself. The towel came off the top and he sucked in a breath. The good apple thing. He tried again, pulling, thinking about how good it would taste. Wondering if Flash would want some, too. He got it all the way to the edge of the stove, then it tilted and slid. Hank grabbed for it, but all he got was a handful of knob. It turned and made a click-click-click sound. The good apple thing slid to the floor. He heard Flash gobbling it.

"No, no, Flash."

The dog didn't listen to him. Just kept gobbling. Hank used the knob as a handhold as he got down from the stool. It turned. The clicking stopped.

His pajama feet stepped in something gushy. He squatted down. The good apple thing. Flash hadn't eaten it all yet, so Hank dug his hand in.

"Ouch."

Still hot in the middle. But he blew on it like his mama did for him. Then he stuffed it in his mouth. The apple thing was good. So good. He scooped up another handful and didn't blow on it. Just pushed it in with the first bite, which he hadn't swallowed yet.

The lights came on in the kitchen.

"Hank Sibley, what are you doing?" his mama said.

He looked up. Her hands were on her hips. She sounded mad, but her face didn't look mad. His daddy was behind her.

"I'll clean him up," his dad said.

"I'll clean the kitchen. No strudel for us in the morning."

Hank's daddy picked him up. "What are we going to do with you, you little bruiser?"

His mama said, "Seriously. What are we going to do? He's going to get himself into real trouble."

"Are we going to have to lock you in your room, son?"

"We can't do that. It doesn't seem safe."

His daddy pointed at the stove and the mess. "This already doesn't look safe."

"We could build him a fence, maybe?"

His daddy raised his eyebrows. "What do you think, Hank? Would you like a gate like we use with the cattle?"

Hank nodded. He liked the cows and the bulls. Maybe if he had a gate, he could pretend to be a bull. He put his fingers by his forehead, like horns.

"Great. I'll pick one up in town this week," his mama said.

"No need for that. Hank and I will build one together in the barn tomorrow."

Hank said, "Yay!" He liked building things with his daddy.

His parents laughed, and his daddy walked down the hall toward the bathroom holding Hank.

CHAPTER TWENTY-FOUR: EVACUATE

Trish

TRISH STARED AT HER TRUCK. It was hard to see through all the flakes falling in her lashes, but the two flat tires were impossible to miss. Her mom's Suburban and her dad's truck had two flats each as well. And of course, the whole reason Wyatt was still with them was the flats on his. She crouched and touched a tire. Ferdinand snuffled around it. The dirty, rubbery smell seemed normal and grounding to her, but the hackles on the dog's neck rose.

Four vehicles with flats? What were the odds? This was the most insane night of her life. Well, second or third most. The first was being kidnapped by Billy Kemecke. The second was the night she'd taken a bus from Denver, trying to catch Ben before he ran away. So far anyway. Tonight was catching up to them fast.

"Do you think the cold caused it?" she asked, doubting it. A girl could hope, though.

Her dad held his .357 Magnum ready as if he expected someone to appear out of the stormy darkness any second. Perry had kept the shotgun and Wyatt had a rifle. They were like a small army. Never mind her superior shooting skills. She didn't want to tote around the shotgun. Let Perry play the hero. It was fine with her.

He said, "Cold does make them deflate some. Air contracts when it cools. But that's not what happened. They were slashed. Like Wyatt's."

That sounded ominous, about like she'd expected. *A maniac is tormenting my family.* She looked around the driveway, but she didn't see anyone but Wyatt, Kelsey, and the Flints. "With a knife?"

"Or something similar."

"Who would do that?"

"Same person who'd throw a brick through a window, I'll bet." Wyatt pointed the barrel of the rife in the air. His voice was strained to a higher pitch and he looked shifty-eyed. Nervous.

"I'm scared." Kelsey sounded like she was about to cry.

Get in line.

"Whoever it is has cost us a bundle. Not to mention the heating issue and the frozen pipes that will probably break before morning." Her dad talked like he was chewing glass.

"And we can't call the police," her mom said. "But more importantly, how are we going to get to the hospital?"

The hospital was their destination. Their intended refuge. While her dad, Wyatt, and Perry had been nailing plywood over the busted window earlier, Trish had tried to flush a toilet. The water wouldn't flow. Her dad said the pipes were probably frozen. With all the chaos, no one had remembered to drip them. That's when he'd announced that they were all going to the hospital where there was heat, food, beds, phones, and functional plumbing. They'd packed in a big hurry. Games. Books. Puzzles. Snacks. Drinks. Changes of clothes. Toothbrushes and toothpaste. Then they'd dressed in their warmest outer gear, sharing extras with Kelsey and Wyatt, and lugged everything out to the cars, only to discover the flats.

"What about the snowmobiles?" Perry moved closer to Kelsey, but both his hands were on the shotgun.

Trish's dad had bought two used snow machines in January, right after he and Perry had fallen in love with the sport on a winter weekend up at Clear Creek Lodge.

"There's six of us," Trish said. "The most we could cram on them would be four. And that's without our bags."

Her dad frowned. "Let's generate some solutions. Maybe two of us could ride ahead to the hospital and get someone back here to pick us up. Wes is supposed to be working tonight."

Trish perked up at the idea. Wes Braten was one of her dad's best friends, and he was also Wyoming tough. Plus, he drove a giant Travelall. They'd all be able to squish into it. Bags, too.

"I can drive one." Perry stood a little taller.

"It would need to be two at a time. No one alone. And I'd like to keep us paired up male/female with one weapon per pair, and only send one pair. I want the bigger group here. In case we, uh, need to get defensive."

"How about Trish and I go?" Wyatt said. "Although what if our snowmobile breaks down?"

"Patrick . . ." Her mom's voice sounded close to frantic. She shook her head. "I don't like it. Bad things always happen when we split up."

Her dad took her mom by the elbow. She pulled it away. Not like jerked it away, more like did it in a way she hoped no one else would notice. "What options do we have? The vehicles are disabled. The only other modes of transportation we have for this weather are snowshoes and cross-country skis." He pointed at the wall, where skis, poles, and snowshoes hung from hooks. Then he frowned and dropped her mom's arm. "Where are my snowshoes?"

Trish counted pairs. Only three. His set—wooden ones with red rope braided through so he could tell them apart from the others—was missing. But misplaced snowshoes seemed like a pretty small problem compared to all the other things they were facing right now.

"In the dark? I can't do those," Kelsey said. "I don't even know how."

Patrick pulled at his chin. "When we were out earlier, the roads had been plowed. We didn't have any trouble getting into town. We only turned back because the interstate was closed. It will be a simple, ten-minute ride to the hospital on a snow machine. That Travelall can handle the conditions. It could be back here in less than half an hour."

Trish thought about riding a snowmobile on the highway in the dark. In this blizzard. With Wyatt, who she barely knew. It sounded scary. But it was better than sitting here waiting for the next move from the wacko who'd slashed their tires and broken their window. "I'll do it. It's not a problem. But we should get going, shouldn't we?"

Trish could see the second her mom gave in. Her forehead creased into elevens between her eyes and she sighed. "Fine."

Her dad and Wyatt pulled out one of the snow machines, checking fuel and head lights, and getting it started. Five minutes later, Trish had her helmet and goggles on and was astride a yellow machine behind Wyatt.

Then she had a thought. A good one. "Wait!" She pulled off her helmet.

Her dad leaned close to her to hear over the engine.

"We've got toboggans. We could tie them behind the snow-mobiles."

His lips moved as he thought about it. "Whoever rode the tobog-gans would eat a lot of snow."

She shrugged. "So, we use a really long rope. Anyway, it's just an idea."

He grinned. "It's a great idea. Hold on." He gathered Perry, Kelsey, and Susanne and told them the new plan, while Trish shouted it in Wyatt's ear. They both got off the machine. Perry and Wyatt ran for toboggans. Her dad secured them with long lengths of rope to the backs of the machines. When he had the toboggans attached, he motioned the whole group to gather a few feet away.

He said, "Wyatt and I are the strongest. We'll be driving. Perry and Trish, I want you in the toboggans, holding our bags. Ferdie will be with you, Perry. Susanne, you can ride behind me, and Kelsey behind Wyatt. I'll take the lead out of here. When we get to the highway, I want us driving side by side, ten feet apart. Wyatt and Kelsey, don't forget to check on Perry and Ferdie frequently. We'll do the same for Trish. If one of us stops, both of us stops. And don't turn off your machine. That yellow one is finicky."

"Yes, sir, sergeant major," Trish's mom muttered.

"What?" her dad said.

"I said, yes, let's get going," she lied. *Mom is pissed at Dad!*

After nods and thumbs up, the group loaded onto the machines and into the toboggans. Trish looked into the pasture. The horses were huddled in their loafing shed munching the extra hay she'd put out for them earlier, exuding calm. Goldie, Trish's palomino, had one of her back legs cocked. Her dad's big blue roan Percheron cross Reno had his eyes closed like he was dozing. And Perry's stout paint, Duke, was chewing as he rubbed his forehead on a fencepost. If there was still an intruder around, they weren't scared of him.

Her dad gripped the throttle and eased the red snowmobile forward. Snow pelted Trish's face. She was glad she had on goggles. But even in the cold and precipitation, she felt a small thrill to be riding at night and a large amount of relief to be leaving their house. She snuggled further between their bags. Air rushed over her face, making her cheeks feel stiff. She leaned her head back and stared at the night sky. To the north toward Sheridan, she saw a clear patch of sky. How could that be in the midst of this storm? There was something different about the sky, though. She peered into the distance. A green glow streaking up toward the heavens. And what was that above it? It almost seemed pink and purple. She'd read about this before, she realized. The aurora borealis. The northern lights. Seeing them was supposed to be very good luck. Then, as quickly as she'd spotted the phenomena, the clouds closed ranks again, and the lights were gone. Good thing, because her cheeks couldn't stand another second with her face into the wind.

She ducked behind the bags for cover. She'd never thought of the hospital as warm and cozy before, but she did now.

CHAPTER TWENTY-FIVE: SALVAGE

Story, Wyoming
Saturday, March 18, 1978, 7:00 p.m.

Ben

BEN KEPT both hands on the wheel and steady, easy pressure on the gas pedal all the way to Story. Ronnie had been right. The plowing of the road was recent, and he had no real trouble, even though it was like driving through an ice tunnel with no visibility, until he got to town. There, he had a decision to make. Go left toward Piney Bottoms or straight northward toward Sheridan.

He slowed, coasting, and peered north. The north didn't look too bad, what he could see of it, which was about one hundred feet. Not much to go on, given that Sheridan was twenty miles away. He almost took it, but at the last second he made a hard left. His tires spun and the truck slid to the right, slightly downhill. He finally found traction in a snowbank on the far side of the road. Or, rather, off of it. But it wasn't deep, and it was better than the compacted, icy snow in the intersection.

He urged the truck forward at its slowest possible speed on the shoulder. It responded. "Come on, come on." After a few inches, the tires lost their grip. He backed up half the distance and tried again. Same result, but he gained some ground. Over and over he repeated the maneuver, working the shoulder until he found himself damp with sweat and finally in the middle of the flat roadway ten minutes later.

Exhaling stale breath, Ben drove through two more white knuckle turns—these without inclines or traction loss, though. He passed an old house with a two-story garage and workshop. The road graded upward. The snow grew deeper. He kept his speed constant. Then a memory hit him. That garage looked familiar. He'd only spent one year living with the Sibleys, but last winter Henry had showed it to him. He kept an old snow machine in it, in case of emergencies. There had been a key hidden outside.

This seemed like an emergency to Ben. But were the key and snowmobile still there?

Without pulling off the empty road, Ben shifted into reverse and backed up slowly. He idled on the street, considering his options for accessing the building. The plowing had created a snow wall about two feet deep between the road and the driveway to the garage. He didn't dare try to back through it. If he couldn't get to the machine and his truck was stuck in the bank, he'd be walking to Piney Bottoms. Or sleeping rough and cold in his cab. *No choice.* So, he parked where he was, somewhat in the street. Come tomorrow, the plow driver would be cursing him, and it was likely that when he returned the truck would have to be dug out of snowbanks on both sides. That was better than getting it stuck on Wagon Box Road where few if any people would come by, or, worse, sliding off road into a ravine or Little Piney Creek.

He clambered out of the truck and through the snowbank, stomping postholes to the garage. He stopped by the door. He recalled the key being under a mat. If he was right, and if the mat was still there, it was now buried under a foot of fresh fall, plus what had fallen from the roof. He kicked around with his feet until he found the lip of something. Sinking to his knees, he flung snow to the sides with both hands. A minute later, his efforts revealed a brown mat with the word COWBOYS in faded yellow. Carefully, he lifted it by one corner.

No key.

He took off one glove and probed the frozen earth. It was practically dark outside, so he closed his eyes, moving slowly. At first, all he found was that he missed the warmth of his fishing glove. The cold was crippling, and his fingers stiffened after only a few seconds. Then he scratched at the edge of something. Rock? No, metal. Whatever it was, the frozen ground had it in a tight grip. He pried at it with his fingers, which now had no feeling. It didn't budge. He found a sharp-edged stone that was loose enough to dig out. A tool. He struck the earth repeatedly around what he hoped was the key, trying to break it free. Chips of icy dirt flew up. One hit him in the teeth. He tasted salty mud.

He aimed the stone against the edge of the metal and levered under it. The ground gave way, and the metal catapulted in the air, and into the snow.

Growling, Ben stuck his bare hand into the powder, sifting through it. A minute later, his fingers touched something of the right hardness. He squeezed it. It was also about the shape he'd expect of a key. By now, his teeth were chattering, and his fingernails felt like spikes had been driven under them. But when he pulled his hand from the snow, he was holding a key. Just barely. He transferred it to his gloved hand and stuck the bare one under his clothes, against his stomach, cradling it wrapped in the hem of his shirt until the needling pain eased and his jaw relaxed. Using his knees and his teeth, he worked his club-like hand back in the glove.

Only then did he give himself a moment of satisfaction. Step one accomplished, despite the odds.

He stood and walked over to the padlock. Tried to insert the key. Met resistance. Of course. Ice? He knelt in front of the lock, holding it in one hand, and exhaled hot breath into the keyhole again and again. The effort made him lightheaded, and he took a break, trying the key again. It slid in. It turned. He pulled the shackle and body in opposite directions, and they parted.

"Heck, yeah." The snow swallowed his excited words.

He tucked the padlock and key into his pocket for safekeeping, then flipped the hasp away from the loop and raised the door. He blinked. The interior of the garage was pitch black. He remembered the matches he kept in his glove box. The ability to light a fire was critical in cold climates, and he never went anywhere without them. He trudged back to the truck and returned to the garage with the full box. He struck one. A tiny light flared, but it was bright enough for him to see the interior.

Five feet away from him stood a dusty black snowmobile. *Now all I have to do is start it and drive it.* He'd only ridden snow machines a few times on the ranch, so that wasn't as easy as it sounded.

The match burned down close to his fingertips. He blew it out, dropped it, ground it with his boot, and lit another. Walking around the snowmobile, he set the switches and turned on the ignition. Lit another match. Found the pull-start. He needed both hands, so he discarded his match and pulled. The cold engine didn't turn over. He pulled again. And again and again and again. For five minutes, Ben pulled, cursed, and prayed, as the engine sputtered but refused to start. When it finally caught and coughed to life, he collapsed on the ground, breathing hard, sweat running down his forehead and back.

No time for rest. He had no idea if the old beast was gassed up. By the light of another match, he checked the tank. The gauge read one quarter full. That was enough, if it was accurate.

Now, to get it turned around. He lifted the back end and swung it a few inches, then did the same with the front in the opposite direction. Repeating the exercise, he had it facing outward in no time. Then he dragged it forward by the runners until the belt was on some snow and the back end had cleared the garage. Finally, he grabbed his emergency backpack from the truck—a survival must in Alaska as well as Wyoming. He locked up his vehicle and the garage.

He took a deep breath. He could do this. He hopped on the machine and pressed the throttle. It spurted forward, and the jubilation he felt was so overwhelming he felt lightheaded.

An hour ago, he'd never wanted to go back to Piney Bottoms again. Now, all he could think about was how good it would feel to be inside the warm house in his soft bed, near three of the people he loved most in the world.

Tomorrow would be soon enough to get back on the road to Alaska.

CHAPTER TWENTY-SIX: ENLIST

Patrick

PATRICK LET off the throttle and steered his snowmobile to a stop on the edge of the hospital parking lot, away from the drop-off area and street traffic, crosshatch to a parking space. He motioned Wyatt beside him, and the youth followed his instructions. Both of them turned off their engines, and Patrick's ears rang in the relative silence. Relative being the key term, as the wind was howling like a banshee.

"Thank God," Susanne whispered.

Patrick shared the sentiment. What a relief to escape the home that usually felt so safe for the sanctuary of the hospital. It wasn't a place he normally associated with warmth and security. Tonight, though, that was exactly what it offered. He pulled off his helmet and turned back to the toboggans, patting her thigh as he did.

Perry, Ferdinand, and Trish looked like ice sculptures.

"Everyone, okay?" he called.

Perry broke the pose and shot the same thumbs up he and his sister had been giving when Patrick had checked on them during the twenty-minute ride over from the house.

"C-c-c-cold," Kelsey said. And she'd been protected by Wyatt's body warmth and substantial wind block, unlike Perry and Trish.

Trish stood, brushing snow off her coat and pants. *There's a girl under there after all.* "I'm all right. Ready for cafeteria hot chocolate."

Hot chocolate sounded perfect. The temperature seemed like it had fallen just during their ride. Patrick glanced at his watch. It was only seven-thirty, but it felt like the middle of the night, and it was nearly that dark out. "Let's put the toboggans between the snow machines and get our bags inside."

He didn't have to ask twice. In less than a minute, the group hustled to the door, toed off their boots, and descended on the waiting room. Behind reception, a woman stood. The new night nurse, a recent graduate who didn't seem much older than Trish. Kathy Bergman.

"May I—oh, Dr. Flint, is that you?" The tall, freckled brunette looked perplexed. "But you're not on until six-thirty. And is that a *dog?*"

Patrick walked over to her while the others settled their belongings along the wall and began taking off their outerwear. "Hello, Kathy. We've had an emergency at our place. No heat, frozen pipes, and an intruder. I couldn't call the police because our phones are down. And the intruder slashed our tires, so we had to caravan on snowmobiles. I couldn't think of anywhere else to come." He grinned apologetically. "Sorry about the dog."

Her mouth hung slack. "Oh, my gosh."

A booming voice made Patrick turn. It was his best buddy, Wes Braten, lab tech slash guru of all things medical in Buffalo. His copper-colored walrus mustache bounced as he said, "Look what the cat dragged in."

"Sno-cat, maybe," Patrick said.

Ferdinand loped over to Wes. The two were old pals.

"Don't tell the snow dog that." Wes leaned his long, lean frame on the reception desk. He winked at Kathy as if bringing her in on his joke. She blushed pink from her cheek down to her collarbone. "Ha. Well, you're not the only refugees here tonight. It's down to zero out there with a minus twenty-five windchill. Some of the patients we're seeing have minimal complaints other than wanting to be somewhere warm and safe. That didn't extend to staff, though. We're running at fifty percent, even with Dr. Farham over from the reservation. We could sure use some extra hands."

"I'm the only pair in my group qualified to provide medical care. But did you say Abraham Farham is here?"

"He's covering while Dr. John is in North Carolina visiting his new grandson. Good thing. The hospital is filled to capacity. The ER is nearly full, too, and we have nowhere to transfer ER patients that need admittance."

Abraham's presence was welcome news to Patrick. He and Abraham—not the doctor's real name—had formed an unlikely friendship when Abraham was on the run in the Bighorn Mountains from SAVAK, the Iranian intelligence and secret police. Patrick had helped the U.S. Secretary of State hide the doctor on the Wind River Indian Reservation under his assumed name. The Northern Arapaho and Shoshone who lived there were chronically underserved with medical care, so Abraham's placement was a blessing to him and to them. Patrick was one of the few people in the world who knew that Abraham was a cousin to the Shah and had been one of his personal physicians, until he'd confronted the Shah with knowledge of the man's cancer. The Shah had sent assassins after Abraham to keep the information quiet.

Patrick said, "That's wonderful. I haven't seen him since he moved there."

Wes nodded. "But back to what we need. Anything with a pulse and a kind heart can do the work. Everything from food prep and delivery to light cleaning and laundry. Think your group can cover that?"

Said group had moved closer, and Patrick beckoned them with a hand. "You guys have been drafted. A lot of the hospital employees haven't been able to make it in. We're going to need your help."

"I thought we were playing board games . . ." Kelsey pouted, an expression that Patrick suspected she thought was cute. It wasn't.

Perry frowned at her. "Maybe later, Kelse."

"Yes, sir, Dr. Flint," Wyatt said. "Do you think I could get community service credit for this on my college application?"

Wes laughed. "You do everything we ask of you tonight, son, and I'll write the letter myself."

"Who do we report to for assignments?" Susanne put a hand on Trish's shoulder.

"And what will Ferdie be doing?" Trish said.

"This ole mutt will be in charge of security." Wes fondled Ferdinand's ears. "Think you can handle that, boy? Or would you rather be our goodwill ambassador?"

Ferdinand flopped to the ground, begging for a belly rub. Everyone laughed.

"I think whatever his role, he'll get to do it from the staff lounge," Patrick said. "Kids, can you get our bags there with him when he goes?"

"Sure, Dad," Trish said.

"Then the dog gets to hang out with Dr. Farham," Kathy said. "He was catching a cat nap in there last time I checked." This time, she winked.

Wes laughed heartily, and the two held eye contact a few extra beats. "How about Kathy coordinates assignments? And, Dr. Flint, don't get your hopes up on the laundry detail. You're still doctoring tonight."

Patrick was thinking first he'd be drinking some coffee, and making sure everyone else did, too. By the time his shift was over tomorrow evening, he'd have worked a double. "I need to call the police. We had some trouble at our place."

Kathy and Wes shared a look of commiseration.

Wes shook his head. "Ah, Sawbones, you're out of luck. Our phones are down."

The lights went out. Kelsey screamed. Then, seconds later, the lights flickered and came back on.

"And now our power is out, too," Wes said. "Thank the good Lord for the generators. I'd better go check on it. Thanks, team." He waved goodbye and loped away down a corridor into the innards of the building.

Patrick knew the backup generators weren't enough to power everything in the hospital. There were some battery backups, like emergency lighting in critical areas. Luckily, the hospital's heating system was largely propane-based, although it sported electronic controls. If the hospital lost generator power, the furnace would shut down.

But to have power and phone problems at the hospital? It was like a dark cloud was hovering over the Flints, following them. In a night where nothing seemed to go right, Patrick wondered what else could go wrong. Then he cringed as if just by thinking it he would doom them to more disaster.

Nah. That's just superstition.

Trish spoke, her voice sounding befuddled. "Is that a horse-drawn sleigh?"

Patrick turned, following her gaze outside the door. Sure enough, a black two-seater sleigh was parked, harnessed to a gray Percheron team. He shrugged. "Well, they work in snow when cars don't."

A man climbed down from the sleigh and fell to his knees, one hand out like he was begging for help.

Patrick said, "Trish, come with me. You secure the horses. I'll help the man."

Patrick ran to the covered entrance, conscious of his daughter behind him. The cold air hit him hard when he opened the door.

"Ugh," Trish said.

"Get your gear," he told her. "The horses can wait a few minutes." Then he knelt to assist the man, only at the last second realizing Ferdinand had joined him. One of the horses snorted and pawed at the snow. He could smell them. The horses. A combination of sweet feed, sweat, and that particularly pleasant yet indescribable horsey scent.

The face that looked up at him was recently familiar. "Dr. Flint? And that infernal dog of yours!"

"Wilfred. Mr. Mitchell. You look hurt."

"It's my blasted arm. I think I broke it. And I sprained my ankle, I guess. I'm feeling a mite lightheaded. But why is the dog here?"

"Long story. Let's get you inside where I can help you. Which one is your good arm?"

Wilfred lifted a hand. "This un."

"I'm going to grab you by that one to hoist you up, okay?"

"That'll do."

Patrick hoisted the man upward. Wilfred groaned and paled, but he managed to stand on one leg, leaning on Patrick.

Patrick saw a fancy cane with a metal eagle's head topper sticking up out of the sleigh. "Do you want your cane?"

"No." Wilfred's answer came out as a snap.

Trish stomped up to them, arms wrapped around herself. "What do you want me to do with the horses?"

"They'll be fine," Wilfred said. "They pasture in worse than this."

Trish's face looked stricken.

Patrick leaned to her ear. "Take their bits out. Lead them around and tie them to one of the posts supporting the roof here, where they're under cover. Offer them some water, but don't leave it out here where it will freeze."

"If you're that all fired concerned about it, I have a bag of sweet feed in the sleigh. But don't give 'em more than a ration each. You'll spoil 'em."

"Yes, sir," she said, her face relieved. "I'll be back after I put Ferdie up." She called the dog and took him inside. *Good call. Horses and strange dogs aren't a good mix.*

"Now, let's get you inside, Wilfred."

"Wait a durn minute. There's something I gotta tell you while we're alone."

Patrick paused. Wilfred didn't appear to be in shock, but he wanted to get him out of the cold. "Can it wait? It's freezing out here."

"It's why I came to your house earlier. I couldn't talk about it in front of that deputy lady. It doesn't paint me in the best light, but I think I figgered out who killed my Leslie Anne, and I've gotta tell somebody."

That held Patrick still. "I appreciate you thinking I might be the right person to tell, but I'm not sure what I can do for you. I'm a doctor."

"People trust you. You help them. And I need your help now. Are you gonna give it to me or not?"

"I'll do my best, Wilfred, but in the end I can't promise you help without involving law enforcement."

"Your best is what I'm asking for."

"All right then. What is it you came to tell me?"

Wilfred glanced in both directions. He nodded at Trish, who was re-emerging from the hospital, his eyes questioning.

"She's okay. I vouch for her."

Wilfred nodded slow, but still he waited for Trish to lead the horses about ten yards away before he spoke, and then in a loud whisper. "My neighbor. Tristan Babcock. He's been pushing down my fence and letting his cattle run amuck on my place."

What had happened to his suspicions about his new hand? Patrick had been sure that was the person Wilfred would name. "Well, now—that's not very neighborly." There was a saying that good fences made good neighbors. The reverse was definitely true. He hoped bad fences was all there was to Wilfred's complaint.

"They're eating up my forage and hay. It's costing me money while his beasts fatten up to his profit."

"I can see that could happen."

"I did something I'm not proud of." He closed his eyes and cradled his arm to his torso. Patrick stayed silent, giving him time to continue. "After I pushed his beasts back where they belonged and fixed my fence for the fourth time, I fed 'em."

Patrick frowned. He wasn't sure what Wilfred meant. "And?"

"I fed 'em something that would make 'em a little sick."

"Ohhh." Tristan's actions might be trespassing. At a stretch, even theft. But poisoning livestock was a whole 'nother level of criminal activity. Wilfred had crossed a line. A very clear line. "Are they okay?"

"I just want 'em to lose the weight I put on 'em. Ain't fair that Tristan profits off me like that."

"I see."

"Now don't you go passing judgment, Dr. Flint. I ain't proud of it. And I hate telling you. But I have to. Because Tristan caught me at it a couple few days ago and I think it's him that killed Leslie Anne. As a way of getting back at me for his cows that died."

"His cows died?"

"Only two or maybe three or four."

Patrick did the math in his head. That was thousands of dollars, compared to the hundreds at most that Tristan had cost Wilfred. This range war was getting out of hand, clearly.

But out of hand enough to drive a man to murder his neighbor's woman?

CHAPTER TWENTY-SEVEN: SPILL

BUFFALO, WYOMING
SATURDAY, MARCH 18, 1978, 8:00 P.M.

Susanne

SUSANNE STOOD in front of reception with the kids as Kathy made work assignments.

The young woman twisted the end of her braid. "Um, Mrs. Flint, would you mind helping in the ER, like, um, keeping things clean, fetching things for people, and, you know, whatever it is the doctors and nurses need?"

Susanne nodded and smiled. No reason to tell Kathy that was basically Susanne's job description at home, too, except only for one doctor. And how sick she was of being told to do it. "Of course."

"The cafeteria is quiet since it's the middle of the night. They may need help in there in a few hours. Right now, we're missing the staff who do their jobs when there are less people in the hospital milling around. Cleaning and laundry mostly." She hesitated.

Susanne nodded. "How about Kelsey and Wyatt work on laundry together, and Perry and Trish can do some cleaning? Just a suggestion."

"That sounds great. If you don't mind keeping an eye on my station, Mrs. Flint, I could get them started and be back in about fifteen or twenty minutes? Since the phones are out, you'd just be taking information from people who walk in and relaying it to the ER staff. And the middle of the night is usually pretty slow."

"Sure." Susanne had absorbed a lot from Patrick over the years, the main thing being to err on the side of caution and always assume the worst in illnesses and injuries until good news proved you wrong. She turned to the young people. "Everyone good with that?"

Trish and Perry said, "Yes, ma'am," almost simultaneously. It made her heart swell. Wyatt echoed them a few beats later.

Kelsey bit her lip. "When will we be done so we can go to sleep?"

Kathy flushed. "Um, yeah. If we can just get the laundry in progress, you could take shifts watching it while one of you naps. I'll show you empty beds where you can sleep. And, obviously, you're not being paid, so I can't force you to finish it. But it usually takes all night."

"I'm fine," Trish said. "And I can drink coffee to stay awake."

"Me, too. Right, Mom?" Perry said.

Susanne didn't usually let either of her kids drink coffee. The stimulant was addictive. "Just for tonight."

Perry pumped a fist.

Kathy ducked her chin, smiling. "The intake forms are on the desk, Susanne."

"Got it."

"Follow me," Kathy said to the kids, shooting Susanne a grateful smile.

"Don't forget Ferdie. And all of our bags. Drop them in the staff room."

The kids detoured across the room, picking up bags while Kathy waited for them. Perry called for Ferdinand. Then the group set off at a slower pace.

Susanne settled at the reception desk and perused a form clipped to a board. The questions looked straightforward. She touched a mug filled with pens, a second clipboard, and a stack of the forms. She had everything she needed.

The door opened and a blast of icy air raced across the room. She eyed her coat laying on a chair with her hat, mittens, and scarf on the other side of the waiting room. *Not now.* Lifting her gaze, she nodded at the two people making their way toward reception. She blanched. A tiny woman was supporting a large man, and he was moving like something was seriously wrong with him, head lolled, gait lurching, shoulders slumped. Her throat and chest tightened. Heart attack? Stroke?

Susanne jumped to her feet. "What's the matter?"

"Drunk as a skunk," the woman said.

Not a heart attack or stroke. Susanne's face crinkled, then she realized that was unprofessional. Even if this wasn't her profession, she owed Kathy and the rest of the staff to treat it like it was. She owed the patients that. This patient that. She pasted a pleasant expression on her face. "Let me help you get him seated."

"Thank you," the woman said.

Susanne approached and pushed her shoulder under the man's armpit. Heavy alcohol fumes laced with vomit blasted in her face. She pulled her head as far away as she could. Working together, she and the woman lowered the man into a chair. Susanne pulled off his hat and gloves. She left the jacket on and buttoned. There was too much vomit on it. She wasn't about to touch it. Volunteerism had just met its limits.

"You're on your own, buddy. I'm out of here." The woman turned to leave.

"Wait!" Susanne said. "Are you not together?"

"If by together, you mean am I responsible for him, the answer is no. I barely know him. I had a few drinks with him at the Ox for blizzard happy hour, and he got way out of control. His drinking and his behavior."

Susanne gave her a sad smile. "Could you possibly help me? It will only take five minutes. I have an intake form." Susanne looked at the man. His eyes were closed, and his chin was on his chest. "I don't think he'll be able to do it."

"His name is Stuart Renwick. He drank half the liquor at the Ox. And he's a disgusting pervert. That's all I know and should be all you need."

"Did you say Stuart Renwick? Professor Stuart Renwick of Sheridan College?"

"That's him. Do you know him?"

Susanne stared at the man. He lifted his face and burped. It *was* him, only so very not the man she knew from school. This man was filthy, rumpled, and oh so very drunk. "I, uh, have a class with him." She couldn't admit she'd tentatively agreed to work for this man only hours ago.

Professor Renwick's eyes seemed to focus on her for a few seconds. His expression went from zoned out to something icky. "Susanne! My new research assistant." The way he said research assistant made it sound dirty.

"Good luck." The woman's voice came from across the room as she headed for the door, but she wasn't too far away to telegraph her disgust.

With me? What did I do? But it didn't matter. Susanne had a job to do. She grabbed the clipboarded form and a pen. She filled in as much as she could then took a seat across from her professor.

"Professor Renwick, I—"

The man fell from the chair, drool running from his mouth. She tried to catch him but only managed to get her wrist caught and twisted between him and the metal arm of the chair.

"Ouch!" She jerked her wrist free. It was abraded and hyperextended. Painful, but not to the level that she would drain medical resources from patients on a night like tonight.

She stared down at Renwick. Did this constitute the sort of emergency that required a medical professional or a janitor? *Err on the side of caution.*

"Professor Renwick—Stuart—hang in there. I'll be right back with help."

"What's going on?" It was her husband's voice.

Susanne felt a hundred times better with him here, even if she was still upset with him. "I have a very drunk patient. I was just about to let the staff know."

"Where's Kathy?"

"Showing the kids their volunteer jobs. I'm filling in."

Patrick set a Styrofoam cup of coffee on a magazine table and squatted by the man. "I'm Dr. Flint. How are you feeling, sir?"

Professor Renwick had eyes only for Susanne's anatomy. "My Susanne," he slurred.

Patrick shot her a look. "Did he just say *my Susanne*?"

"Unfortunately, yes."

Patrick's eyebrows didn't lower as he examined the man. "How much have you had to drink?"

Renwick sneered. "Not so much. Hit me hard tonight."

"Beer?"

"Do I look like a beer drinker?" He patted his flat belly.

Patrick shot Susanne a withering look over his shoulder. "What's your poison?"

"Glenlivet. Single malt scotch. Top shelf." His slurring made it hard to understand him, but his superiority and condescension transcended his drunkenness.

Patrick eased back Renwick's eyelids and peered into his eyes. He took out a pen light and shone it into them, then asked Renwick to track the light. "Did you fall down any tonight? Hit your head on anything?"

"No, sir, I dinnot." Renwick muttered something about his "good-looking mama in research," then appeared to nod off.

Patrick sighed. "We need to start him on fluids with some vitamins and glucose. Maybe oxygen therapy. And monitor him. I'll take him back and get him started. It appears that he's had so much alcohol that he might be in danger of alcohol poisoning."

"Is that dangerous?" Susanne said.

"Very."

Out of nowhere, Wes appeared, grinning. "Well then, good thing I'm here," he said. "With a wheelchair. You want a blood and urine test, too?"

"Of course." Patrick stood. "What, now you're a mind reader on top of a wiseacre?"

Wes grinned. He parked the wheelchair. "I saw him come in. Help me load him up?"

Patrick took one side of Renwick. Wes took the other. They set him in the chair.

Renwick swatted at their hands. "Waz goin' on? Waddya doin' to me?"

"We're taking you to a comfortable room where we can make you feel better," Wes said.

Renwick shook his head. "Coffee. Need coffee and sleep."

"What we've got is even better. You're going to love it. Luckily, these things come with seat belts." Wes strapped him in. "What's your name, sir?"

Renwick's head fell to the side. His mouth opened and emitted a loud snore.

Patrick cocked his head and looked at Susanne.

She hated that she knew the answer. "Stuart Renwick." To Patrick she added, "He's one of my professors."

"Aha," her husband said, but he didn't look satisfied yet.

"All right, Stuart. Let's go see if we can keep the demon drink from doing you in tonight." Wes pushed Renwick away, his long strides eating up the floor, and the two men disappeared into the corridor leading toward the ER.

Susanne pushed her hair away from her face. Maybe Patrick

wouldn't ask her. Maybe he'd just follow Wes and go do his doctoring.

"Care to fill me in on the details, good-looking mama?" Patrick's voice was dry, with an edge.

Susanne winced. Or maybe not.

CHAPTER TWENTY-EIGHT: DISCOVER

Ben

BEN STOOD on the runners of the snowmobile as he goosed it over the cattle guard at the gate to Piney Bottoms. Relief coursed through him. Even though sliding and getting stuck had been less of a problem on the snow machine than in his truck, the darkness and snow had made it difficult to keep his bearings. More than once, he'd thought he was in the center of the road only to find himself bearing down on a fence post. He roared up the entrance road. The loud machine heralded his arrival, ensuring he wouldn't be sneaking up on anyone. That was good. He didn't want to be met at the door by Henry with a shotgun. Henry could look out the window and watch his own snowmobile cruise up to the house. He'd be pretty surprised when he realized it was Ben.

So, when Ben parked beside Henry's and Vangie's snow-covered vehicles, he took off his hat to be sure he was recognizable. He watched the house, expecting the porch light to switch on, but it didn't. At the front door, he knocked and rang the bell. A smile tugged at the corner of his mouth. He hated that he might wake up Hank, but, then again, he couldn't wait to see the little guy. For not having wanted to come here, he couldn't control his happiness now that he was.

No one answered.

"Lazy bums." He took out his keys. The one to the house was still on his ring.

Opening the door, he shouted, "Anyone home? It's Ben."

No one called out to him. Maybe they were out of town? But if so, why were both their vehicles here?

He toed the snow off his boots and stepped inside. The place smelled a little like rotten eggs, and he wondered if Vangie had a cooking "oops." Most of the time, she was a great cook and even better baker, but she liked to experiment, and Flash ended up eating anything that went awry.

A cold breeze hit his face as he walked down the hallway toward the bedrooms, thinking about the shotgun Henry kept above the master door. The hall window was open, something Henry did every year for ventilation as soon as they started using the heating system. He kept calling out to Henry and Vangie. He decided to go to their bedroom first. It would scare them to death if they got up and found an unexpected man in Hank's bedroom.

"It's Ben." He knocked on their door, rattling it. "Home from Alaska. Wake up."

No answer.

Unease flickered in his belly. He tried the doorknob. It turned easily. He flung the door open and turned on the light.

"It's Ben," he repeated.

Henry was on his back, Vangie's head nestled on his shoulder. They didn't move.

The flicker turned into a brush fire. He ran to the bed and shook Henry, who was nearest to him. "Henry. Wake up. Henry. Henry!"

Henry groaned but didn't open his eyes.

Ben repeated the shaking and calling out with Vangie. She didn't respond at all. He checked for a pulse and found one. *Thank God.* What was wrong with them? And what about Hank?

Ben sprinted back to the little boy's room, opened the door, and yelled his name. He didn't waste time shaking and pulse checking, just picked Hank up and rocked him back and forth frantically.

Think. Think. Think. What is wrong with them?

CHAPTER TWENTY-NINE: CHEW

Patrick

"Care to fill me in on the details, good-looking mama?" Patrick said to his wife, quoting the very drunk patient Wes had just wheeled away to the ER.

Susanne winced. "I went to meet with Professor Renwick at his office this morning. That's why I asked for your help."

"Great," Patrick said, his voice too heavy on the sarcasm. But he was angry. Susanne had met with this man this morning without telling him about it, and now the guy was in Patrick's ER talking about her in a familiar way that Patrick didn't like. This was not okay.

"Don't use that tone on me, Patrick Flint, or you won't hear another word." Her eyes bore into him.

How had she gone from calm to enraged so quickly? His anger rose to meet hers. "He was awfully *familiar* with you Susanne."

Her voice rose. "He was awfully *inappropriate* about me, Patrick. I am not the cause of his bad choices and actions."

Patrick looked around the reception area to ensure they were still alone. "He sure implied there was more to your relationship than professor and student."

"Because there is. He offered me a job as his research assistant. It's a very prestigious opportunity, and quite flattering."

"And you took the job without talking to me about it first? We're already stretched too thin!"

"I tried to talk to you about it, but you were late to the Sibleys. After not checking on Perry or Trish. After breaking your commitment as my partner. And, no, I didn't take it. I told him that I would have to think about it and talk to you."

"You want to talk about commitments? You committed to raising the kids. Now you've changed our plan, and you expect me to do your job for you."

"No, Patrick, I expect you to be a partner in parenting our kids, not to spend your every free moment chasing after whatever the latest thing it is that you have your heart set on."

"What's that supposed to mean?"

"Mountain climbing? Really? Was that part of our plan? That I'd be locked into being your maid and personal assistant so you could spend our time and money chasing the Seven Summits? And that it would make me so happy that I'd still be your Madonna by day and your Mata Hari by night? Think again. Your activities don't leave me any room at all to become the woman I was meant to be."

Red blurred Patrick's vision. He couldn't believe the things Susanne was saying to him. He started to defend himself, then changed his mind and went on the attack. "We don't need the piddly money you'd make working as a research assistant. Or as a teacher for that matter. It's a waste of our time. And if you're so unhappy with how I spend mine, just remember you'd have more if you hadn't decided to pile school and now a job on top of the portion of the load you committed to carrying. I sure hope this is a migraine talking and not my wife."

For three long seconds, Susanne stared at him without speaking. Her lips were pressed in a thin white line. Her fists were clenched. Her pupils were dilated like a wild animal, her chest was heaving, and her nostrils were flared. Suddenly, Patrick wanted to take everything he'd said back. He'd been angry. He opened his mouth to speak, but she beat him to it.

"You selfish, selfish man. I do not have a migraine. My head is clear. It's all about your needs. Your hobbies. They come before any of the rest of us."

"Susanne, I'm—"

Heavy footsteps sounded close by. Patrick stopped speaking in mid-sentence. They weren't alone.

Then a soft voice with a faint accent said, "Patrick, Susanne. What a treat to see you."

The familiar voice. Patrick turned. The swarthy, friendly face and dark hair. The medical scrubs. It was Abraham. Patrick looked back at Susanne. Hesitated a second before tearing his eyes from his wife's pale, slack face. The timing was horrible. He hated leaving their conversation like this. The things he'd said. He needed to apologize. He needed to listen. He could see in her eyes that she was hurting. That he'd made her feel that way.

But it was too late now. Later. Later he'd have to make things right.

Patrick licked his lips, stuck out his hand, and took Abraham's. "Great to see you."

The men leaned in and clapped each other on the shoulders.

"Hello, Abraham," Susanne said.

Abraham nodded at Susanne. He didn't touch her, but he radiated warmth.

"How are things at Wind River?" Patrick asked.

"I have no complaints. The work is good, the people are grateful, and the scenery is magnificent."

"Good to hear."

"And you and your family?"

Before Patrick could answer, a vehicle honked from the entrance. Whoever it was didn't let up, just kept the horn pressed down so that it blared endlessly. Abraham and Patrick shared a glance, then ran for the door. As they burst out of it, the horn let up and a truck threw snow up behind it as it sped away from the unloading area. Wilfred's horses snorted and pawed.

"This patient needs a stretcher," Abraham said. "He appears to have head injuries."

"Grab one. I'll stay with him." Patrick knelt by the man on the ground.

Abraham disappeared into the hospital. The man groaned and kicked out with one foot. Patrick leaned closer to see his head. The main point of injury—or at least bleeding—appeared to be his mouth, and it was clear the man had been hit more than once. Patrick frowned. A chill passed through him, one from more than the frigid temperatures and wind. It looked similar to the wound he'd seen across Leslie Anne's orbital region that morning. A flattening at the point of impact with diagonal indentations running through.

Had the same weapon that killed Leslie Anne been used on this man?

CHAPTER THIRTY: RESCUE

Ben

BEN'S BRAIN churned as he hurried out of Hank's room with the limp little boy in his arms. What was wrong with his family? A nagging headache had come over him, sudden and intense, and it was making it hard to think. A wave of nausea passed through him. Why did he feel sick now—was it from something in the house? Was it going to make him pass out too or was he just scared? He staggered, dizzy and almost falling, catching himself against the hallway wall with one hand, and hanging on to Hank with the other.

Then it came to him. The smell of rotten eggs when he'd first come into the house. The headache. *Propane leak.* The Sibleys used propane for their furnace, for their oven, for their stove. *Thank God they always left the window at the end of the hall cracked open for ventilation. Even more that they'd all been sleeping with their doors closed and that the kitchen was so far from the bedrooms.* He had to get everyone out of the house. But that would take time. Time when they would still be breathing the propane in. Panic licked at him like a red-hot flame. They needed fresh air. *Now.*

He stumbled into the master bedroom, set Hank on the bed, and ran to the largest window. He unlatched it and tried to raise it. It wouldn't budge. Ran to the next one. Did the same. Same result. *No!* Henry had complained that summer that Vangie had closed the windows too soon after she'd given the frames a fresh coat of paint and now they were stuck. He tried each one again, pulling upward with all his strength.

They didn't move.

There was no more time to waste. Ben looked around the room, searching for something to use as a club. *The shotgun.* He stumbled to the door, reached up for the gun, and hefted it off its pegs. Staggered quickly back to the larger window, reared the gun back by the stock, and swung the barrel at the glass like he was Hank Aaron or something. CRACK. The window exploded into the yard sending shards of glass flying outward and a few to the carpet below Ben's feet. He hurried to the other window and repeated his batting exercise.

Cold air rushed into the bedroom. It was below zero outside. Far colder with the wind chill. How quickly would hypothermia overtake Henry and Vangie in their condition? Because he needed their comforter. Little Hank was going out into the storm. *Please, God, don't let this be a mistake.* He ripped the comforter off Henry and Vangie and wrapped Hank in it. He would bring back blankets for them from the closet. He would need to wrap them up good when he got them outside.

And not to pass out himself.

Outside, outside, outside. Time to get outside.

He sprinted blindly down the hall, through the front room, and to the entry, somehow managing not to crush himself and Hank against a wall. He flung open the front door and left it ajar. Snow was still coming down sideways.

Now what?

They needed shelter and body heat. His truck was too small. So was Henry's. But Vangie's station wagon would be big enough for all of them. He stomped through the snow and tried the back door. *Unlocked.* Finally, something going right. He yanked the door open and set the boy on the back seat. His own face felt wet. He touched it. He was crying.

No time for that.

He tucked the comforter tightly around Hank and sprinted back toward the house. Slipped on the front steps. Fell to his knees. The pain was like a hot poker. He ignored it. Got back up and ran inside. The smell of rotten eggs was still there, but not as bad as before. Maybe the open windows and door were helping.

He stopped at the linen closet for blankets, ripping them off the built-in shelves and out onto the floor. He picked the thickest one up, hopped over the pile, and went for Vangie. She was just as he'd left her, lying on her back. He spread the blanket beside her then reached for her. Her skin was cold to the touch, but her chest was rising and falling. *That's good. But hurry.* He rolled her over into the blanket and bundled her up. The woman was so tiny. He lifted her over his shoulder, holding the blanket closed. She was so light. Carrying her was easy, running with her effortless—until he tripped over the blankets, sprawling on them and on her. Pain shot through his knee and up his thigh from his earlier fall.

Vangie groaned.

"I'm sorry. So sorry." His tears had turned to sobs, and the words barely came out.

He struggled to his feet without letting go of her, ignoring his knee. It was a reminder that he was awake, he hadn't succumbed to the fumes. He had time to save his family. Out the door he ran, down the steps, across the yard, through the snow, and straight onto the backseat with Hank. He took a moment to nestle them together for body heat.

One more time. Just one more time.

For a moment as he was bent over them, everything went dark.

No, no, no.

He held himself up. His breathing was shallow. His head light. But his vision came back. There was no time to worry about himself. Back inside he went, skipping the blankets, heading straight for Henry. The rancher was a head shorter than Ben. Spare, but strong. Much harder to lift than Vangie. Ben crouched and threw Henry over his shoulder. Running was difficult. His balance was off. He rammed into the bedroom door frame. The pain in his shoulder was intense, but he shook it off and pinballed down the hallway, this time skirting the blanket pile. He'd come back for the blankets. Right now he just needed to get Henry into the fresh air.

As he passed Hank's room he heard a whimper. He frowned as he ran on. What was the whimper? He had everyone. He slowed as he went through the door, more careful on the steps with his heavier load. Crossing the yard was easier, the snow stomped down from his earlier trips. At the car, he took the time to sit Vangie up and put Henry in beside her, pressed against her, then Hank across their laps.

But the whimper . . .

He headed back in, nervous. Walked into Hank's room. The sound had stopped.

Maybe it had been his imagination? Maybe the sound had come from him?

Turning on the light, he looked around quickly. Just one scan, and then he'd go. But what he saw nearly stopped his heart. A brown, black, and white ball of fur was curled up at the head of the crib.

Flash.

Ben cried out. How had he forgotten about the dog? The dog that had slept with him in the room next to Hank's, gone fishing with him, rode shotgun in his truck around the ranch? Been his best friend besides Trish.

"I'm sorry, boy. So sorry." He scooped the animal into his arms, running, praying he wasn't too late. Too late for Flash. Too late for all of them.

In less than a minute, he set the beagle next to Hank in Henry and Vangie's laps. The family was huddled together. Ben was heaving for breath.

What next?

More blankets. Coats. Gloves. Hats.

Car keys.

God, I hate going back in there.

Should he call for an ambulance?

Yes. The phone was in the house.

But shouldn't he turn off the propane first? *Yes.*

He had to slow down. Think. Where did the propane come into the house? A memory surfaced of a propane truck parked on the side of the house filling a giant white cylinder. *Yes.* He ran to it, but he couldn't see anything. Wished he had turned on the outside lights. Wished he had a flashlight. A lantern. Any light.

But he still had the matches in his pocket.

He pulled them out and was about to strike one when it occurred to him that flame and propane were not a good mix. Safer to take the time to turn on the lights than to die and leave his family to freeze to death. Back inside he ran, flipping on all the switches by the front door. He returned to the tank. The front lights weren't great, but they were enough. On top of the tank, there was a dome. He twisted it, yanked it, then pushed it. It opened on a hinge, revealing a valve. A valve, just like the valves on the outdoor water faucets. He grasped the valve and tried to rotate it in the off direction.

It turned. He continued until it stopped, panting, sweating, scared. But had this solved the problem? He had no way of knowing. It didn't matter. He had no choice but to go back in that house to use the phone.

CHAPTER THIRTY-ONE: STARTLE

Perry

PINE-SCENTED WATER SLOSHED over the edge as Perry pushed the mop bucket down the hall. He didn't care. His mom would have said he was in a snit. Whatever it was called, he didn't like Kelsey and Wyatt being off alone together doing laundry. Not one bit. And their job put them in the same room the whole time. He'd seen the room. It was tight quarters. They'd even been given access to a private place to sleep. Just thinking about it made his stomach hurt. Meanwhile, his job was to follow Trish, mopping floors after she swept them. He couldn't keep an eye on Kelsey. Couldn't go back to check on her at all. And he sure wasn't being given nap time.

Mopping was exhausting, too, something he never would have imagined. He suddenly had a little grudging respect for his mom and the school janitors who cleaned up after him and his friends in the cafeteria.

At least he and Trish were moving into the emergency area, where maybe he would have something to distract him. The ER was a lot more interesting than the cafeteria and the chapel, where they'd started. Those areas were boring and empty. Kathy had told them to stay out of the staff's way and not to create slipping hazards in busy areas. *Whoops. Slipping hazard.* He took a few steps back and mopped up the spilled water. But when was the ER not busy? It was so busy that there was a hum to it. Like raw energy. He imagined when they moved into the actual patient rooms in the hospital it would be quieter.

Trish stopped short of an exam area with a closed curtain. She spoke in a low voice. "Should we do the floors where there are patients?"

Kathy had told them to sweep and mop the exam rooms. But she hadn't said what to do if there were patients in them. How was he supposed to know? "Maybe?"

Trish rolled her eyes at him. "How about we do, but only if there aren't doctors or nurses with them. And let's be fast."

She slipped behind the curtain. Perry followed. A wrinkly old guy slept on the exam table, his mouth oozing blood. *Yuck.* It seemed like his face was a funny shape, too. Flat around his mouth. And his teeth were all broken. He wasn't tied in, but the rails were raised on both sides, and he looked dead. A machine beeped from the corner, which is the only reason Perry didn't think he was.

"What do you think you're doing in here?" a woman said, her voice commanding and a little scary.

Perry dropped his mop. It hit the ground with a THWAP. He sunk to his knees to grab it. When he looked up, he relaxed some. It was Ronnie. She could be terrifying when she needed to be, but he wasn't doing anything wrong.

"Hey, Ronnie." Trish stood up straight, holding the broom to her chest. "We're volunteering. They've got us on sweep and mop duty. Do you think it's ok that we came in here? I mean, he is asleep and all."

Ronnie smiled at them and beckoned them outside the curtain. "I'm sure it's okay. I just got a little worried when I saw people in here with Mr. Babcock. The hospital radioed me, and I came to keep an eye on him." She lowered her voice. "Someone hit him earlier. Lucky for him he stayed conscious long enough to call a friend to bring him to the hospital or he would have died out in this storm."

"Hit him like with a car?" Trish asked.

"Like with a blunt instrument to the mouth. Which at best is assault and battery and at worst attempted murder."

Perry's eyes flew so wide it felt like he was stretching them. "Is that why you're here, to protect him?"

Ronnie laughed. "More like to be here to talk to him when he wakes up. Don't worry. This weather will keep the bad guys away."

Perry hoped she was right. An image of the guy in the backyard flashed into his mind. The weird thing he'd said from the Bible about not lusting after the beauty of her eyes or something. It had probably been him that slashed their tires and threw the brick through the window. Or maybe not. If there was one thing he'd learned in the last few years it was that there are a lot of bad guys doing a lot of bad things. But a lot of good people, too. He wondered if his dad had talked to Ronnie about the things that had happened at their house yet.

He stared at the beaten-up old guy. Better to be in the hospital. For him, and for the Flints.

CHAPTER THIRTY-TWO: CHURN

Trish

RONNIE POPPED her neck in one direction and then the other as Trish studied her.

The deputy was so pretty, even if right now her eyes were puffy with dark circles. She was athletic, too. Trish wondered if she'd been a cheerleader in high school. She'd probably been too busy with rodeo and working on her family ranch to do anything frivolous. Was Trish making a big mistake trying out with Marcy? It wasn't too late to back out. To do something more serious with her time. Ronnie was doing a hard, important job, like Trish wanted to do one day, although Trish wanted to go into wildlife biology and work for the forest service. Ronnie was tough and strong. Trish didn't feel worried about whoever had hit this old man with Ronnie here.

Ronnie said, "I'll let you two get back to work. I'm about ready to call it a night, whenever Radish gets here. It's been a long night and day . . . and another night." She turned to go, then stopped. "Hey, Trish. Good to see Ben back in town."

Every thought in Trish's head blanked out. Her body felt like someone had just stuck a thousand needles in her. "You saw Ben?"

"Yep. He was headed north on the interstate from Buffalo to Piney Bottoms when I was out there closing it down. Are you two back together?"

Trish stared at her, unsure of what to say, of how to form coherent words. She wasn't even sure she could keep standing up. Any second, her body would puddle into the floor.

"Never mind. I didn't mean to put you on the spot. None of my beeswax." Ronnie winked. "I'll be calling soon. Jeff and I need a babysitter for next weekend if you're available."

Trish rallied. "Sure. I'd love to see Will." *Ben was here? Why hadn't she seen him? Why was she just now hearing about it because he'd run into Ronnie and Ronnie had run into her?*

"And he'd love to see you. Tell your parents hello for me."

When Trish didn't respond, Perry gave her a funny look and said, "We will."

And then Ronnie was gone.

Perry started questioning her like a machine gun. "What was she talking about? Did Ben come to see you? I thought you were at cheerleading clinic and then a party with Wyatt? Why didn't you tell me?"

Trish snapped back to life. Perry could irritate the dead. "I wasn't *with* Wyatt anywhere. I was at the clinic and then at a party with Marcy. Wyatt gave me a ride home to our house. I never saw Ben." Trish knew she sounded snappy. She felt snappy. She didn't care.

"But Ben's in town?"

"I don't know, Perry. I guess so. That's the first I've heard about it."

"Don't bite my head off. I just figured you knew, that's all."

"Well, I don't."

"Maybe Ronnie had him confused with someone else. You know. In the dark and the snow."

Trish put her fist to her mouth. *Maybe. Would she rather that than Ben coming to Buffalo and not to see her?* But that was crazy. She had prayed for him to come back and to know he was safe. Shouldn't she be thankful that if he was here, he clearly was? *I'm not. If he doesn't want to see me, how can I be happy about anything?* She'd been happier when her prayers went unanswered.

"There you are."

Trish and Perry turned to the voice at the same time. Their mother.

"Hi, Mom," Perry said. "We just saw Ronnie and she said B—"

Trish interrupted him. "She said to tell you and Dad hello."

Perry frowned a question at her. Trish glared at him, trying to send a *keep your mouth shut about Ben* answer telepathically.

"I just saw her. She said you guys were in here." She made a sad face at the old man in the bed. Trish and Perry had accidentally left the curtain open. "Wow. It's terrible seeing Mr. Babcock like that. He's such a big, strong man. And so healthy, too. He must be eighty, and his only infirmity was using a cane. And even that was only because a horse fell on his leg. Are you two done with his room?"

Trish pulled the curtain shut. She thought it was funny that her mom called it a room. It wasn't a room. All the exam areas were just curtains, running back and forth on tracks in the ceiling. Tracks that went in every direction. An upside-down Hot Wheels car track. The place probably looked like a basketball gym when the curtains were all open.

"We just finished," Trish said.

"All right." Their mom nodded. "Then move along. Lots more floors to clean."

Trish poised her broom to sweep, moving on autopilot. Already her mind was back on Ronnie's news. On Ben.

Ronnie had to be mistaken.

CHAPTER THIRTY-THREE: DISLIKE

BUFFALO, WYOMING
SATURDAY, MARCH 18, 1978, 8:55 P.M.

Patrick

THE STENCH of vomit still hung in the air as Patrick tried not to stomp like a petulant child on his way from *Professor* Stuart Renwick to his next patient in the ER. He wasn't sure he'd been successful, though. The man was infuriating. Even hooked to an IV and oxygen tank and in between bouts of stupor, he was continuing to mumble inappropriate comments about Susanne. Patrick found himself wishing he didn't have a duty to provide care to everyone who came to the hospital. As soon as the guy's blood pressure and respiration were up to normal and the alcohol was out of his system, Patrick would be happy to see him on his way. But then he remembered the weather. He wondered how many patients were going to need to overstay because they were stuck here.

Just as long as it wasn't this one.

But the man probably didn't have a vehicle. *Great.* And Patrick was spending time on him when he could be checking back in on the old guy with the mouth busted up like Leslie Anne's eyes. Tristan Babcock, he'd learned, when they'd looked at the man's license. There was nothing he could do for Tristan right now, though. He and Abraham had done the best they could to make him comfortable and insure that he didn't have any other injuries. The entire staff would check on him every chance they got. He was just glad Kathy had radioed law enforcement. He had a feeling when this guy woke up, he'd be pointing his finger at a killer.

Still, if he was honest with himself—and that was no fun, but occasionally necessary, he'd admit that the real thing bothering him was his fight with his wife. He couldn't believe she was actually considering going to work for the lecherous drunk, Renwick. *Not if I have anything to say about it.* But he wondered if he did right now. She wasn't happy with him. His ears still burned from the chewing out she'd given him half an hour before. The things she'd said would be hard to forget. That he was selfish. That he put his own needs before anyone else's in the family. That he expected her to be his maid and personal assistant, a Madonna by day and a Mata Hari by night, and that he didn't leave room for her to become the woman she was meant to be. Honestly, he didn't even know what she meant. It had smarted. He had gotten mad. Maybe said a few things back. But he was having second thoughts about his reaction. Somehow, without meaning to, he'd made her feel . . . bad. Worse than bad. It was the last thing he wanted.

They needed to have a talk. A serious talk. One that included his apology. He knew they did. But when?

Abraham stuck his head out of an exam area. "Patrick? A word?" He shut the curtain behind him and walked into the corridor.

"Certainly." Expecting to be consulted on a medical issue, Patrick moved to the side of the hall.

Abraham lowered his voice to a whisper. He was normally soft-spoken, but now Patrick had to lean in to hear him. "The patient in that exam room has refused to let me treat him."

Patrick frowned. "What's the problem? Is he trying to leave against medical advice?"

"No. That's not it. It seems," Abraham gritted his teeth and closed his eyes for a moment, "that there is an objection to my heritage and appearance."

Patrick's mouth could have caught flies. Abraham was born, raised, and educated in California. His father was Caucasian. But his mother was Iranian, and Abraham had lived in Iran for several years as an adult after the death of his father. He did look Middle Eastern, and his voice carried a hint of the Farsi accent he'd acquired from his family and time there. But heritage and appearance had nothing to do with the quality of medical care. He didn't understand people who objected to others at face value. "What did they say to you?"

"It does not bear repeating. The patient's injuries are significant. He needs care. I am hoping you will provide it."

He put a hand on Abraham's shoulder. "I'm sorry my friend. People can be ignorant and unkind."

"And others can be quite wonderful. It is one of the mysteries of life, how different some are on the inside." Abraham bowed his head and shoulders slightly. "Thank you. I will check in with Kathy to let her know I will take the next patient and that you have taken mine."

Patrick pulled back the curtain to the room Abraham had come from. From one irritating patient to another. But as a physician he had no right to base care on whether he liked the patients or not. He would give his best to this person. And he would circle back with Abraham later. He hated that his friend had been mistreated in his town. His hospital.

Inside, he found two men. One was seated in a chair. He was the older, with heavy lines on his face that suggested fifty or more years in the sun and wind, or sixty plus if he worked an office job. But everything about his attire proclaimed outdoor work. Dusty boots and jeans. A flannel shirt layered over a long john top. A smudged cowboy hat in his lap. The man on the exam table was harder to peg, mainly because his face was a bloody mess, and he was slumped over, holding his left side.

"I'm Dr. Flint." He approached the man in the chair, hand extended.

The man shook Patrick's hand. "Roger Compton. This here's my boy, Andrew."

"Nice to meet you." Andrew croaked the words out, wincing and wheezy.

"You gonna take care of him instead of that Ay-rab fella?" Roger said.

Patrick clenched his teeth. Deflect and move on quickly. "I'll be caring for him." He suspected the younger man had broken ribs, but as beat up as Andrew looked, he'd have to rule out organ damage, too. Spleen especially. "Andrew, what happened to you?"

The two men shared a long look, Andrew through a slitted eye that would be black, blue, and green the next day.

"A wreck."

Patrick knew he'd just been fed a line of hooey. This man had been beaten. "Was the wreck with a large animal or a person?"

Andrew shook his head.

"If it was a car accident, the police will need to be notified. And if it wasn't a car accident, I still need to contact them unless you got these injuries from a run-in with livestock."

Roger's eyebrows shot up. "Let's just agree it was a one-car accident and leave the police out of it."

Patrick let the subject drop. For now. He stepped closer to Andrew and began inventorying his injuries. The ear had borne the worst of it. A few other blows to the head and face. Ribs. "Are you gentlemen from hereabouts?"

"Not really. We live east near Moorcroft. Are you familiar with the area?"

Moorcroft. Like Leslie Anne and the father and brother Ronnie had seen arguing earlier with Wilfred. What were the chances this was a coincidence? *Zero to none.* He palpated Andrew below his left ribs. Not hard or swollen. The man winced. Patrick worked his way up to the rib area. Andrew cried out and nearly leapt from the table. The spleen area was tender, but it could be radiating from the rib injury. Might need a CT scan. "Any dizziness or fainting?"

"No."

"Nausea?"

"No."

"Left shoulder pain?"

"No. My right one hurts, but I got whacked there."

Getting whacked was not consistent with a vehicle accident, but Patrick let it slide. He turned to Roger. "Has Andrew seemed confused since the . . . accident?"

"No. Just madder than a wet hen."

"Does he look pale to you, compared to normal?" He didn't seem pale to Patrick, but everything needed to be evaluated against the patient's personal baseline, when possible.

"No. He's always a pasty one."

Patrick nodded. To Andrew he said, "Blood in your urine?"

"No."

"Difficulty breathing?"

"Hurts like crazy on my left side, but that's all."

Patrick pulled out his stethoscope. First, he listened to the lungs. No sounds of punctures. He moved to Andrew's heartbeat, then took his pulse from his wrist. Within normal range for someone post-injury. He'd expect the pulse to be elevated from pain and stress. Next, he took the man's blood pressure. If anything, it was a little higher than he would have expected. They'd have to keep a close eye for low blood pressure and a fast heart rate, but, for now, he didn't see evidence the spleen was ruptured. Or really of any severe internal injuries.

Patrick began cleaning the wounds. The man would need a few stitches, although the injury to the ear was pulpy. There wasn't much to do with it except clean it, treat it with antibiotics, and cover it. "What brings you to Buffalo?"

Again, the two men looked at each other before Roger answered. "We came to visit my daughter."

Bingo. "Leslie Anne?"

Roger drew back, his face wary. "You knew her?"

"Not exactly. I tried to save her this morning. My condolences to you for your loss."

Andrew shrugged. "My sister was a shrew. Anybody would have wanted to kill her if she opened her mouth around them. But it wasn't their business to do so."

Patrick fought not to recoil at the harsh words. Instead, he focused on the injury to Andrew's ear. He frowned, his eyes blurring as he stared harder, in disbelief. This was the third time he'd seen this same pattern in one day. A flattening at the point of impact with diagonal indentations running through. Leslie Anne, Tristan, and now Andrew. What was going on here? Who was attacking these people?

"But she was a hard worker, son. We needed her back home. We're going to miss her, mark my words."

"I ain't arguing that point. I just ain't gonna miss her mouth."

"Bottom line, she was our'n, not his'n. Now, she won't do nobody no good."

Andrew snorted. "Except the worms and maggots."

Patrick looked at the injury on Andrew's right shoulder. It had already started to bruise, but it had not broken the skin. He rotated the shoulder and asked a few questions about Andrew's range of motion and pain. Andrew's answers didn't cause him concern. But the pattern of the injury did. It was a clear imprint of what he thought he'd seen in the head wounds of Leslie Anne, Tristan, and Andrew. The indent. The diagonal lines. He blew out, vibrating his lips.

"What is it, doctor?" Roger asked.

He wanted to tell them the problem was that they were rotten people and take them to task about how they were talking about Leslie Anne and what they'd said to Abraham. But that wouldn't do any good. He wished that Ronnie were here so he could relay his fears to her, but she wasn't. So, he focused on his medical findings.

"These injuries. I've seen them before," he said.

"Really? Where?"

Patrick hesitated, unsure whether to divulge what he knew. "Tell me the truth. What were you hit with? This could be important information."

"I already told you doctor. A car," Andrew said.

Patrick shook his head. "I'm sorry. But unless a car came into the field at Wilfred's ranch and struck your sister across the eye sockets, that's just not true."

"What are you saying?"

Patrick pinched the bridge of his nose. "I'm saying that whatever hit you hit her, too. And that I think you need to talk to the police."

CHAPTER THIRTY-FOUR: HOPE

Ben

Ben piled blankets on Hank, Vangie, Henry, and Flash. He pulled caps on their heads. Put mittens on their hands. Started the car and turned on the heater to full blast. Sat in the driver's seat, trying to decide what to do.

He'd done everything he could think of. He'd tried to call 911 but the phones weren't working. He'd opened all the doors and windows in the entire house. Turned off the propane heating system, just to make sure. He'd even checked the stove in the kitchen, and found one of the burners turned on but not lit. He'd turned it off. Already, though, the smell had gone away. His headache was still there and his stomach unsure, but he imagined it to be getting better.

How long had it been since he'd found them? An hour maybe? Indecision wracked him. Should he stay here, try to make it back to the hospital in Buffalo, or maybe wake up the hands and see if any of them knew what to do?

Because Ben had no idea what to do to help his family. They'd been poisoned. He couldn't make that go away.

Before he could make up his mind, a raspy voice from the back-seat said, "Ben? Is that you?"

He turned, hope surging.

Henry's eyes were open. And then they closed.

A moan. Vangie. A wail. Hank crying. A howl. Flash. They were still alive. For now.

Ben wiped away the tears streaming down his face. He put the car in reverse and backed in a half circle, then pulled away from the house.

CHAPTER THIRTY-FIVE: FEAR

Buffalo, Wyoming
Saturday, March 18, 1978, 9:15 p.m.

Patrick

PATRICK SPLASHED his face with cold water in the men's bathroom. He'd been unable to convince the Comptons to tell him what weapon had been used on Andrew. He needed to talk to Ronnie about the three similar injuries. It was important. It had to be. And it made him extremely uncomfortable to have two of those three injured parties in the ER at once. Bad things came in threes, he'd always heard, and they'd already had their third.

At least he'd managed to stall Andrew, insisting that he stay for observation of his spleen. He wouldn't be able to hold the man and his father against their will, though. The Comptons could walk out whenever they felt like it. He couldn't imagine they would want to with the roads out of Buffalo closed and the weather like it was.

He stared at himself in the mirror. The man he saw was death warmed over, and the night had barely begun. His actual shift didn't even start for nine more hours. Catnaps during lulls tonight were going to be critical. The emotional turmoil of the day and of the fight with Susanne was already taking a toll on him.

Wes walked in. "That bad, Sawbones?"

"Pretty bad. Wish we had phones. I need to call Ronnie, and I think she's at home. I'll have to get Kathy to help me with the radio when we both have a chance. Maybe someone can go out to her place and send her in."

"Sounds important. But Ronnie's here somewhere. Or she was."

"What?"

"Yeah. Kathy radioed for help after Mr. Babcock arrived, and Ronnie came. She was waiting for him to wake up so she could talk to him."

Patrick rubbed his forehead. "I've been back and forth past his room over and over since he got here. How did I miss her?"

"You are a little oblivious at times, Doc. But maybe she was in the women's room. Or getting coffee. What's the problem anyway?"

Patrick peeked under the two stalls. No feet. "Something troubling is going on. This morning, I found a woman who'd been murdered. Leslie Anne Compton. Girlfriend of Wilfred Mitchell."

"I heard about it."

"I think we're going to hear from the coroner that she died of a blow to the head. Or, more specifically, to the face."

Wes cringed. "Her face?"

"Her eyes."

"My God, it just keeps getting worse. Who did it to her?"

"Ronnie doesn't know yet. And Wilfred—who is here now, with a busted arm and sprained ankle—told me he believes it was his neighbor who killed her."

"Why?"

"A dispute over cattle and grazing."

"Who's his neighbor?"

"Tristan Babcock."

"What? And now he's in here with a facial injury."

"Yes. His mouth. And it looks a lot like the blow to Leslie Anne. The pattern is pretty distinctive."

"He was hit on the head, too."

"Yes. Same as Leslie Anne. But his mouth took the worst of it. Same as Leslie Anne's eyes."

"So, the same person hit them both?"

"I don't know about that. But a similar weapon was used, at least. And the timing seems . . ."

"The timing makes them seem connected."

"Yes."

"But whoever hit Tristan dropped him at our door and took off. Doesn't seem like they wanted to kill him."

Patrick mulled that over. "Who's to say they meant to kill Leslie Anne?"

"True."

"And to top it all off, Leslie Anne's father and brother were in town today, and they argued with Wilfred after her death. Ronnie saw it and thinks they believe Wilfred killed her."

Wes made a rolling motion for Patrick to continue his story.

"The Comptons are here. Now. In the ER. The brother, Andrew, has an injury to his ear that—"

"Don't tell me it looks like the one to Leslie Anne's eyes and Tristan's mouth."

Patrick nodded.

"Like see no evil, hear no evil, speak no evil?"

Patrick grunted. He hadn't thought of that. "Or meaningless and just use of a similar weapon, either by the same or a different person."

"I like my explanation better."

The door to the bathroom opened a crack. A female voice said, "Patrick, are you in there?"

His wife. His heart leapt. Maybe she'd forgiven him. They'd both said things in the heat of the moment that they regretted before. They'd gotten past it. They would this time, too.

Wes beat him to a response. "Hi, Susanne. We're having boy talk."

Susanne didn't seem to notice Wes's jovial response. "There's a patient you need to see. He's just been put in the exam room nearest the waiting room. We're trying to isolate him from the other patients."

"Why?"

"Just come on out."

Patrick raised his eyebrows at Wes.

"Go. I'll find Ronnie and update her, if she's still here, Sawbones."

"Thanks." Patrick left the bathroom.

Susanne moved to the side of the hall, avoiding contact with him. His heart sank.

Trying to think of something he could say—anything to establish a dialog between them—he said, "Have you seen the kids?"

She nodded but didn't look at him. "Trish and Perry were hard at work. I need to check on Wyatt and Kelsey. Now, I think you need to go."

"Okay." Patrick started walking backward toward the new patient's exam room.

Susanne turned without another word and walked in the opposite direction.

Patrick tried to remove the frown on his face before he drew back the curtain. It took a Herculean effort, but he managed to get it to a neutral position, then he walked in to see the new patient. "I'm Dr. Flint. What seems to be the problem?"

The man on the exam table looked like a refugee from Siberia. Tattered, heavy clothes, in layer upon layer. A wool cap with ear covers tied on top. Thick facial hair. Dull, sunken eyes that lifted halfway to his. The man scowled. "You're the man with the dog."

Patrick didn't bat an eye at the odd, unfriendly greeting. "What?"

"Your dog is a witness."

His insides flip flopped. "A witness to what?"

"She died."

"You mean Leslie Anne Compton?"

The man didn't answer.

"How did you hear that?"

"The police."

"A blonde deputy?"

No answer.

"They talked to you?"

He slow nodded. "Somebody did bad things at your house."

The hair rose all over Patrick's body. "You were at our house?"

"Not me. A boy in a truck. Dark hair. He was mad."

"How do you know he was mad?"

"He wouldn't give me a ride."

The conversation was difficult, frustrating, and a little bit terrifying. It got worse when he heard Trish behind him.

"What boy in a truck? What was his name?" she said. Her voice was shrill and demanding.

The man didn't even look at her.

"Was his name Ben?" She advanced on the patient.

Patrick put a hand on her arm, holding her back. "Ben is in Alaska honey. I've been meaning to tell you. The investigator thinks he went to Ketchikan."

"He's not. He's here."

"Trish . . ."

"Ask Ronnie. She saw him."

"Ronnie? When?"

"Heading to Piney Bottoms. When she was closing the interstate."

"When did you talk to Ronnie?"

"Earlier. I was sweeping in some guy's room that she's waiting to talk to."

Patrick didn't know how to respond.

"He was mad," the man said again.

Trish sounded desperate now. "Why was he mad? Was he mad at me?"

Patrick lowered his voice. "Trish, I don't think—"

"He looked in the window."

Trish clapped a hand over her mouth, holding a broom in the other. "Wyatt. He saw me with Wyatt."

"You don't know it was him, Trish. And Ben would never do bad things to our house and vehicles." Again, Patrick lowered his voice. "We don't even know if Ben was really there."

"I know he was. I know it was him. I need Mom." She burst into tears and fled.

Patrick agreed she needed her mother, but he hated that he didn't have the foggiest idea what to do in these types of situations. He was a good father. He felt certain of that. But he believed it took two parents to come up with a whole range of the necessary skills for raising kids. If anything ever happened to Susanne, he'd do his best, but he didn't know how single parents managed. He felt sure he'd screw it up. Heck, according to Susanne, he was already screwing it up when he had her here to help him.

His younger child's voice was next. Perry, standing in the open curtain. "That's him, Dad. That's the guy from our backyard."

The man's voice was a monotone. "That boy told me to go away. I warned him. Do not lust in your heart after her beauty or let her captivate you with her eyes."

Patrick backed up. The man hadn't said what bad things he'd seen done at their house. He might not be their saboteur. But he had definitely been there, and he gave off glaring signals of mental illness. Mental illness didn't equate to violent or criminal behavior. There was a correlation for some people, but not nearly everyone who suffered from mental illness also broke the law or hurt other people. He needed to ignore what Perry had told him, get help, and treat this man. Although what condition he'd come in for, he didn't have a clue.

"Dad. Did you hear me?"

"I heard you. Can you get Wes for me? Tell him we have a

patient that needs immediate attention. Leave the curtain open as you go, please."

"But, Dad . . ."

Patrick used his sternest voice. "Perry. Now."

"Yes, sir." Perry's sounded resistant, but he left.

Patrick kept his eyes trained on the man. "What's your name, sir?"

No answer.

"Why were you at my home earlier?"

"I was looking for a place to stay."

"But you didn't ask for one."

"Your young'un sent me off."

Patrick felt the presence of another person. Wes had arrived.

"What's up, Sawbones?" Wes's eyes said he knew.

"We have a patient. Sir, this is Wes. Can you tell us what brought you in to the ER tonight?" Patrick said.

The man looked at his feet. "My face hurts. I'm cold. And dizzy."

Patrick motioned forward, indicating that Wes should approach the man with him. They stood on either side of him. "Show me where it hurts on your face."

The man gestured clumsily at his nose and cheeks. "It was stinging."

Patrick pressed on the hard, waxy skin of the man's cheek, in the center of a white patch. The man didn't react. "Does it still sting?"

"I didn't feel nothing then."

"Have you been outside all day?"

The man nodded.

"How did you get to the hospital from my house?"

The man shrugged.

Patrick looked around the exam room. A backpack and a pair of snowshoes leaned against the wall. *My snowshoes.*

Patrick gritted his teeth and nodded at Wes. "Could you start him on an IV for dehydration? We'll need to warm that frostbitten skin slowly, too. And he'll probably need a painkiller."

"No problem, Doc."

Patrick gestured for Wes to join him in the hall. When they were alone, he said, "This man is acting very strangely. He knew Ferdie found Leslie Anne's body this morning. He was at my house earlier and scared Perry. He knew that 'bad things' had been done there. We need law enforcement."

"I couldn't find Ronnie. She'd mentioned Radish would be spelling her, but I haven't seen him either."

"And still no phones?"

"That's the situation."

"I feel like I'm about to violate every ethical canon of the medical profession, but I think this man is potentially a threat to others. I think we should give him something to sedate him until we can get the police or someone from the sheriff's office here."

Wes nodded in agreement. "Just tell me what you want, Sawbones. Full sedation?"

Patrick wrestled briefly with his conscience, moving his lips with no sound coming out. "Yes. Diazepam. With morphine, since he'll need a pain-killer anyway. That should keep him down and us safe. Just keep an eye on his breathing and make sure he's monitored."

Recognizing the expression of angst on his friend's face, Wes added, "Desperate times call for desperate measures. Are you armed?"

Patrick didn't usually carry his .357 Magnum into the hospital, but he'd worn it tonight because of the problems at their house. It was in a holster at the small of his back, his pocketknife in a small holster at his waist. "I am. You?"

"Always."

"I have a shotgun and a rifle in my locker in the staff room, too. We brought them with us on the snowmobiles and sleds because of the trouble at home."

"Expect the best and prepare for the worst."

"Exactly."

"I'll take care of him, Doc."

"Also, let's ask the rest of the staff not to go in his exam room."

"Good thinking. I guess that's why you get paid the big bucks."

Patrick snorted. Working with his friend gave him a sense of comfort and hope that his worry about the strange man was for nothing.

CHAPTER THIRTY-SIX: BUST

Wyatt

WYATT LET his eyes linger on Kelsey. She was young, but she was really cute. Great smile, which she'd been using a lot on him since they'd been on laundry detail together. Not as pretty as Trish, but Trish put the "cold" in "cold fish". Kelsey seemed a lot more hot to trot.

He liked hot to trot.

She caught him looking at her and smiled. "I've never done laundry before. My mom always does it at our house."

He believed it. She sucked at it. He bumped her with his hip. "Here. I do it all the time."

"But you're a boy." She giggled.

"And you're a girl." Her cheeks flushed. "Yeah. I noticed."

"I don't know what to say to that."

He grinned wide. He knew it gave him dimples, and lately he'd discovered that girls liked dimples. "How about, 'Thanks, Wyatt. And I've noticed you, too.'"

"I can't say that! I mean, I can say thank you, but not the other. So, um, thanks, Wyatt."

"So, you haven't noticed me?" He winked at her.

The flush flamed from pink to scarlet.

Wyatt piled the bedding into a wheeled hamper. Kathy had asked them to distribute clean gowns to the ER as soon as possible. This was their first dry, folded load. He grasped the handle. "Are you coming with me or taking a nap?"

Kelsey's cheeks were still rosy. "I'll come with you."

"Good."

She opened the door, and he pushed the cart out. They walked side by side a few steps down the hallway.

Wyatt said, "Is Perry your boyfriend?" He glanced over at her.

Kelsey's mouth made an O.

"Cat got your tongue?"

"I wouldn't call him my *boyfriend*. We've been close since our friend John died last fall."

"I'm sorry. I heard about that."

"Yeah. It was awful."

"Help me understand what 'close' means. Because what I'm hearing from you is that it's okay if I ask you out. That Flint isn't gonna challenge me to a fight and make me whup his ass."

Her smile spread from ear to ear. "Nothing like that. But please don't beat him up. He's a nice guy."

"I'll try not to. What about you? Do you want me to ask you out?"

Kelsey bit her lip. It was even cuter than her smile. Then she took a deep breath. "I think that would be far out."

He stopped. She did, too. He let go of the cart and stepped toward her. It was quiet. They were alone.

He touched her cheek. "What about if I wanted to kiss you?"

"But we haven't been on a date yet!" she said, her voice high and nervous.

He closed half the distance between them. She hadn't said no. "You've never kissed a boy, have you, Kelsey Jones?"

"I have, too."

"Then you know kissing is no big deal. It's not like it would ruin your reputation."

"I know that."

"Besides, no one can see us back here." He slid his hand to the nape of her neck.

"I know that, too."

"And I am going to ask you out. Right after I kiss you."

She lifted her chin, presenting him with red, bow lips.

He leaned down and kissed her. He'd expected wooden lips and that she would end the kiss quickly. Instead, she rose on her tiptoes and put both her hands on his chest.

"Talk about far out," he whispered, without moving his lips from hers.

The kiss deepened. Kelsey looped her hands around his neck. Wyatt's drifted down to her hips. *I may make it to second base!*

A woman's sharp voice startled them. "What's going on here?"

Kelsey jumped, her teeth cutting Wyatt's lip. "Mrs. Flint!"

Wyatt clapped his hand over his mouth. He tasted blood.

Mrs. Flint's eyes were sad and mad at the same time. "I am responsible for the two of you tonight. I trusted you. This is a violation of my trust."

"I'm sorry," Kelsey said. Then she blurted, "Please don't tell Perry."

"Don't tell Perry" sounds pretty darn close. But then what was she doing kissing me?

"You can tell him yourself. It's not my business."

"I apologize, Mrs. Flint," Wyatt said. "It won't happen again."

"Oh, you can be sure it won't. It appears you have laundry to deliver?"

"Yes, ma'am, we do," Wyatt said in his most polite voice.

"Kelsey, you'll work with me. Wyatt, you'll handle the rest of the laundry delivery by yourself."

And the fun is over. "Yes, ma'am."

Pounding footsteps approached. "Mom." It was Trish. She was bawling. Had she seen him kiss Kelsey? She couldn't have. But she wouldn't have cared anyway. "Mom, I need to talk to you."

"We can talk in here." Mrs. Flint pointed down the hall. "Wyatt, go. Kelsey, wait out here. I'll be right behind you."

Wyatt and Kelsey shared a look of regret, then he pushed the laundry buggy toward the ER.

CHAPTER THIRTY-SEVEN: GROUSE

Buffalo, Wyoming
Saturday, March 18, 1978, 9:30 p.m.

Patrick

PATRICK STOOD outside Wilfred's exam room, hands on a cart handle. On the cart were the materials he'd assembled to cast the man's arm. The liner. The casting material. A dish of water. Since they were short-staffed, he'd have to do it himself. This wasn't going to be pretty. But Wilfred wasn't the kind of person who seemed to worry about his appearance.

He looked up. Kathy was escorting a skinny older woman down the hall. The woman was elevating a bloody, homemade bandaged hand at shoulder height, supporting it with her other hand. If they had more than a couple more patients show up, the ER would be at capacity. *Is it a full moon out tonight in addition to the blizzard?*

Wilfred approached from the opposite direction, hobbling back toward his designated area holding his injured arm. *Why isn't he in his room?* Patrick hoped he didn't catch sight of Tristan Babcock, the neighbor Wilfred suspected had killed Leslie Anne. Or the Compton father and son duo, whom he hated. If he did, they might have to lasso the rancher and hogtie him to keep him from going after them, hurt arm notwithstanding.

Wilfred spoke in what Patrick was coming to think of as his usual cranky tone. "Wanda, what fool thing have you gone and done to yourself?"

Wanda. A familiar name. Patrick took a closer look at her face. Yes. He'd seen her earlier that day when Ronnie had been interviewing Wilfred. She had unusual eyes. Strabismus. What some people called wall-eyed.

Wanda stopped short, her face lighting up. "Wilfred! I was shoveling the steps at the church and fell. I cut my hand on the edge of my shovel." She made a moue of her face, like she was a much younger woman. "My condolences again on the loss of your . . . Leslie Anne."

Kathy turned around. She was twenty feet ahead of Wanda. "Ms. Carmichael? Are you coming?"

Wilfred grunted and limped into his exam room where he hoisted himself onto the table with one arm, his face clenched in pain.

Wanda glided past Patrick, into Wilfred's curtained area, acting like she owned the place. "You know, you didn't need that easy woman in the first place. I'm here. Always have been. I can take care of you."

Patrick followed her in, ready to shoo her out, but the conversation progressed too rapidly for him to interrupt.

"Don't speak ill of the dead. Especially not about the woman I loved." Wilfred chewed and spat his words. "And you and me? It ain't happening. Not in this lifetime or the next."

Wanda huffed, looking miffed but not particularly discouraged. "She's only been gone a day and you're already a mess without a woman to look after you. What brought you in here?"

"None of your business."

Wanda eyed the way Wilfred was cradling one arm in the other.

It was fairly obvious what he was in for, but her hungry expression said that was far less information than she was looking for.

Kathy entered the crowded space, in pursuit of her patient. "Ms. Carmichael, over here. I have your exam room ready. We need to get you stitched up. And I need to attend to other patients, too."

"Yes, yes." Wanda tore her gaze from Wilfred and followed Kathy out.

Patrick pulled the curtains shut around Wilfred.

"That woman is the kind who gives church a bad name," Wilfred muttered.

The last thing Patrick wanted to do was gossip about or badmouth one patient with another. And if he let Wilfred get started, there wasn't a patient in here he didn't have a beef with. The grousing could continue all night.

Patrick redirected Wilfred to his injury. "The X-rays confirmed that your arm is broken. I need to cast it, but it's a clean fracture. No malalignment. I won't even have to set it, and it should heal well. As for your ankle, it's not broken, as you suspected. You ready to tell me how this happened?" Wilfred had steadfastly refused to discuss it when he'd first been examined.

"There ain't nothing to tell. I'm a stupid old man. Busted arms is what happens to stupid old men in blizzards." Wilfred scowled at Patrick like the break was his fault. "How long do I have to wear a cast for?"

"You can come back in six weeks. We'll x-ray it again. If it looks good, we'll take the cast off then."

"How'm I supposed to get my work done in the meantime?" Wilfred said, his voice a surly growl.

"I'm sure it will be hard. Don't you have a hand you can lean on? You mentioned him earlier."

"Dabbo. Dabbo Kern. If you see him, tell the whippersnapper to get his keister back to my ranch or he's out of a job."

"He still hasn't turned up?"

"Isn't that what I just said?"

As unlikeable as Wilfred was, Patrick was beginning to suspect that his animosity toward other people might be due to their natural reactions to him. Then he remembered how despicably the Comptons had behaved. Still, dark drew dark, and light drew light in his experience.

He placed a stockinette over Wilfred's hand and forearm and began wrapping a soft liner around and around. "Maybe he was caught in the weather," Patrick said.

"The weather was just fine this morning when he didn't show up. He's been sparking a girl too young for the likes of him. I wouldn't be surprised if he was chasing her around."

"Oh?"

"She came around the ranch looking for him, wearing nothing but a tiny cheerleading skirt. Hussy. And him a man in his twenties."

A high school cheerleader? Nausea roiled through Patrick. Trish was trying out for the squad. He hoped the girl that chased after grown men was graduating. He shook off the thought. He dipped the cast material in the water, squeezed out the excess water, then applied it over the liner. It should take six layers, which he would then have to mold, so he'd be at this for a while.

Layer after layer of plaster, Patrick thought about Leslie Anne's death while Wilfred sunk into blessed silence. He wondered if Ronnie had found Dabbo. He was positive she would have wanted to interview him about Leslie Anne's death. Earlier, Wilfred had insinuated the hand was sweet on Leslie Anne. Maybe he'd made an advance and she'd rebuffed it. A certain kind of man didn't take things like that well. What if Dabbo was that kind of man? What if he was the killing kind? Yet now Wilfred was singing a different tune, one about Dabbo dating an inappropriately young girl, not making passes at a much older woman. A thought lodged in his brain. What if it was the other way around? What if Leslie Anne had been the one sweet on Dabbo, and he had rebuffed her? He'd have to ask Ronnie about Dabbo when he caught up with her. Run his thoughts past her. Brainstorming crazy ideas could lead to the good ones sometimes. Hopefully he'd talk to her soon, since he still needed to report the intruder at the Flints' house, who just might be sleeping a few curtains down.

Patrick smoothed the last layer of plaster casting. "Now I've got to ask you to hold still and not mess with this while it dries."

"And how long is that?"

"It will start to dry in ten or fifteen minutes, but it won't be finished drying for a day or two. You'll need to take it easy. It will be important to keep the swelling down. I'm giving you some anti-inflammatories and a prescription to refill them when the storm blows over and things reopen. You need to keep your arm elevated above your heart as much as possible for the next twenty-four hours, too."

"Gotta take care of my livestock."

"You'll either be doing that with one arm over your head or you'll hire some help if Dabbo doesn't show up. I'm serious, now. You'll end up out of commission for far longer if you don't protect this arm. And your ankle won't thank you for it either if you don't take some time off."

"Have you ever tried to drive a sleigh team with one arm?"

"Between my wife, daughter, and I, we'll find a way to get those horses home. You'll be riding in a closed vehicle. And I don't want to hear any more arguing about it. I have other patients to see, and we can discuss this later. For now, lay still, don't touch it, and try to go to sleep."

"Hurts too durn bad to sleep."

"I'll send Kathy back in with more pain medication, then. I expect it will continue hurting for a few days. Worse if you use it or don't take the anti-inflammatories."

"So, I can leave when the cast dries?"

"Normally, yes. But you'll need to stay here until we can get you a ride home."

"My horses need tending."

"I can put them up at my place in the morning, until we can bring them back to yours."

Wilfred nodded, his expression slightly less petulant. "Fine."

"All right. I'll check back in on you in a few hours, and the nurse on duty will pop in from time to time if you need something." Patrick paused before leaving. "Any questions for me?"

Wilfred shook his head.

This was normally the time at which a patient expressed gratitude. But if Wilfred felt any, he was keeping it to himself. Slightly amused, Patrick left the man to his own bad company.

Just as he stepped back into the corridor, the lights went out.

CHAPTER THIRTY-EIGHT: SABOTAGE

.

Kelsey

KELSEY FIDGETED in the hallway outside the supply closet. Trish and Mrs. Flint were in there talking. About her, she bet. She was so embarrassed that Mrs. Flint had seen her kiss Wyatt. She wasn't sure what had come over her. Wyatt was so handsome. Tall and strong, with those dimples. All the girls at school thought he was a fox. And he was going to be a senior and probably captain of the football team. No matter how much she liked Perry, she couldn't pass up a chance with Wyatt. What girl would, really? But there was a problem, besides that she didn't like the idea of hurting Perry's feelings. She wasn't a mean person. Perry had been her friend before he was her . . . um, before they were close. He'd been really, really good to her when she was sad about John.

No, the problem was that Wyatt hadn't asked her out.

He'd *said* he was going to, after he kissed her. But then Mrs. Flint had showed up and ruined everything. Now, if Wyatt didn't want her to be his girlfriend, she may have messed things up with Perry. Perry would be a good boyfriend. It's just that Wyatt would be a better one. But was she going to end up with neither of them, all because of bad timing? Kelsey would be like the last one standing in musical chairs. She shifted from foot to foot. *Not good, not good.*

From inside the closet, she heard Trish crying. Kelsey pushed her hair back from her ear and leaned against the door. If they were talking about her, she wanted to hear it. Although, come to think of it, Trish had been crying before she talked to her mom. She might not even know what Kelsey had done. Kelsey hoped Mrs. Flint never told her. Or anyone.

Trish said, "Ronnie thinks Ben was in Buffalo today."

Kelsey's mouth dropped. Ben, the cute older boy who had dumped Trish and run off? He was dangerous. He'd been in juvie. *A bad boy.* Perry told her that Ben was a nice guy, but hadn't he helped kidnap Trish? And then he'd gotten into trouble over drugs in Laramie his first day at the University of Wyoming. She edged closer to the door. This was getting good.

"Is she sure?" Mrs. Flint asked.

"I was too embarrassed to ask her any questions. Mom, he didn't call me. He didn't write. He didn't tell me he was coming to town. But what if he came to our house to see me and saw Wyatt there?"

"That's really unlikely, Trish."

"But it could have happened. Why did Wyatt have to stay?" Trish was really wailing now.

"It wasn't his fault. He was trying to help you."

"I'm not interested in him. He should have taken the hint."

"I don't think him being interested in you is going to be a problem anymore."

"What do you mean?"

Kelsey winced. *No, Mrs. Flint. Nooooooo.* Mrs. Flint sighed and lowered her voice. Kelsey couldn't hear what she said, but she heard Trish's answer.

"Oh, my gosh. Poor Perry."

She'd done it. She'd told Trish. Now everyone would know. Perry .
. .

"He'll survive. Better to find out now how Kelsey is than later after he was really attached to her."

Kelsey's mouth fell open. *How Kelsey is? What was that supposed to mean?*

"You're right. He's better off."

No! He is not better off! She was a catch. Wyatt seemed to think so. She hoped.

"Everything is going to be okay, Trish. You can call out to Piney Bottoms when the phones are working. If he's there, and if you're right about what happened, you can explain and work it out."

"I can't stand this."

Kelsey balled her fists. She was so mad at Mrs. Flint for telling Trish and for what she said. She'd said it wasn't her business. And then what Trish had said. Oh! She was so steamed. Kelsey wanted to tell them both how she felt, too, but she knew she wouldn't. Mrs. Flint was a grown up. She couldn't disrespect her elders, no matter how bad she wanted to. Trish was going to be a senior. She might make the cheerleading squad. But she didn't have to keep what Trish had said about Ben being in town a secret. She might have if Mrs. Flint and Trish hadn't talked behind her back. All bets were off now.

There was a CLICK and suddenly all the lights went out. It was pitch dark in the hallway.

Kelsey screamed. "Mrs. Flint! What happened? Why are there no lights?"

Mrs. Flint opened the closet door. It bumped into Kelsey, and she yelped. Then she smelled expensive, spicy perfume and a cold hand grabbed her arm.

"The power must have gone out," Mrs. Flint said.

"Aren't there emergency lights or, like, night lights or something?" Trish said.

"There should be battery-powered back-ups. We just need to move closer to where people are. Let's head toward the ER."

"How? It's pitch dark!" Kelsey said.

"I know the way. I'll keep my hand on a wall and walk in front of you girls."

"Don't let go of me, Mrs. Flint!"

"Why don't you hold on to the back of my sweater? I need my hands in front of me, so we don't run into anything. Trish, what about you?"

"I'm fine," Trish said. Her tone was condescending.

What a snot. Kelsey had gotten along with Perry's sister just fine until a few seconds ago. As scared as she was, she still seethed with anger at Trish. Perry was better off without Kelsey? How dare she.

Mrs. Flint moved Kelsey's hand to grasp the back hem of her sweater and started moving forward. Trish's footfalls were behind Kelsey. *Where she can stab me in the back better.* A few times, metal clanged as Mrs. Flint ran into equipment stored in the hallways. Each time, she guided the girls around them. When they reached the end of the corridor, they came upon an open door. Light glowed and bangs, clangs, and clacks sounded from inside it.

"Who's there?" Mrs. Flint said.

The noises stopped. No one answered.

"I said who's there?" she repeated.

Kelsey sucked in a panicked breath and shrank back, stepping on Trish's foot. *Could it be someone dangerous, like in* The Texas Chainsaw Massacre? She knew she shouldn't watch horror movies. They gave her nightmares and crazy ideas. But she loved them.

"Ouch." Trish didn't sound scared.

"Sorry."

A direct beam of light was suddenly pointed at them. Kelsey threw up a hand to cover her eyes, letting go of Mrs. Flint's sweater. Touching no one, she felt isolated. Vulnerable.

"Susanne? Who is that with you?" A man's voice.

Kelsey groaned. The killer was always a man in the horror movies.

"Wes! I have Trish and Kelsey. We got caught near the laundry room when the lights went out. What's the problem?"

The flashlight beam lowered to their feet. There was still enough light that Kelsey could see the man. She recognized him from earlier. Not that she knew him. The Flints did. But he was practically a stranger to her. As far as she could tell, though, he wasn't carrying an ax or a chainsaw. She tried to relax.

"The generator quit. Patrick went to check on it. I was grabbing some flashlights and battery powered lanterns that we keep stashed in here. There's more light just around the corner. At least the battery-powered backup lights came on near the exits and stairwells."

"Why would the generator go out?" Mrs. Flint asked.

"Oh, it could be it's out of fuel. Or maybe it just died and needs to be restarted."

Heavy, quick footsteps approached. Kelsey's throat clenched. She pressed a hand to her chest, holding her breath. A large figure stepped into the edges of the light from the flashlight. She prepared herself to scream her lungs out.

"What did you find, Doc?" Wes said.

Kelsey exhaled and sucked in a greedy breath. Dr. Flint.

"Who all is here?" Dr. Flint's voice sounded funny. Like her own dad's did when he was really upset about something but trying not to admit it.

Mrs. Flint said, "Trish, Kelsey, and me."

"Hi, ladies. Why don't we give you some lights and meet you in the ER?" he said.

Kelsey knew something was wrong now. He was trying to get rid of them. *Uh uh. No way.* If there was a killer on the loose, she wanted to know about it right now.

Apparently, Mrs. Flint agreed with Kelsey because she said, "Whatever it is, Patrick, we'll all find out sooner or later."

Dr. Flint didn't say anything for a long time. When he finally did, he sounded bummed. "The generator is broken."

"Is there a mechanic or maintenance person on staff that can fix it?" Mrs. Flint said.

The Wes guy shook his head, which looked spooky in the flashlight beams. "During the day. At night, they're on call. Which means not tonight, since the phones are down."

"It wouldn't matter, anyway." Dr. Flint sighed. "The only fix for this generator is replacement."

"Why's that, Doc?"

"Because someone sabotaged it."

Mrs. Flint gasped. "What? How?"

"It looks like it was beaten with a five iron. Or a sledgehammer."

Kelsey hadn't seen a movie with either of those weapons in it, but it didn't matter. They sounded terrifying. She gasped and sank to her knees.

CHAPTER THIRTY-NINE: BREATHE

Perry

Up until the lights went out, Perry was doing both the sweeping and the mopping. Which was three hundred percent unfair. Trish had dumped it on him after Ronnie got her all worked up about Ben. Then Trish had gone running off when she heard the creepy backpacker patient talking about someone she thought was Ben. She got it in her head that Ben had come to their house. That's when she went looking for their mom, howling. Literally, howling. Anyway, the only good things to come of the mopping were the workouts. His shoulders, from the heavy, wet mop, and his frustration, about his mom sending Kelsey off with Wyatt.

But with no light, he couldn't keep working. He'd stood there in the dark for a second, waiting for them to come back on. He'd heard his dad, Abraham, and Wes discuss checking on the power and getting some extra lanterns and stuff. At the time, Perry had been mopping in an empty exam room. The only empty one. He hopped up onto the table. From exam rooms up and down the hall, people were hollering for answers about what was going on and some were even crying. Perry thought it was pretty obvious what was wrong. Duh, no lights.

Then Kathy had started talking really loud, so everyone could hear her. "Hello, everyone? No need to worry. Just a little power outage. It's normal in storms. Just like at your homes. If anyone needs something, call out for me. But it will only be me and Dr. Farham in here for a bit while the others go to fix the power. We'll do our best." Her voice sounded young. Like she was still in high school.

Was she scared? *Should I be scared?* Maybe not scared, but he should definitely help. Everyone else in here was hurt or sick. It would give him something to do besides sit in the dark anyway.

Perry got down from the table and walked with his hands outstretched. His eyes weren't adjusted to the dark yet. He remembered his dad teaching him about how to access his night vision like an Indian. Owl eyes, he called it. The gist of it was to use your peripheral vision and blink a lot. Like owls did. Perry tried it. It seemed to help a little bit. His dad said that all the other senses improved in the dark, too. Perry believed it. The bucket of mop water smelled like the dirtiest socks ever now and he'd barely noticed it before. No more pine scent. He'd have to change the water and add cleaner.

When his hands touched the curtains, he pushed them aside and stepped into the hall. "Kathy? This is Perry Flint. I can help if you need me to."

"Over here," she said.

He followed the sound of her voice. By the time he reached her, he could see the outline of her body with his side vision. He stopped before he ran into her. A bigger body was standing beside her. Dr. Farham.

"Young Mr. Flint. We appreciate your offer of assistance," the doctor said.

"Uh, sure."

"It is better for the two of you to remain here with the patients. I will be returning shortly with additional warm blankets. It will get colder quickly." The doctor disappeared into the darkness.

"What can I do?" Perry asked.

Kathy said, "Why don't you start at one end of the ER, and I'll go to the other. We can just check on people one by one. We need to reassure them that everything will be okay."

Perry whispered, "But will the machines work? You know, like the monitors and stuff?"

She matched his volume. "Not without electricity."

Perry thought about the unconscious man with the caved in mouth and the beeping machine that had been beside him. How many more people were there like that in the hospital? He hoped none of them died because of the storm and loss of power. It was sad to think about.

"Okay."

Kathy moved off down the corridor. Perry felt very alone. It was hard to believe he was responsible for talking to patients. How could he reassure them? He was just a kid. The doctor would have been better suited for this job and Perry to get the blankets. He didn't understand why he'd been given this role. He wished he had said so when he had a chance. Now he was stuck with it.

He was able to walk fairly quickly using owl eyes to see where he was going. At the first exam room, he paused to breathe deeply a few times, like he did before every football game. It helped calm his nerves. And he did feel nervous. He didn't know how he could make people feel like everything would be okay when he had no idea if that was true. But he had to try. He knew from personal experience that getting upset only made things harder.

He drew back the curtain. A woman older than either of his grandmothers was reclining on the exam table.

He cleared his throat. "Um, ma'am? Hi. I'm Perry Flint. I'm here to check on you."

Her voice was wobbly. "Come closer, young man."

He did, until he was about three feet from her. He tried not to stare, which was weird anyway, because how can you stare when you're not looking at someone straight on? But he could see her plainly. *Dad is pretty smart.* There was something wrong with her eyes. Was it worse to look at her eyes or to not look at them? He opted for looking at her chin.

"Can you tell me what happened, Perry Flint?"

"We, uh, we lost power."

"I know that. Do you know why?"

"No, ma'am. But my dad and Wes have gone to fix it."

"Who is your dad?"

"Dr. Flint?"

"Is Dr. Flint an electrician?"

"No, ma'am. But he's pretty handy. He says that being a doctor is one part science, one part art, and one part mechanics. He's good at the mechanical stuff."

"All right. Well, I'm fine for now. I'm waiting to get some stitches in my hand, but I don't want anyone poking me with needles when they can't see what they're doing."

"Yes, ma'am."

"You're very polite. Who taught you your manners? Your father or your mother?"

"Mostly my mom, but whenever she gets upset with us about them or anything, she turns it over to my dad for the consequences."

The old woman cackled, witch-like. The sound made the hair on Perry's arms stand up.

From the other side of the curtain in the next exam area, someone said, "Um, like, help?"

It was Wyatt.

"Excuse me, ma'am."

"Um hm," she said. "Sounds like he's got bigger problems than me over there."

"I'm serious. Hurry." Wyatt's voice was a panicked hiss. More than the-lights-aren't-working panic.

"I'm coming." Perry chucked back the curtain and moved as fast he dared. He didn't want to plow into a patient and make things worse. "What is it?"

He could see well enough to catch the skeptical look on Wyatt's face.

"Dude, no offense, but I need help. From someone who works here."

"My dad and Wes went to try to fix the power. Dr. Farham is getting blankets. Kathy is all the way at the other end of the ER. If you want her, you're going to have to go get her. Otherwise, I'm the only one you've got right now."

"Whatever. I didn't want to be in here anyway. I was minding my own business, delivering clean laundry, when I found him like this."

"Him?" *And where is Kelsey?*

Wyatt pointed at the exam table. "He's not breathing. You hear it?"

Perry heard nothing, which he guessed was the point. He inched closer. It was the shape of a man. Silent machines loomed next to him in the dark. With a flood of recognition, Perry got his bearings. This was the exam room with the guy who had a busted mouth. He'd been unconscious earlier, but definitely breathing then. Just because he couldn't hear breaths didn't necessarily mean the person wasn't breathing. Breathing could be very quiet. But then again, it might mean that. He'd seen dead people before. The worst time was when John was murdered by some mob guys on the trail down from Black Tooth Mountain. This wouldn't be as bad. He knew he could handle it. He just didn't want to.

But was this guy only alive because of the machines? And now he isn't breathing because they aren't working?

He had to know for sure. If the old guy wasn't dead, he could help him. Or get help. Perry was close enough to touch him now. Something about the shape of his face and head seemed very wrong.

Perry leaned over. Reached out. His fingers met something soft. Not skin soft. Fabric soft.

Cloth?

No cloth should be over his face. It could suffocate him.

He pulled on it.

It wasn't a cloth. It was a pillow.

Perry lifted it away, his movement jerky. Why would there be a pillow on this man's face? It made no sense. Except that maybe it did. He shivered. Someone would have had to put it there deliberately. There was no good reason. It was to smother him. To kill him.

With the pillow removed, he strained to hear breaths that might have only been muffled before. But he heard nothing. He looked for a rise and fall of the man's chest. Nothing there either.

Wyatt might be right. This guy might be dead. And if he was, it was murder. A murderer might be here in this dark hospital with them right now.

Perry put a finger to his lips.

"Why do I need to be quiet?" Wyatt said. But Perry noticed he was still whispering.

"Because I don't want whoever did this to him coming after me. Do you?"

Wyatt must have agreed because he shut his trap.

"I've got to find my dad."

Wyatt backed toward the curtain door. "I'm not staying here alone with him. I'm coming with you."

Perry wasn't crazy about Wyatt, but he didn't mind bigger, stronger company right now, and he motioned him to follow.

CHAPTER FORTY: FACE

BUFFALO, WYOMING
SATURDAY, MARCH 18, 1978, 10:20 P.M.

Patrick

PATRICK LIFTED his hands from Tristan Babcock's chest. "Time of death: ten-twenty p.m."

He'd done everything he could for the old man—CPR only, sadly, since there were no shock paddles due to the loss of power—but he'd likely died half an hour before. The temperature in the ER, though falling, was still in the sixties. Yet there had been a cooling to the man's skin, barely perceptible, but there.

Abraham, Wes, and Kathy stood by his side.

Wes whispered, "Can you confirm he was smothered with a pillow?"

Patrick put his hands on his hips. "No. But I can't think of any other reason he'd have one over his face."

Kathy wrung her hands, one in the other, then switching sides and repeating. "I don't get it. If someone did this, why did they leave the pillow? If they hadn't, we'd have thought he just passed from his wounds."

"Maybe they were startled and left in a hurry?" Wes suggested.

"A pillow is easy to remove quickly," Abraham said. "I would guess the person or persons want us to know what happened."

"But why? It doesn't make sense to me." Kathy's voice shook. Her competence made it easy to forget her age. Patrick suspected her past didn't include exposure to the dark side of humanity that his kids had experienced, either.

He turned to Abraham. The men exchanged unspoken agreement, and Patrick said, "It feels like it was intended to scare us."

"It's working."

"I wonder if it's the same person who broke the generator?" Wes said.

"I sure hope so." The thought that there might be more than one lunatic in this building with them was too much for Patrick to contemplate.

"But who?" Kathy's voice dropped to a level so soft it was little more than vibrations.

Patrick motioned them closer. "We know it's not the four of us. Or anyone we were with at the time."

"But what time is that? Perry and I didn't leave the ER." Her voice caught. "It probably happened while we were in here."

Patrick couldn't argue with her logic. "When's the last time any of us saw Tristan alive?"

Abraham spoke calmly. His voice had a soothing, musical quality. "Mr. Babcock was on a monitor, so we didn't have to see him. If he'd died before we lost power, it would have set off the alarm on his monitor."

Patrick nodded. "Good thinking."

"After the power went out." Wes pulled at one side of his mustache. "That knocks out Susanne, Trish, and Perry's friend. Kelsey. They wouldn't have been around to see anything. They were together near the laundry room. I saw them on their way back to the ER when I was gathering lights."

"What about Wyatt and Perry?" Patrick said.

Kathy frowned in concentration. "Perry was mopping. I walked by and saw him in an empty exam room right when the power went out. Then he came out and helped me. I wasn't with him, but he was checking on patients, starting at the far end with Ms. Carmichael."

"Right next to Tristan."

"And that other teenage boy—"

"Wyatt."

"He came in right before the outage pushing a laundry buggy. He was the one who found Tristan."

Wes grimaced. "So, Perry didn't see anything, most likely. But we don't know about this Wyatt kid."

"Let's approach it from a different perspective. Who had a reason to want Tristan dead?" Patrick said.

Kathy shrugged, her eyes wide. "I guess whoever hit him in the head in the first place would be a suspect."

"True. But we don't know who that was. If we assume it had to be someone here in the ER with us—"

"But can we assume that?" Wes bunched his forehead, thinking. "Could someone have come in, sabotaged the generator, run from there to the ER, and done this?"

That silenced the group for a minute. Patrick's mind chased around the possibility. It wasn't likely, but they couldn't rule it out.

Finally, Kathy spoke. "Wouldn't we have noticed someone hurrying around? And I think that goes double for someone I hadn't checked in at reception. I didn't see any strangers or anyone in a hurry."

Patrick rubbed his forehead. "True. I think it's best to focus on the people we know are here, for now. Did any of them have a reason to hurt Tristan?" He lowered his voice until it was barely audible. "I know of at least one person who believed they did."

Kathy, Wes, and Abraham stepped closer.

"Who?" Abraham whispered.

Even more softly, Patrick said, "Wilfred Mitchell. He told me when he arrived that he and Tristan were in a mini-range war that had escalated to Wilfred poisoning some of Tristan's cattle."

"Oh, my," Kathy breathed.

"Even worse, Wilfred believes Tristan killed his girlfriend, Leslie Anne, in retaliation."

Kathy's eyes were wide and the whites glowing. "Oh, my God. Wilfred did this."

"Maybe," Patrick said, his volume increasing slightly. His brain snagged on a memory, like a hook into the side of fish. He tried to reel it in, but it came loose before it surfaced. "Although we have a nearly full ER tonight and the hospital is over capacity and without power as well. We don't know what interactions or issues any of the rest of them may have had with Tristan. Whoever it is, though, our first duty is to keep our patients safe. I'd like to say that extends to my family and their friends."

Abraham was nodding fast. "Of course, of course."

"But how?" Kathy said.

"Possibly we should lock the entrances and exits?" Abraham said. "So that no one else can get in who may intend harm?"

"That makes me nervous, Dr. Farham. Fire and the like. Trapping people in here feels inhumane." Wes sounded regretful.

"Not to mention what if we lock the murderer inside with us?" Kathy said.

"You are right," Abraham said. "The doors must remain as they are."

Dear God, how I wish we had law enforcement here. Or phones. "Let's try radioing for help again. Then, I'd say it's strength in numbers," Patrick said. "Armed numbers."

CHAPTER FORTY-ONE: PLOT

Susanne

When Perry had told Susanne about the murder of Tristan Babcock, she assumed he was mistaken. Even given the sabotage of the generator, smothering an old man seemed a big stretch. She'd huddled with the kids under an emergency light in the corridor outside the ER, waiting for a reliable version of events. From a grown-up. Then Patrick had joined them, a lantern swinging from his hands. The look on his face told her it was true.

Murder! In the hospital, while they were here!

"We need to talk. Let's go to the staff lounge," he announced without even breaking stride, just motioning for them to follow. He blew by with his fast walk. The one he used hiking, hunting, or when he was upset.

The kids shared wide-eyed looks. Kelsey's eyes went to Wyatt's while Perry's went to Kelsey. She wanted to strangle the fickle young woman. *The little climber.* Later, though. After this horrible night was over. She fell in behind the teenagers, like a herding dog ready to push the stragglers or cut off any that strayed. They had a hard time keeping pace with Patrick, but he waited for them inside the lounge. Susanne trailed her last charge in where Ferdinand was greeting each of them like an enthusiastic host. The whole staff room smelled like dog now, and he'd only been there a few hours.

Patrick shut and locked the door. "Have a seat."

There were four chairs at a round table in the kitchen nook. The kids took them. Rather than sit alone on the couch across the room, Susanne stood with her hand on Perry's shoulder.

"What is it, Patrick?" she said. Had they really had the worst fight of their marriage only an hour ago? She felt the echoes of her anger, but it was receding. They had much bigger problems than which of them felt more taken for granted and taken advantage of.

Patrick inhaled deeply, then exhaled a sigh. "One of our patients, Mr. Babcock, is dead. Perry probably already told you that it looks like he was murdered." Everyone nodded. "We think it happened shortly after the power went out. And, of course, the power went out because someone beat the generator to death."

Susanne swallowed down words that wouldn't help, about her belief that murder didn't even occur in Wyoming anymore without zeroing in on the location of the Flints. They were a nice family. All she wanted was a peaceful life. But it didn't look like she was going to get it today. She needed to be part of a solution. So, she said, "Okay. What else do you know?"

"Nothing for sure. But Wes and I are armed." He touched the .357 Magnum at his waist. And we have the shotgun and rifle, right?"

Perry jumped up. "We put them in your locker." He went to the locker, which wasn't locked. None of them were. It might not be the way people did things in the big city, but in Wyoming vehicles, houses, and lockers were usually left unsecured. Perry threw it open. He turned stricken eyes to them. "I thought we put them here."

Wyatt frowned. "Dude, we did. Where are they?"

Susanne looked at her husband. His eyes were closed. He was rubbing his forehead. His lips were moving fast and furious.

Then he opened them, and his expression was steely. "We still have my gun and my knife."

Trish ran to the kitchen drawers and threw them open one after another. "There's nothing sharp in here. Plastic ware." She slammed the last one in disgust.

Perry was opening and closing lockers, shining a flashlight into them. "Nobody else brought guns to work today. Or at least they're not in the lockers if they did."

Patrick said, "Susanne, can I leave the gun with you?"

Her wrist. She hadn't told anyone about it. But there was no way she could shoot a gun. The pain had gotten worse. It was swollen, too. She lifted it up and pulled back her sleeve.

"Well, you can't handle a gun with that." Patrick's voice was harsh. "What happened?"

She knew it wasn't like her not to have told him. But between their fight and the unusual circumstances, nothing was like it usually was. "A patient fell on it."

"You need to get ice on it. We can do an X-ray later. I think there are anti-inflammatories in one of the kitchen drawers."

Trish pulled one open and pulled out a bottle of ibuprofen. "Will this work?"

"Yes."

She opened it and handed it to Susanne.

Susanne went to the sink and filled a paper cup with water and downed two of the chalky tasting pills, then threw away the cup and returned the bottle to the drawers. She felt an irrational, embarrassed anger that her injury had been discovered. And that it was keeping her from protecting her family.

Patrick pointed at Trish. "You're the best shot in the family. Can you pull the trigger if you need to?"

Trish's mouth dropped open.

Wyatt stood. "But, Dr. Flint, sir—I'm an excellent shot."

Susanne said, "Patrick, that's too much—"

Trish nodded, her demeanor cool and calm. "Yes, sir. I can."

Susanne snapped, her voice giving away her frustration and emotions. "Why don't we just take the kids on the snowmobiles and go . . . go . . . somewhere."

"Because there is an ER full of helpless people here. It is my duty to care for them. If you'd rather take the snowmobiles and go, you can, but you'll have to face that blizzard and a town without phones, power, or lights, in the middle of the night. But staying together matters. I hate the thought of you going where I can't help you. If you stay in here, this is the only door to the staff room. Guard it with the gun—don't let anyone in but Wes, Kathy, Abraham, or me. You'll be just as safe here as on the road. More so."

Susanne thought of times in the past where they'd been separated when trouble struck. When Trish had been kidnapped from Walker Prairie and taken up Dome Mountain. The time Patrick had gone to the Wind River Reservation without them and been poisoned. When Barb Lamkin had taken Susanne and the kids up Highway 16 intending to burn down a cabin with them inside. On the Gros Ventre River, when Susanne's niece Bunny and Trish had been lost, Perry injured, and the river wild. The time Patrick had rescued plane crash survivors and Trish and Perry had fled from mobsters at the base of Black Tooth Mountain. And most recently, when Susanne was in Denver and Trish ran away after Ben at the same time that Patrick and Perry were snowmobiling in the mountains and saved Abraham from assassins.

He had a point. Separation always led to further disaster. But why did she still feel so unsettled about it? She nodded in grudging agreement. "Okay."

Patrick unbuckled his holster and handed it to Trish with the gun pointed at the floor. His holster held his extra rounds. "It's loaded. I need to go back to the ER and help Abraham bring patients in here. Right now, Wes is standing guard with Kathy."

"What about a weapon for you?" Susanne said.

"I have my knife."

"It's no match for a gun. Two of them. Our guns."

Patrick licked his lips. "Whoever did this didn't use a gun before. I'm hoping they only took ours so we couldn't either."

"Do you know who did this, Dad?" Perry asked.

A flicker of something crossed Patrick's face. "No. Anyone not in this room besides Wes, Abraham, and Kathy is a suspect."

"What aren't you saying?" Susanne said.

"We have a suspect. We just don't have any way to prove it."

"Tell us so we can be prepared. So we don't let him in."

Again, his lips moved in a spirited conversation with himself. When the warring sides of his brain had worked it out, he said, "Be careful of Wilfred Mitchell."

And then he was gone.

CHAPTER FORTY-TWO: DOMINO

BUFFALO, WYOMING
SATURDAY, MARCH 18, 1978, 10:50 P.M.

Wes

WHAT IS TAKING *Doc so long?*

Wes fingered the safety on his old M1911 .45 caliber service pistol. The scent of the gun oil was comforting, a scent he'd grown fond of in many years of caring for the weapon. He hadn't been this nervous nor felt this trapped since Vietnam. That wasn't his best six years, but he'd gotten training as a medic and then gone to lab school on the Army dime. And he'd come back alive, with his seven-shot. He still had nightmares—waking and sleeping—but not like some of his buddies who ranged from barely functional to societal dropouts. The worst of it was that his girl had married an oil field worker and moved to Gillette while he was gone. He had a good job, he had friends, he owned his own house, and he owned his Travelall free and clear. Yet he hadn't been able to keep a good woman since.

He grimaced. No family. That was his regret. He envied Doc and Susanne, their relationship, their kids.

Kathy made a tiny sound, like she had started to speak and then swallowed it back. The young woman had impressed him tonight. Sure, she was scared. She'd be a fool not to be. But she was holding it together, like he'd expect of a ranch kid from Upton. Sensible for her age. That's why he'd voted to hire her. Kids who grew up working the land and the animals with their family, learning to do without, seemed to turn out better than the city kids. Or even the town kids. She was pretty, too. Something he'd tried not to notice, since they were coworkers, and he had a decade on her.

"You okay?" he asked her.

"Yes. Although I wish we still had the radio and that I could have reached the police after all this started." It had been beaten to smithereens like the generator. Now there was no way to contact the world outside the hospital. "I was about to ask you the same thing," she said.

The dark had an impact on him that was hard to describe. It brought back the memories of night marches and skirmishes. But it also created a strange intimacy. Some of the truest friends of his life he'd made during its worst moments—sharing terrors, discomfort, and meager rations.

Maybe that's why he was feeling drawn to Kathy. She deserved better than him to act the fool with a schoolboy crush. He scooted a few inches back.

She closed the distance with a hand on his arm. It was small, warm, and, he imagined, soft. "What is it?"

"Just wondering about Doc." *Amongst other things.*

A voice interrupted them, making Kathy gasp and Wes jump. He was glad he'd left his safety on, or he might've just had an accidental discharge.

"I know something has happened. Not just the power." It was a mature man's voice.

Wes shined his flashlight at what he hoped was the fellow's chest height. He'd nearly blinded Susanne and the girls earlier and felt bad about it. He prided himself on common sense and practicality. He was no neophyte to night vision, but he'd had a bad vibe since the power went out, and it was getting to him. His beam shed a ghostly illumination on the man's face. It was the father with the injured adult son. The Comptons. He couldn't remember the guy's name.

"Well, sir, we're evaluating locations to move everyone." Wes wondered where Abraham was. It had been his job to let all the patients know they would be moved. Wes and Kathy were guarding the door.

"Why?" His voice and eyes crackled.

Wes cleared his throat. "Warmth. Consolidation of light. Ease of care in the dark. Safety."

"There was a commotion earlier. Those teenage boys sounded upset."

Wes nodded. "You're right about that. They surely were. Sadly, they were the ones to discover we'd lost a patient. He was in rough shape when he came in, and he didn't make it." It wasn't all of the truth, but true enough that he didn't feel too bad about the telling of it.

The man stared at him for long, silent seconds. Then he turned his gaze on Kathy. "What part of the story am I not getting from him?"

Kathy tensed. Wes put a hand on the middle of her back. Before she could answer, there was a crash from an exam room. The man startled, then seemed to relax.

"We have to go check on that, sir. Please return to your son's exam room." Wes applied gentle pressure to Kathy's back, and she walked ahead of him, in the light he pointed in front of her feet.

The noise came from a few rooms down. Clangs and crashes were still emanating from it. With his long arms, Wes reached above Kathy's head—he was a good foot taller than her, not an uncommon difference for him with women, except for Ronnie Harcourt—and parted the curtains. He moved his beam around until it landed on a plastic bed pan on the floor. The man crouching beside it had knocked over his IV stand. The drunk professor.

"What's the problem, sir?" Kathy asked.

"Needed to take a piss." He sounded clearer than he had earlier. The alcohol was working its way through his system. "And I heard that sonuvabitch talking."

"Who?" Wes said.

"The jerk who totaled my car yesterday. Wanted to kick my ass for it when it was his own damn fault. Him and that hussy."

"Disgusting." It was father Compton. He'd followed and was standing behind them in the corridor.

"Please respect the privacy of other patients and return to your son's room." Wes shut the curtain with a snap of rings on metal. "Let's get you back up on the table, sir. I'll help you with the bed pan."

"Wanna go to the loo." His voice was demanding. Disagreeable.

Kathy righted the IV stand. She touched the patient's wrist, reaching to check his IV. He snatched his hand away.

Wes had done his share of drinking and drugging overseas, but, as a general rule, he didn't love it when people abused their bodies and then siphoned away medical resources from other patients. Some people needed help breaking away from their demons. He understood that. Others didn't want it. Experience told him this guy fell into the latter category.

"No can do, my friend. The power is out, and we don't have any lights, nor do we have the manpower to get you there. You're going to have to use the pan."

Belligerence darkened the man's features. "Let me speak to your supervisor." His voice was a shout.

Wes heard footsteps, then Patrick's voice. *Thank the good Lord and the good doc.*

The curtains slid open. "Professor Renwick, we need you back on that table. You're going to pull out your IV."

"This jackwipe won't lemme go to the bathroom."

Patrick leaned over to Wes. "Where's Abraham?"

"I was just about to ask you that."

Patrick shook his head. "We can't worry about that now. Time to start evacuating patients to the staff lounge. Everyone in there is up to speed. I've told them not to let anyone in but you two and Abraham. Trish has my gun. She's guarding the door. It's locked. But our other weapons were missing from my locker."

"Son of a . . ."

"I couldn't agree more."

"Are you even listening to me? Do you know who I am?" Renwick said.

A wail prickled Wes's scalp. Kathy grabbed his hand. He didn't resist.

"You go check on that. Together. I've got the professor." Patrick pointed at the bed and was addressing the patient as Wes and Kathy hustled out. "Get on the table now, or I'll have to put you there myself, Renwick."

Wes moved recklessly in the darkness, still clutching Kathy's hand. "This way."

"It sounded like it came from one of the rooms in the middle."

But with only curtains as walls, what constituted a room was hard to discern by sound alone. A new noise reverberated through the entire ER, sounding like it came from the same place. It was a guttural cry that lasted several seconds until it broke and became a harsh sob. Wes followed it into an open room. The elder Compton was prostrate across the exam table.

"Sir, what's wrong?" Kathy said.

Wes stopped a few feet away, training the flashlight beam on the two figures on the table.

The father stood and turned toward them. His hands and face were covered in blood.

CHAPTER FORTY-THREE: BLUDGEON

Patrick

PATRICK STUDIED the wound where Andrew Compton's ear had been. No doubt this was murder. He wanted to tell his colleagues, but Abraham was missing, and Wes and Kathy were placating the other patients. He'd asked them to start the evacuations, too, one at a time, Wanda Carmichael first. *Women, children, and old people first.* She qualified twice. There was no time to waste.

Son of a biscuit. He spoke aloud, though mostly to himself, even though Roger Compton was in the room, too. "It's in the same place as the injury was earlier. Like someone came to finish off the job."

Was it the same weapon, though? It was hard to tell in the dark, but this one looked like a puncture wound. Like someone had ground a spike into Andrew's brain.

Patrick shuddered.

"How did he find us here?" Roger Compton paced around the bed like a caged predator.

"How did *who* find you?"

Roger Compton's voice rose to a shout, and he stabbed his finger to emphasize his words. "Mitchell. Wilfred Mitchell."

Patrick's blood turned to ice in his veins. He whispered, "Please keep your voice down."

The other patients were terrified and probably listening to every word, their hearing enhanced by their lack of vision in the dark. One of them could be the killer—whether Wilfred, or someone else.

Roger didn't respond verbally, but the sneer on his face spoke volumes.

"What makes you think Wilfred did this?" Patrick asked.

"It's either him or that Ay-rab doctor who got his feelings hurt because I wouldn't let him touch my son. But my money's on Wilfred." Roger moved close. Patrick was surprised when Roger's voice came out as soft as his. "We feuded over Leslie Anne. The man refused to pay me a proper settlement, even though we had to go out and hire a girl when she left. He claimed Leslie Anne had made her choice, that I hadn't sold her to him." He spat on the floor, and Patrick grit his teeth to hide his distaste. "So, we came to town to visit with him about it. I think he killed her."

"Why is that?"

"Could be he didn't want to pay. Or maybe he found out she was still seeing her old beau on the side."

The name came back to Patrick. "Bull Folske? Here in Buffalo?"

Roger nodded, looking surprised. "Bull's the one who found her in the first place and called me."

For some reason, Patrick thought Wilfred had said that Leslie Anne had been in touch with her mother. Or maybe that was just what she told Wilfred. If she was still seeing Bull behind Wilfred's back, where the heck was the man? And did that make it more or less likely that she'd been interested in Dabbo Kern? Again, he wished he could run his thoughts by Ronnie.

"Was your son's fight earlier with Wilfred?"

"Fight? Attack is more like it. We went back to his ranch to talk to Wilfred after law enforcement cleared out. It weren't our fault Leslie Anne died. He still owed me cash money."

Patrick's fists balled. Exercising equal compassion for all his patients was more challenging than usual tonight. Luckily, Roger wasn't a patient. But he had just lost his son, so Patrick held back his thoughts, as well as the fact that the man Roger was accusing of two murders was lying in a bed thirty feet away. *If he's still there.* Patrick hadn't checked on him since before the power outage.

Roger was still talking. "Andrew told him to pay up. Wilfred picked up a cane and came at him, swinging it around his head like one of them samurais, you know, like from Japan? He whacked Andrew a few times. I pulled Wilfred off, and when we left, he was just sitting on the ground, staring into the sky. Good thing we left when we did, too, because the roads were nigh impassable. That's when we came here."

Patrick frowned. An image formed. Wilfred, that morning, charging at Ronnie and him across his pasture. He hadn't been using a walking stick. He hadn't even limped. He felt a whirring sensation in his head. His brain was looking for something that it expected to find in there, but it was coming up empty. If there was another fact or memory related to Wilfred, Patrick couldn't retrieve it.

"Did Andrew get a lick in with Wilfred?"

"You kidding me? With that metal head on that cane carving up the air? He was lucky to have sur- . . . sur- . . . survived it." His face crumpled. "Didn't do much good in the end. A few more hours, that's all."

"Where were you when this happened to your son tonight?" Patrick waved at Andrew's body.

"I went to ask your people what's going on that you aren't telling nobody. That tall man and the short girl."

"Did you see anyone coming or going from this room?"

"Ain't no room. All there is between us and the people around us is a coupla flimsy pieces of fabric."

"Is that a yes or a no?"

"It's a no. I didn't see no one, I didn't hear no one. I came back—with no answers, mind you—and found my son dead. I wasn't gone but five minutes."

That narrows down the time of death. Another victim with a beef with Wilfred, dead. They had to do something about Wilfred. But Patrick wasn't judge and jury. He had suspicions but no witnesses. No evidence. *The safety of everyone else comes first. You have to do this.* He felt sure that together he, Abraham, and Wes could restrain him, especially given his broken arm. If they could find him.

"Abraham?" he said, projecting his voice.

The doctor didn't respond. Patrick was beginning to worry about him. A lot.

"Wes?" he called.

There was no answer.

"Kathy?"

No answer.

The two of them were probably delivering Wanda to the staff lounge.

"Okay, Mr. Compton. Thank you. Could you stay with your son for a little while? We're going to evacuate everyone one by one to the staff lounge."

"That's what your man said."

"I'll be back for you just as soon as I can."

"My wife died last year. Leslie Anne was supposed to take her place, but she ran off. Andrew was my only other surviving child and my heir. I'd rather stay with him."

"We'd feel better if you came with the group, Mr. Compton."

"Not until I say my goodbyes. His spirit is on its way to his maker. I got to send him off right."

"Whoever did this to your son could still be here. You could be at risk."

"He doesn't want nothing with me."

"Why do you say that?"

Roger narrowed his eyes. "Because Andrew provoked him. Told him about Leslie Anne and Bull. Insulted his manhood. It's Andrew's way. I kept quiet. When we left, I told him I'd withdraw my claim for a settlement. Andrew was hurt. I didn't want no more trouble. Besides, if Wilfred owes me, so does that other man she was carrying on with. Maybe he'll be easier to collect from."

It was plausible. "Be vigilant."

Roger nodded, then bowed his head over Andrew and began praying.

Patrick backed away. He didn't like the thought of leaving the man alone. But for the good of everyone, he had to find Wilfred and restrain him. He couldn't let another person die on his watch. He opened all the curtains around Andrew and Roger. Maybe if he kept Roger open to public view, he'd stay safe.

As he walked off, it hit him. Who did Roger want to collect a settlement from—Bull, or someone else?

CHAPTER FORTY-FOUR: KNOCK

Buffalo, Wyoming
Saturday, March 18, 1978, 11:00 p.m.

Trish

Trish leaned her back and head against the wall just to the side of the door, her arm and the gun in her hand hanging at her side. Her mom had locked it when her dad left the staff lounge, but that hadn't been enough to ease their apprehension. Perry and Wyatt had shoved a couch against the door, wedged under the handle. It seemed to help Kelsey, but Trish knew it was only for show. As easily as the couch had slid across the terrazzo floor, it wasn't a serious impediment to anyone getting in the room. But if it kept Kelsey calm, that was a good thing. Not because Trish cared much about the girl's feelings after what she'd done to Perry, but because, honestly, she didn't want to deal with any drama from her.

A sharp KNOCK KNOCK KNOCK sounded on the door.

Trish jumped, keeping a tight hold on the gun, then sucked in a breath.

"Who's there?" her mom asked.

"It's Wes and Kathy with Wanda Carmichael," a man said.

Trish recognized Wes' voice. She exhaled, hard.

Her mom whispered to Trish. "Be on the alert, just in case. Wilfred could be behind them. Or they could be his hostages."

Trish nodded. It was a horrible thought. But Ferdinand wasn't growling. In fact, he was standing with his front feet on the couch, tail wagging. That was good. But now she wished they'd established an "all clear" code word.

Her mom motioned to the boys. Perry and Wyatt pulled the couch back, and Ferdinand scrambled to make room. Kelsey cowered by the refrigerator, out of the way at least. Trish's mom unlocked the door and opened it a few inches. Trish cocked the hammer, ready, but pointing the barrel at the floor. She was able to see people through the crack.

Lantern light bathed Wes from behind. He was helping a gray-haired woman climb off a gurney. "Mrs. Sawbones, we've got a guest for you. If you could find a comfortable place for her, we'd appreciate it."

The scent of baby powder and hair spray preceded the woman into the room.

Trish's mom took the woman's elbow. "I'm Susanne Flint. Come in and get comfortable."

"Wanda Carmichael. And be careful of my arm. I came in for stitches and still haven't been attended to." She sniffed.

Trish wanted to congratulate her that at least she hadn't been murdered. Instead, she said, "Luckily a wound can be sewn up for nearly twenty-four hours after an injury." *Things girls learned when a parent is a doctor.*

"Why are you holding a gun, young lady? This is a hospital." She turned back to Wes. "Is she some kind of juvenile delinquent?"

An exuberant Ferdinand, who Perry had been restraining, broke free and rushed Ms. Carmichael. Trish's mom intercepted the dog, who still lunged against his collar, appearing to have sized Ms. Carmichael up as a new best friend.

"What is a dog doing in a hospital?" Ms. Carmichael's voice was nearly a shriek.

Wes winked at Trish out of Ms. Carmichael's line of sight. "Ferdinand is in charge of morale and security. Now, Mrs. Flint will explain everything to you. I need to bring the rest of the patients from the ER." He turned to Kathy. "Kathy, why don't you stay here with Ms. Carmichael?"

Kathy crossed her arms over her chest, her expression pure bulldog. "Not until we've got all the patients delivered safely."

"What could I say to change your mind?"

Kathy stared up at him, gaze steady, not speaking.

Trish smiled. Wes was a big guy. Kathy had moxie.

"Forget I asked," he said. "All right everyone. Be sure to lock up after us."

"Of course," Trish's mom said.

He leaned over to her. "There's been another," he whispered, within Trish's earshot.

"Did Wilfred do it?"

"It's our best guess." Wes saluted Trish and her mom, and he and Kathy left. For a few seconds, Trish could see the swaying light of their lantern before they turned a corner.

"What's that about Wilfred?" Ms. Carmichael said.

Her mom shut and locked the door and moved back into the kitchen. Trish uncocked the gun and stayed to the side of the door. No one answered Ms. Carmichael.

Ms. Carmichael took a seat at the table. "Well?"

There was another knock at the door.

"Who's there?" Trish asked.

No one answered her. A cold dread seeped over her.

Trish raised her voice. "Who's out there?"

After a few seconds of silence, a man answered in a grouchy tone. "This is Wilfred Mitchell."

Trish re-cocked the pistol. Her mouth was dry. She was scared. But her hands weren't shaking. She took a deep breath in through her nose, then blew it out with her mouth, something her dad had taught her do to reduce tension. "What are you doing here, Mr. Mitchell?"

"I was, uh, coming back from the bathroom. I saw Wanda go through this door. What's going on in there?"

Trish's mom walked back to stand by Trish. She put her hand on Trish's back and said, "This is the staff lounge. Go back to the ER, Mr. Mitchell."

"Let him in this instant!" Ms. Carmichael got to her feet. When no one did as she had ordered, the woman made a move for the door.

Trish's mom intercepted her, blocking the doorknob. It rattled, and Kelsey screamed.

Wilfred's grouchy tone turned downright nasty. "It ain't right how you're treating me. I heard Wanda's voice. Something's going on, and I dadgum know it."

Trish's mom put a finger over her lips then leaned close to Ms. Carmichael and whispered to the woman. "Hush. I'm not asking you, I'm telling you. I'll explain in a moment."

Ms. Carmichael gave her a snarly look and opened her mouth to speak.

Trish's mom cut her off. "Don't make me gag you, Ms. Carmichael.

The woman's mouth snapped shut.

"You'll be sorry. All of you," Mr. Mitchell said.

Trish's heart was pounding. Mr. Mitchell might have the rifle and the shotgun. He could shoot them through the door. He could blow the doorknob right off it and force his way in.

After a few seconds of silence, Mr. Mitchell spoke again. "It don't make no sense you not lettin' me in."

"Talk to Dr. Flint in the ER," Trish's mom said in her no-nonsense voice, the one she used as her last warning before she grounded Trish or Perry.

Trish hated that they were sending Mr. Mitchell back to her dad.

Were they being cowards not dealing with him themselves? She had a gun. She could use it. But it was wrong to shoot a man who hadn't attacked someone first. For all she knew, he was going to give himself up. Maybe the killings had been accidents. He might feel remorse. It wasn't for her to decide what to do about him. Her job was to protect the group in case of attack. So that is what she would do. Nothing more.

Mr. Mitchell was quiet for several seconds. Finally, he said, "Fine." But he didn't sound like he meant it. His tone sent chills down her spine.

She listened for the sound of his footsteps and didn't draw a normal breath until she heard him walk away.

CHAPTER FORTY-FIVE: SURPRISE

Patrick

Back in the ER, Patrick opened the curtain to Wilfred's exam room, his knife hidden in his closed hand and a smile on his face. "Mr. Mitchell, thanks for your patience. We . . ." His voice trailed off.

Wilfred wasn't in the room.

Damn. He whirled in a circle, his eyes raking the shadows and corners of the space, but they only verified that, indeed, Wilfred was not there. Patrick swallowed. *Be calm.* Where would the man go? *Other than into Tristan's and Andrew's rooms to kill them?* Patrick tried to reason it out. Where would he go if he'd just murdered two people? *Nowhere. Because I never would.*

"He'd run," Patrick said to himself in a soft voice. *Unless he's not done here.*

If Wilfred had made a break for it, Patrick wasn't about to go after him in the storm. But if he was still inside, well, then Patrick had to find him before he killed again. He wished he had a gun, but it was more important that Trish have it so his family could stay safe. He was capable with the knife. It would be enough. He would make sure it was.

Since his family was armed and behind a locked door, the first place to look was here in the ER, where his patients were. He'd make sure the area was clear. Wes and Kathy should be back any moment, and they could take the last of the patients—and Rick Compton, if he'd leave his son's body—to the staff lounge then. If there was still no sign of Wilfred, so be it. Patrick would join them there. *Where is Abraham, though?* He took a moment to whisper a prayer that his friend was all right. He was beginning to have his doubts, and the fear and sadness lapped at him. He couldn't let emotion derail him, though.

What he needed to do first was think. He had to be efficient and avoid an ambush by Wilfred, and that meant a systematic search. Work one end of the ER to the other. Open all the curtains and doors and leave them open. By the time he was done, he intended to be able to see the length of the ER with no hiding places left.

He unfolded his knife, holding it at the ready, and started with Wanda's vacated space. Curtains open. Cabinets open. No sign of Wilfred.

He strode through the side curtain to the exam table where Tristan's body lay. Opened the curtains. Opened the cabinets. Stared at Tristan's body. Noticed traces of the smell of death. Guilt stabbed him. He hated leaving the man out in the open like this. He deserved privacy. Dignity. Normally, someone would have taken him into the morgue while his next of kin was notified. He'd wait in cold storage for pick up from a funeral home. That wasn't going to happen tonight. At least with the heat off and the temperature falling, rigor mortis would be slowed. It would be better for him. And for Andrew.

He turned away from Tristan. No sign of Wilfred.

Patrick repeated the curtain and door opening process in the next exam room. Searched it. Found it empty.

And the next one. Open. Search. Empty—this had been Wilfred's room.

The next one. Open. Not empty. Professor Renwick. Patrick did a double take. The professor was ripping out his IV and lunging off the table. At Patrick.

Patrick threw up his hands to ward Renwick off, cocking his wrist back to protect the man from the knife blade. The professor was still drunk, and he bounced off Patrick's hands and against the cabinets and countertop. Bottles crashed to the floor and shattered. The strong scent of rubbing alcohol filled the air. Renwick's inebriation must have made him less susceptible to pain because he merely growled, then stood, and attacked again. Patrick feinted and the man flew past, bumping him to the side, but not knocking him down. Patrick wheeled in time to hear an "oomph," and see Renwick collapse over the table in the next bay. Snarling, he stood and turned back at Patrick.

This time, Patrick was ready for him. Knees flexed, knife hand up and slightly back, shoulders and hips squared.

"Stop," Patrick yelled. "Professor Renwick, What are you doing? This is Dr. Patrick Flint. You don't want to hurt me."

Renwick panted, but he didn't move. "Doctor?"

"Yes. You've attacked me. You need to stop immediately."

"You're not him?"

"Him who?"

"A man came sneaking through here. At first I thought it was a doctor or a nurse. Then he was gone behind the curtain, and I heard a noise. A shout. And some kind of awful gurgle. It sounded like someone was dying. Or being killed. And I thought you were . . . him." Renwick's voice was less slurred than it had been earlier. Less drunk. Practically sober.

A gurgle. That sounded bad. Patrick rose to a normal stance. "Who was it?"

"I don't know."

"What did he look like?"

"I don't know."

The two men stared at each other, both still wary.

Then footsteps close by and a voice. "Hey, y'all, where is everybody?"

The unfamiliar voice startled Patrick. He whirled, crouching into a defensive stance again, knife raised and ready.

Renwick dove behind the exam table. He made a whimpering sound.

"Whoa, whoa, whoa." A young, good-looking man Patrick had never seen before threw his hands up in the air. Cowboy-like with a bushy mustache and felt cowboy hat, but muscular instead of ropey. "I don't want no trouble. I'm just looking for my boss."

Patrick didn't trust anyone or their ready excuses. Not now with the body count in the hospital piling up. "Where did you come from?"

Before the newcomer could answer him, Wes and Kathy appeared, pushing a gurney back down the hallway into the ER, visible with the curtains all thrown aside in their direction. Wes jerked his head at the newcomer and released the gurney to put his hands in a "who's this?" gesture, then parked the gurney. He stepped in front of Kathy, hand on the gun in his holster.

Without taking his eyes off the young man, Patrick said, "We were just working on an answer to that question. But I've got this. Could you check on Roger Compton?" At Wes's blank look, Patrick added, "Father of our deceased patient, Andrew."

Wes frowned. "Is something the matter? And what is the patient doing behind the table?"

"Yes." Patrick didn't elaborate or bother answering the second question.

Kathy and Wes turned and walked quickly toward the few remaining curtained exam areas. Renwick peered over the edge of the table.

Patrick said, "You were about to tell me where you came from. I need to know that, your name, how long you've been here, and how you got here in the middle of this blizzard. And I need to know it quickly."

"You're scaring me, man," the newcomer said.

Patrick didn't have time for evasions. He didn't have time for anything. He rushed the man, knife out, stopping three feet in front of him. "Answer me!" he bellowed. *Be cool. Be cool.*

But before he could regain any semblance of cool, he heard a loud, feminine moan.

Wes shouted, "We've got another one, Doc."

CHAPTER FORTY-SIX: LANCE

BUFFALO, WYOMING
SATURDAY, MARCH 18, 1978, 11:15 P.M.

Patrick

PATRICK GRABBED the newcomer by the arm and frog marched him toward Wes and Kathy.

"What the hell?" the man said. "Who are you? What's going on?"

"Don't expect any answers until you start giving them to me first." Patrick pushed him into the exam room. The side curtains were still drawn, but the door area was wide open.

"Oh, God. Stop. No," the man said, shielding his eyes.

Behind them, a young female voice said, "Dabbo? I couldn't wait for you out there. It was too dark and scary. Are you okay?" Then she screamed. "Oh, my God!"

Patrick didn't even startle at the entrance of another person. He was transfixed with horror at the sight in front of him.

Kathy and Wes stood on either side of a body. Roger Compton's body, head lolled to the side. His body was somehow affixed to the wall with a lance protruding from his bleeding chest. A lance. In a hospital in Buffalo, Wyoming. It didn't make sense.

Patrick released the man he was holding. *I left Roger alone. He asked me to, but this is my fault.* But he didn't have time for self-indulgent recrimination. He barked, "Everyone, all the patients, all of us, need to get to the staff lounge. Right now."

"What about him?" Kathy's eyes were on Roger. Her eyes were like saucers, bright with unshed tears.

Patrick took a brief second to examine Roger. He stepped closer. *It isn't a lance. But what the heck is it?* The end closest to him was an ornate metal eagle. A cane head. A cane was impaled through Roger. But how did someone shove the foot of a cane through a man's body?

"You're sure he's dead?" Patrick asked. "You checked him for vitals?"

"Very," Wes said. "Yes."

"What's going on, man?" The newcomer said.

Patrick turned to face him. He'd forgotten about him. Now he saw that the man had his arm around a girl's shoulders. A girl about Trish's age. Short, red-haired. Terrified. But the guy looked too young to be her father.

"We don't know," Patrick said. "But we're going to find out. Starting with you. And her."

"No way. This is too freaky." His voice shook. Suddenly, he whirled and tried to run, dragging the girl with him.

Patrick and Wes were on him in an instant, each grabbing an arm. The girl started screaming. Long, ear-splitting screams that reverberated in the now open ER.

"Calm down, buddy," Wes said. "We just need to talk to you."

"What's wrong with you people? Let me go!"

"We can't do that. We're taking the two of you and the rest of our patients somewhere safe."

Patrick shook his head. "He's not going near my family yet. He owes us some answers first. So does she, for that matter. But I'll start.

I'm Dr. Patrick Flint, this is Wes Braten, he works here, and so does Kathy Bergman. She's a nurse. Now, speak."

"Are you, like, Trish Flint's dad?" the girl said. "I know her from school. Encyclopedia Flint."

Patrick felt his forehead bunch up, but he nodded.

"She's probably going to make cheerleader, so you'll be seeing a lot of me."

"I'm Dabbo Kern. This is Jillian Tupelo, my girlfriend. I, uh, we came looking for my boss."

The elusive Dabbo Kern. Who Wilfred suspected was interested in Leslie Anne. So, this must be his high school-age cheerleader girlfriend. Great. "Is your boss Wilfred Mitchell?"

Dabbo frowned. "How did you know that?"

"He said you didn't show up for work today."

The man groaned. "He's going to fire me. I was in Sheridan. With Jillian." His expression changed. He winked. "We went out to the ranch, to explain, but by the time we got going, the roads had gone to shit. Excuse my French."

Jillian giggled.

I wouldn't want a man cursing in front of my daughter. But I'm not this girl's daddy. "Go on," Patrick said.

"We got out to the ranch, barely. I found a note. From Wilfred. It said that Leslie Anne . . . that Leslie . . . that she was dead." Tears filled his eyes. *That's a surprise.* He swiped them away with a corduroy sleeve.

Patrick glanced at Jillian. Maybe she didn't know Leslie Anne, but she looked unmoved. Even a little smug.

Dabbo continued. "She was a special lady. Good to me. Nicer than Wilfred, although that isn't saying much. Anyway, the note said that he took the team into the hospital because he was hurt. I drove out in my own tracks. Took us forever to get here. Musta got stuck five times." He exhaled a noisy breath. "So, is he here? Is Wilfred okay?"

CHAPTER FORTY-SEVEN: JOIN

Patrick

Patrick's brain raced around like a chicken with its head cut off. But he was out of thinking time. It was time to act, and Dabbo and Jillian were in danger if they left them alone out here. If Dabbo was a threat, it was unlikely he'd act on it in an armed group. If he did, they could deal with him together.

"We'll bring them," Patrick said to Wes and Kathy. "Besides the drunk professor, is there anyone else left in here?"

"I don't think so," Kathy said. "But everything about tonight feels like a month. I don't trust my recall right now."

"I cleared back that way." Patrick pointed in the direction he'd come. "Let's just throw open the rest of the curtains, take whoever is here, and clear it out."

"I'll open the curtains," Kathy offered.

"Stay where we can see you. Please," Wes said.

She smiled at him and started walking and opening.

Wes leaned to Patrick and whispered in his ear. "I don't like it that Abraham's missing."

"Me either. I'm very worried about him," Patrick said.

"Are we sure it's Wilfred doing this? Abraham has been through some really traumatic stuff. Trauma can do terrible things to a person."

"What are you saying?" Patrick asked.

"I'm saying he's been missing, and things have been happening. We can't rule it out."

His words cut Patrick to the quick. Abraham was his friend. He fought the impulse to lash out at Wes. Because Wes was his friend, too. And he was right. They knew nothing for sure. Patrick gave Wes a curt nod. "Noted. But I hope you're wrong."

"Me, too."

Patrick raised his voice. "Renwick?" The curtains were open toward Renwick's area, but the professor was nowhere to be seen.

"I don't like what I'm hearing, Dr. Flint." His voice was muffled, like he was hiding.

Patrick shone his flashlight toward the voice. "Walk into the open. We're going to the staff lounge. We'll come get you."

Renwick crawled out from a supply cabinet. Patrick led him into the corridor with the flashlight beam. "Can you guarantee my safety?" The professor sounded like a cultured snob instead of a drunk.

With his back to Renwick, Patrick closed his eyes and sighed. "Will you keep an eye on Dabbo and Jillian?" Patrick said to Wes.

"No problem, Doc."

Patrick released Dabbo's arm and went for Renwick.

The professor stood erect. He was several inches taller than Patrick. Thin and less fit. That didn't stop him from looking down his nose at Patrick. "Where's my Susanne? Tell me she got out?"

Something in Patrick snapped. Never mind that this was a patient. He grabbed the professor by his tweedy shoulders and slammed him into the wall on the far side of the open space. Supplies rattled on their shelves. In a tone more dangerous than Patrick knew he was capable of, he snarled at Renwick. "She is not your Susanne. She's my Susanne. My *wife*. If you ever forget that and speak about her like that again, or to her other than in a required professional manner, I will find you, and I will make sure it never slips your mind again."

Renwick twisted in his grip, but Patrick didn't release him. "Stop it. You're a doctor. You can't hurt me."

Wes called, "Everything under control Patrick?"

"It is now." Patrick gave Renwick another hard shake. "March. Ahead of me."

Kathy returned, her face aglow in the lantern she was carrying at her side. "Done with the curtains. I didn't find anyone else."

Patrick, Renwick, Kathy, Wes, and his two charges walked toward the opposite side of the room, through the openings Kathy had created. Then the caravan made their way silently through the long, eerie hallway to the staff lounge. Overhead, one of the battery-powered emergency backup lights flickered, went out, then came back on. They might be nearing the end of their battery life. Patrick had no idea how long to expect them to last.

Wes knocked. "We're back. Patrick, Kathy, and Wes, with three folks from the ER."

Patrick wouldn't have classified Dabbo and Jillian as folks from the ER. He didn't know what he'd call them. A surprise? At least that.

There was a scraping noise from inside the door. A woof. The sound of the lock disengaging. Then the door opened.

Susanne peeked out at them. Ferdinand rushed the door and planted his front paws on Patrick's thighs. For once, Patrick didn't knee him in the chest and holler at him to get down. He just ruffled the dog's ears. "Hey, boy. I'm fine."

And he was fine. The sight of his wife's beautiful face made everything ten thousand percent better. He wished he could take back every word of their fight, and that he could have a do-over for that morning. He'd show her that he would partner with her on the less glamorous side of parenting and their household. But he couldn't change the past. He'd just have to change the future. He tried to convey everything he was thinking and feeling in a split second with his eyes. She didn't look away. He took that as a good sign.

Then he refocused on his responsibilities. "Is everyone in here okay?"

"We're good." She moved back to let them in, narrowing her eyes at Renwick.

"My . . . not my . . . I mean, Dr. Flint's Susanne, glad to see you're well," the professor said.

Susanne raised her eyebrows at her husband.

"We had a discussion." Patrick didn't elaborate.

"Just Susanne will do," she said to Renwick.

He nodded and walked over to the others in the lounge. The rest of the party from the ER entered behind him. Everyone started talking at once.

Trish stood behind her mother with the gun in her hand pointed at the floor. She scowled and spoke directly to Jillian. "What are you doing here?"

The red-haired teenager tossed her hair. "Hey, Trish. Oh, Wyatt, hi. I'm here with my boyfriend. Dabbo. You might have met him at my place?"

Wyatt lifted a hand in greeting.

"I saw him there," Trish said. Her voice was tight.

"Where's Abraham?" Susanne paused at the door, one hand on the knob.

Patrick shook his head. "We haven't seen him. Hopefully he'll show up." And not be responsible for any of this. But he'd given up hope of a good ending for Abraham. He'd either fallen victim to a killer, or—but Patrick couldn't even finish the thought. It was too horrible. After he saw to it that everyone in the lounge was settled, he'd have to look for him. If there was a chance he was alive, injured, and uninvolved, helping him to safety would be Patrick's next order of business now that he had all the patients, other co-workers, and his family and their friends secured.

Susanne's eyes widened.

"I'll find him. Soon," Patrick said, his voice low. "Lock up for now."

She flipped the dead bolt, and the teenage boys pushed the couch back against it under the knob. Patrick hugged his kids, patted Kelsey and Wyatt, then drew Susanne in for a long embrace. *Oh, the smell of her.* Always familiar, always home, yet always exciting. Her strawberry shampoo. The last remnants of Chanel N° 5. And an earthy, fresh scent all her own.

"I'm so glad you're okay," Susanne said, her lips next to his ear. "We had a visitor."

Patrick leaned back, still holding on to her. "Abraham?"

"No. Wilfred was here. We sent him to the ER to find you."

Patrick raised his voice. "Wes, Kathy, did you see Wilfred?"

"No," they said, nearly in unison.

From her perch at the table, Wanda said, "I told you that you should have let him in."

Susanne rolled her eyes at Patrick. "Did you have any other problems?"

Patrick released his wife. This was news the whole group had a right to hear. "We lost another. Roger Compton. Leslie Anne's father."

"Those people were trash." Wanda looked defiant, like she was begging someone to disagree.

Kathy flew at her, stopping just short of contact. Her voice was taut with fury. "Who do you think you are? They were human beings. Roger Compton was slaughtered like an animal and left hanging from the wall. No one deserves to be murdered. To die like that."

Wanda shrank back. Kelsey gasped, then started to cry. Both Perry and Wyatt went toward her. Wyatt stopped. Perry put his arm around her.

Wes eased up to Kathy and squeezed her arm. He leaned down and whispered something in her ear. Kathy drew a deep shuddering breath, then turned and put her face in Wes's chest. He patted her back.

"You're Wilfred's new hand," Wanda said to Dabbo. "I've seen you but haven't met you. I used to be a regular visitor to Wilfred's ranch before he . . . before . . . when he wasn't with Leslie Anne."

"Dabbo Kern." Dabbo looked around the room. "I've worked for Wilfred a coupla few months now."

The air grew heavy. Unease and suspicion was etched across face after face. No one else in the room introduced themselves to Dabbo.

Jillian stepped forward. "Hey, everyone. I'm Jillian. Dabbo's girlfriend."

"Oh, sorry," Dabbo said.

"Wilfred is the reason Dabbo and Jillian are here," Patrick told Susanne. "Wilfred left a note at the ranch that he was headed here." He raised his eyebrows at Susanne, signaling his trepidation about the additions to the group.

Susanne nodded. She might not know the details, but she'd received his message about Dabbo loud and clear.

Patrick cleared his throat. "I looked for Wilfred, but after we found Roger, we decided to just bring everyone here." He rubbed his forehead. *After we found Roger's body.* He couldn't believe three people had been murdered in the ER. On his watch. Hopefully it wasn't four. It was time to search for Abraham.

From the corner of the room, Patrick heard what sounded like a door squeaking open. Then the sound of something heavy falling to the floor. The door slammed shut. Everyone stared at the corner in silence. *Could that be in here with us? But there's only one entrance.* Besides, the bunks where staff caught naps while on shift were in the opposite direction, and they were separated from the lounge with curtains, not doors. The sound couldn't be in the lounge.

A new noise started and repeated. Thump. Thump. Thump. Thump.

Wes held a hand up as if asking for everyone's attention. "There's a small supply room out in the hall that backs up to that corner. We keep bedding, towels, pillows, and blankets in it. Things for the staff bunks."

"Something's in there," Trish said. Her hand went to the .357 on her hip. "Or someone."

Patrick walked over to her. "Thanks for protecting the group. How about I take the weapon responsibility off you for now?"

Trish sighed. "Gladly." She unfastened the holster and passed it over to him.

The thumping restarted.

Patrick strode to the corner. He tried to project more confidence than he felt, for the sake of the group. "Hello? Is anyone in there?"

The thumping grew louder. Faster.

"Stop if you hear me."

The thumping stopped.

"I'd say that's a yes, Doc," Wes said.

Patrick nodded. "I've got to go check it out."

Just as he was heading to the door, Perry spoke. He was still comforting Kelsey, but Kelsey was looking at Wyatt. *What's going on there?*

"Where's that backpacker dude that checked into the ER earlier?" Perry said.

Patrick, Wes, and Kathy shared a stricken look.

Patrick groaned. "I forgot about him. He should've been out cold, but he wasn't there when we cleared the ER. It could be him out there."

Wes walked over to stand beside him. "You can't go alone, Sawbones."

"I'd prefer if you stayed in here. You can cover me from the doorway." Ferdinand pressed himself against Patrick's leg. "You're not coming, big boy."

Trish grabbed him by the collar. "I'll hold him."

Patrick nodded. "All right. Let's do this. There's a person in that closet unable to talk. Possibly in need of medical attention."

"Or maybe choosing not to talk." Susanne joined her husband and Wes. She took Patrick's hand. "I don't like this, Patrick."

"I'll be right outside and right back." He kissed her forehead, inhaling the sweet scent of her. *I hope I'll be right back.* "Could someone move the couch?"

Perry and Wyatt ran over. They dragged the couch back. Susanne unlocked the door.

Wanda shouted. "Don't you go hurting Wilfred now. You got no call. You doctors think you're God, but you're not."

Patrick checked to see if the gun was loaded. It was. He cocked it. *Be ready but not reactive.* Then he answered Wanda. "I promise, I don't intend to hurt anyone. The only way that will happen is if I have to defend myself." He nodded at Wes.

Wes opened the door a crack, keeping his big body directly behind it. He peered to the right and the left in the hallway. "Clear," he said, his voice low.

Patrick drew in a deep breath, then exhaled it forcibly. He slipped into the hall and turned left, back toward the ER. He saw the closet door about ten feet away, under the blinking emergency light. He stopped at it. Drew in another deep breath, this time holding it, and opened the door much like Wes had. Body out of the line of fire. *Someone* was in this closet. Whether friend or foe, he was about to find out. He just hoped the thumping hadn't been a ruse to get them to open the lounge door.

As the door swung outward, an odor in the closet hit him full force. Fresh, coppery blood. He abandoned caution and threw it fully open. Wilfred's lifeless eyes stared back at him. Underneath his chin, a garish red smile marked his throat. *Someone slit it.* Patrick stepped forward. His foot connected with something on the floor and kicked it forward. It clattered against the door frame. He looked down.

A bloody scalpel.

His training took over. After he uncocked and holstered his gun,

Patrick reached out fumbling for Wilfred's arm, lifted it, and pressed two fingers to the underside of his wrist, searching for a sign of life. *Why is he so high? It's like his body is stacked on a pile of something.*

Just as he was about to announce Wilfred's death to Wes, the thumping started again, faster than ever. With the closet door open, it was impossibly loud.

Patrick dropped Wilfred's arm. The man was dead. It couldn't be him.

Wilfred was suddenly flying toward him.

Impossible. Yet, happening.

"Argh!" Patrick yelled, jumping back and away.

He pulled his revolver, cocked it, and was about to fire when he realized that Wilfred had fallen forward, face down in the hall, unmoving. Someone else was moving, though, on the floor of the closet.

"What is it, Sawbones?" Wes said. "What's that on the ground?"

Patrick aimed at the figure. He fully expected it to leap at him using Wilfred as a shield. To kill him with his own shotgun at point blank range. Just as he was about to shoot, the figure writhed and bucked its way out of the closet.

Not figure. Figures. Two of them.

He saw gagged mouths. Bound hands. Bound feet. One of them had a partially disassembled coronet of long blonde braids. The other, a swarthy complexion and short, dark hair.

Their faces. It was Ronnie Harcourt. And Abraham Farham.

CHAPTER FORTY-EIGHT: RELEASE

Patrick

PATRICK'S HEART was pounding out of his chest, and his brain was short-circuiting. *Wilfred, dead. Ronnie and Abraham, captured but alive.* He felt confusion. Joy. And an electrifying fear. They'd been wrong. All wrong. Wilfred was a victim, not a killer.

He sunk to his knees and pulled his friends out of the closet. "It's Ronnie and Abraham," he shouted to Wes.

He pulled the gag down from Ronnie's mouth, then started to untie her hands. Her eyes were wild with panic. Up close, he could smell it along with sweat and Wilfred's blood. "Are you okay?" If he could get them loose from their wrist bindings, they could help him with their ankles. And they needed out of this hallway. They were sitting ducks for a sadistic killer right now.

"Is she dead?" Wes said. His voice was low.

"I'm alive.' Her voice was raspy. "And I need to find that son of a buzzard."

Patrick finished with her wrists.

She rubbed them each with her hands. "Thanks." She set to work on her ankles.

Patrick freed Abraham from his gag. Abraham gasped and shuddered. "Thank you."

Suddenly, Ferdinand burst out the door with a roaring growl. He sprinted down the hall, away from Patrick, Ronnie, and Abraham, baying, barking, and growling all at once.

"Ferdie!" Trish screamed. She appeared in the doorway, fighting to go after her dog.

Wes caught her around the waist. "You can't."

"No! Ferdie! No!"

Patrick turned back to Abraham. His eyes were wide, begging him to hurry. He fumbled with the coarse rope around his wrists. For a moment, he thought about using his knife. But the rope was too thick for quick work. He just needed to calm down and he'd be able to untie the knots with his fingers. He breathed in deeply through his nose and out through his mouth. Finally, he got it off. Abraham massaged life back into his hands while Patrick started on his feet. He'd be able to untie them faster than his friend could. He was still working on Abraham's ankles when Ronnie spoke in a hoarse whisper.

"I was watching Tristan Babcock. Someone snuck up on me." She touched her head. "Knocked me out with something. I didn't even see who it was until he dropped Wilfred Mitchell on top of me. Us, I guess, because Abraham was on top of me. But Wilfred's weight must have woken me up."

"You saw him," Patrick said.

"Yes. But it was dark. All that really registered was that it was a man wearing a large backpack."

Patrick had feared as much. He felt at fault. He'd recognized the mental instability of the man. He thought he'd taken care of it, though. How had the sedative not wiped the man out? But that didn't matter right now. The safety of his friends and family did. "What about you, Abraham?"

Abraham shook his head. "Nothing. I wish I had something of use to tell you. As with Ronnie, I woke up in the closet. I feel so foolish. I already knew there was a murderer in the building, but he still managed to take me by surprise."

"Not just you. At least now we know who it is."

"And? Who is it?" Ronnie pushed wisps of hair out of hair face.

"Not who, really. But he was in here earlier as a patient, so we know of him. He wouldn't give us a name."

Patrick finished with the rope on Abraham's feet just as Ronnie kicked the ties off her own ankles. Patrick grabbed her hand, pulling her to her feet. She wobbled, then leaned over and vomited.

"You've got a concussion," he said to her.

"I've got a murderer on the loose."

"You don't know the half of it," Patrick said.

He helped Abraham stand. The doctor rotated his neck and batted his eyes. "I still feel quite groggy."

Ronnie patted her hips. "My weapons. They're gone." She turned back to the closet.

"Forget them." Patrick tugged her arm. "Neither of you is one hundred percent. Let's go. Now. Into the staff lounge. Everyone who's left is holed up in there."

She glared at him. "Everyone who's left?"

"Wilfred is our fourth death. He also killed Roger and Andrew Compton—Leslie Anne's father and brother—and Tristan Mitchell. The real mystery is why he didn't kill you guys, too, when he had the chance. We don't want to give him a chance to reverse his decision. We've got to get you to safety."

She held out her hand. "No way. Give me your gun. I'm going after him."

He shook his head.

"Patrick Flint, as a Johnson County Deputy, I am ordering you to surrender your weapon."

Patrick stared at her. She had every right. But she needed backup. The woman had a concussion. She'd been tied up, unconscious, for hours in a closet. He unfastened the holster and handed it over. "Okay. But I'm going with you."

"I'll call for backup."

"The phones are dead. The radio was destroyed. And I wasn't asking permission." Patrick turned to Abraham. "Please. Go in the lounge with the group. Keep my family safe."

"Of course," he said.

"Fine, Patrick. But you'll have to keep up." Ronnie skirted Wilfred's body and started down the hall at a run, in the direction Ferdinand had gone.

Patrick ran silently after her.

CHAPTER FORTY-NINE: CONFRONT

Patrick

PATRICK AND RONNIE approached a hallway intersection. Ronnie stopped and held out her arm for Patrick to do the same. Then she crouched in a shooting stance, checking in every direction. "Clear."

"Ferdie," Patrick whispered. "Here, Ferdie."

There was no answering woof. *Please let him be okay.*

"Left or right?" Ronnie said.

"Left is to maintenance and mechanical. Right connects us to the lab. We know he's already been to mechanical once when he sabotaged the generator."

"That must have been after he put me to sleep in the closet. But it explains why it's so dark and cold in here. This place is like a post-apocalyptic nightmare."

A yelp sounded from the left. *Ferdinand.*

Ronnie ran toward it without another word. Patrick sprinted after her. He fought to silence his breathing, but he was already gasping for breath. He'd been offended when she'd told him he had to be able to keep up earlier. He was training to climb the world's tallest mountain peaks. He'd run half marathons the year before. But Ronnie was smoking him. Had the woman been a sprinter in her youth? He corrected himself. Had the woman always been a sprinter? Because she still had it. With a concussion no less.

They approached the door to the large room that held the HVAC, electrical, and water systems. It was open.

"Is this it?" she whispered.

He nodded.

"Stay out of my line of fire," she said. "And don't get yourself caught. You're here as a witness in case he gets me. Not as a bargaining chip for him or to die alongside me."

Patrick didn't bother arguing with her. Ronnie had put her life on the line for his family multiple times. He was here as her partner, whether she liked it or not.

She slipped into the room, her head whipping from side to side, her body hugging the wall as she circumvented the equipment in the center of the room, going to the left. *Father protect us.* Patrick went in after her, thankful to see the spill of blessed emergency light on the far end of the space.

The room, normally noisy with the hum of electrical, the whoosh of air through fans, and the soft rush of water through pipes, was silent. Until Ferdinand bellowed with rage.

An atonal voice said, "Stop. I don't want to hurt you. You're just a dog. But you followed me. You know too much. You saw too much. More than the cop and the doctor."

Patrick's eyes widened. "Ronnie, he's going to kill Ferdie," he whispered.

She put a finger to her lips.

The man continued, and Patrick listened, dumbstruck. "I loved her, you know. You have to understand that, dog. You're the only one who knew it was me that killed her, but I loved her. She did things with me, dirty things, but then she told me she never wanted to see me again. After she'd lured me with her eyes. The Bible tells us, 'Do not lust in your heart after her beauty or let her captivate you with her eyes.' But I did. Stupid."

Patrick stole a glance at Ronnie. Her head was nodding. Her eyes lost focus. *Her concussion.* He shook her, and she snapped to alertness again.

"I risked so much to be near her. Fooled that stupid old man she was living with. He thought I was a vagrant." He laughed. "Me. Bull Folske. I've worked all my life. I have plenty of money. I was here to free her from him."

Bull Folske! The old boyfriend. The one who had told the Comptons Leslie Anne was here.

"But she asked me to do it. You can see that, can't you? She didn't want to see me anymore. She didn't want to *see.* I took the crazy neighbor's cane. He left it outside by the fence when he came to let his cows onto Wilfred's land. And it was perfect. An eagle. Eagles are free. They fly away, so high they can't see what's down below. When she came to meet me, I gave her what she asked for. She flew with the eagle, and now she'll never see me again."

Bull began to weep. Patrick dared to move where he could look toward the voice from between two boilers. He could see him. Bull had Ferdinand in a chokehold, but he was rocking back and forth, crying and crooning to the dog.

"But when I went to take the cane back, the old neighbor man saw me with it. He tried to take it. I didn't want to hurt him. I just had to get away. I only hit him hard enough in the mouth that he wouldn't tell what he saw. I ran back to the ranch where Leslie Anne had lived. I dropped the cane there. I went inside Wilfred's house. I looked up your master's address in the phone book. I hitchhiked to town and came looking for you and your master. I needed to make sure you didn't come after me. You see that, don't you? That's all I wanted. For you not to follow me."

Patrick didn't see how in Bull's twisted mind that made sense.

Bull was still rocking Ferdinand, swaying side to side. "I slashed the tires on the truck so they couldn't drive. But then your master saw me. So, I threw a brick through the window to get him to come outside. Just him. I didn't want to hurt you. You're a dog. You're innocent. But he didn't come out. What choice did I have? I cut the other tires and waited for morning. But then everyone came out in the night and drove away on the snow machines. I heard them say they were going to the hospital. I knew it would be hard, but I had taken the snowshoes so I followed them."

My snowshoes. The insult of the man using Patrick's equipment stung more than it should, like a personal affront.

Bull's voice was singsong. "A snow plower stopped and gave me a ride. I came here and saw Wilfred's sleigh. And the cane. I found out that everyone who had conspired against me was here. Wilfred. Roger and Andrew who only wanted to reunite us so she would come with me, and they could steal her back again. Andrew, who wouldn't listen to reason. Roger, who had no heart. That weak hand who had fallen prey to Leslie Anne's eyes, too. He showed up. But he was her victim, like me. The crazy old neighbor who would tell people who I was when he woke up. That I had his cane and had hit him with it. They had to be stopped first. So, I pretended to take the sleep medicine—they thought I didn't know their plans to drug me, but I'm not stupid—and I got the cane from the sleigh. I did what I had to do. But I didn't hurt anyone I didn't have to. Even that cop and the doctor. I didn't kill them because they hadn't seen me. Hadn't done me any harm. You see that, don't you?"

Ferdinand struggled in Bull's arms. Sweat rolled down Patrick's forehead. He needed to save his dog. He couldn't let what was coming happen to Ferdinand.

"Stop fighting me, dog. Can't you see it pains me to hurt you? I don't kill innocents. If I knew you wouldn't betray me, if you could promise never to tell what you know, I could let you live. Promise me. Let me hear you say it." Bull sounded strident. Desperate.

Ferdinand lay very still. Had Bull choked him out? Patrick pulled his knife from its small holster. It was now or never. He had to save his dog.

Without releasing Ferdinand, Bull reached down and lifted a shotgun. One handed, he worked the action, loading a shell into the chamber. Then he propped it between his feet. "I thought I'd be okay, but I don't want to live without her. We'll go together, dog."

He lost his grip on Ferdinand. The dog suddenly barked. He writhed out of Bull's grip.

"No!" Bull shouted.

Ferdinand scrambled to his feet and ran straight for Patrick's hiding place. A few feet away, Patrick heard a rustling and a soft thump. He glanced back. Ronnie had crumpled to the ground. *I'm sorry, Ronnie. I'll help you just as soon as I save Ferdie.*

Bull jumped to his feet, jerking the shotgun up, swinging it around, and pressing it to his shoulder. "I'm sorry, dog." He flicked off the safety.

Patrick drew back and hurled the knife at Bull.

A shot rang out.

Bull crumpled to the ground.

Ferdinand crashed into Patrick. Patrick fell to his rump then to his back as ninety pounds of Irish wolfhound landed on his chest and licked his face with pure joy.

CHAPTER FIFTY: RECONCILE

Ben

BEN SAT beside three beds in the hospital. The papa bear bed held Henry, mama bear for Vangie, and Hank was asleep in a baby bear sized bed. Ben had spent the last few hours pacing the hospital corridors while the medical staff provided emergency treatment to his family. Oddly, they'd been diverted from the ER to the main hospital at first because of some kind of situation. There'd been cops everywhere, despite the weather, and the power had been out. But about half an hour after he'd arrived, the power was restored, and the lights had come back on.

"You saved us all, son. God's perfect timing." Henry's face was pale, but his smile was wide.

Ben hadn't told his foster parents he almost hadn't come home at all. But the circumstances of his arrival made Henry's words ring even more true to Ben. "I've never been so scared in my life. I didn't know what was wrong. I didn't know what to do. All of you. So still."

Henry reached over and grasped Ben's hand, squeezing tight for a few seconds. "But you figured it out, and you did it. I'm proud of you."

A tear leaked down Ben's cheek as he thought about the dog who had died on their harrowing midnight drive to the hospital. He moved closer to Vangie and grasped her hand. "I wish I could have saved Flash." He lowered his forehead to the mattress.

Henry cleared his throat. "Flash didn't make it?"

"No, sir." Ben's words were muffled.

"Well, that's a shame, but you saved us and Hank. We'll miss Flash, but we're proud of you."

"You were amazing, Ben. And to see you now—it's like a dream. Your hair has gotten long. I barely recognized you. I'm so, so glad you're here." Ben sat up, and Vangie pushed hair off his forehead. "Why didn't you tell us you were coming?"

"I, uh, I wanted it to be a surprise." It hurt Ben that he wasn't telling them the whole truth, but he didn't want to cause them any more pain than he already had. "And then I almost didn't make it to Piney Bottoms because of the storm. I picked up the snowmobile at the garage in Story. I'm glad I did, because I was able to drive you guys to town in the sled track, then on to the interstate and here to the hospital. I'm not sure I would have made it otherwise."

Henry nodded. "Smart thinking."

"Are you back for good?" Vangie's eyes were full of naked hope.

"No, ma'am. I have a good job in Alaska. I'm working on a fishing boat out of Ketchikan. I really like it. I mean, I miss you guys. But it's right for me."

Vangie and Henry shared a long, sad look.

"Does Trish know you're here?" Vangie asked. The naked hope had turned to unmasked pain.

"No."

"She'll be so excited."

"I don't want her to know." *But she'll find out from Ronnie.* He couldn't worry about that now.

"Why not?"

"It's just best."

Vangie frowned. "I thought . . . Well, that's your business. But she's been very down since you left. We've been worried about her."

Ben snorted softly. "I don't want to talk about it."

Henry cleared his throat. "Your case in Laramie was dismissed."

Ben felt a rush of heat in his face. Good heat. "What?"

"Your roommate was dealing drugs. He had multiple arrests for possession and one for intent to distribute. The police found quite a stash in his car. He's in jail now."

"That's great." Ben leaned forward, elbows on his knees.

"The attorney we hired worked things out with the court when you skipped town, too. We all owe him one."

Vangie nodded, smiling. "You can visit us anytime now. No need to worry about legal trouble. You can even go back to the University of Wyoming."

Ben shook his head. "College isn't for me. But thank you. For everything"

Her face sagged and she suddenly looked ten years older. "We miss you. It was hard. You leaving. Not knowing if you were all right. Not being able to get in touch with you. And the thought of you going back now—I'm not going to pretend it's easy. You'll be so far away. Can we come visit you?"

"I, um, I guess. Yeah."

Henry rubbed his temples. "You know, we went in with the Flints and hired a private investigator to find you."

Ben sat back, legs splayed. "You did?"

"He tracked you part of the way. He was about to come looking in Ketchikan."

"No need now. You know where I live. I'll give you a mailing address and everything. Just as long as you promise not to give it to the Flints."

Henry sighed. "You're putting us in an awkward position. Is there someone else in Ketchikan? A girl you're dating?"

Ben pictured his monastic life as he struggled to chew his mouthful. The barren room he'd rented by the week. Trish sitting next to that jerk Wyatt in the Flints' kitchen as he draped his jacket over her shoulders. Finally, he swallowed, then said, "Yeah. There's someone else."

Vangie rolled her lips, then said, "What do we tell the Flints? We'll be calling off the search for you."

Ben wrapped his hands on his mug and stared at them. "I don't know. Just don't tell them I was here, and don't tell them where I am. Now, can I hold Hank? I've missed him."

Vangie and Henry shared a smile. Then Vangie nodded.

Ben grinned, nervous. He was anxious to get on the road. He couldn't tell them he was about to leave again. And he wouldn't leave without this.

Ben gathered the only little brother he'd ever known into his arms and held him close.

CHAPTER FIFTY-ONE: ABANDON

Ben

BEN PULLED to the shoulder outside Big Timber, Montana. The roads were plowed and clear of snow. He rolled down the window, breathing in the clean, crisp air. He'd filled the previous hours working at Piney Bottoms. Nailing plywood from the barn over the broken windows in the master bedroom. Turning off the water main, which was like shutting the barn door after the cows were already out, because he'd looked in the window and seen frozen water at the end of the kitchen faucet. The pipes had burst. Fixing that wasn't going to be fun. When his work was done, he'd napped in his truck before getting on the road.

He thought about the tentative plans the Sibleys had made to visit him in the fall. That was a long way off, but it gave him something to look forward to. He'd refused to discuss Trish and the Flints for the rest of his two hours with them in the hospital, other than to eavesdrop on conversations amongst the hospital staff about the murders in the ER, and how the Flints had worked together with Wes to save themselves, Wyatt, Kelsey, and the other patients. It had devastated him. Not just knowing the danger Trish had been in, but hearing that Wyatt was with her.

Wyatt.

Trish.

Trish had been in the ER being interviewed by law enforcement while he was in the hospital with his family. So close, and yet not.

Ben pounded the steering wheel. He was making the right choice to leave instead of staying and humiliating himself. He'd been honest with Henry and Vangie about heading back to steady work. But he'd told one lie, and that was that he needed to be back quickly. Cap was on a break. Ben had two weeks to kill.

He opened his glove box and spread the map in his lap. Much like last Saturday night, he was at a crossroads. If he went the most direct route north back to Ketchikan, he knew what he'd see. What he'd do. What he'd find there. He traced it with his finger. Then he traced a different line. If he kept driving westward, the road would take him all the way out to Seattle and the ocean. He could head north from there. Up through Vancouver. He had time and money. He could even take the ferry over to the San Juan Islands. Maybe even Victoria.

It left him plenty of time to rejoin Cap and the crew for spring fishing.

Or he could turn around and drive back to Buffalo. Beat Wyatt to a pulp. Give Trish a piece of his mind. Maybe even beg her to take him back.

He shook his head. He'd never put himself at risk of this kind of pain again. From now on, he was a solo operator. He put the truck in drive. Passed the turn to Calgary and headed west.

CHAPTER FIFTY-TWO: UNCOVER

Patrick

PATRICK AND RONNIE stood side-by-side staring at Bull Folske's body on the stainless-steel autopsy table. Ronnie was bent over on her knees. Despite the mentholated rub on her chest and under her nose and the mask over her face, she was fighting nausea.

"Sorry," she said again.

"You don't get many autopsies in Johnson County." The forensic pathologist was washing his hands. "It's a smell that takes some getting used to."

"I don't think I ever want to get used to it, Dr. Evans. No offense."

Dr. Evans dried his hands on some paper towels and tossed them in the garbage. Then he removed a hair tie from his curly gray hair. It fell around his face like a stringy Brillo pad. "None taken. I know you've both been anxious to hear which one of you caused the death of Bull Folske." Because even though she had fallen from the effects of her concussion, Ronnie was only down, not out. She had grabbed Patrick's gun and shot Bull, just as Patrick had thrown his knife. "Not that it matters much. He was about to die anyway."

"What?" Patrick said. "I don't understand." He felt out of place in the cold sterility of the autopsy suite. Maybe it had him discombobulated. Because he thought Dr. Evans had just said Bull was about to die before Ronnie shot him through the heart and Patrick embedded a knife in the man's temple.

"Mr. Folske had a malignant brain tumor. I literally don't know how he was still functioning."

"Could it have caused mental instability?" Patrick knew that depending on size and location, a brain tumor could completely change a personality in the patient's waning days, leaving someone in unbearable pain and robbing them of their sanity. "Like the kind that causes someone to kill five people and then attempt suicide?"

"I'd say it's possible." Dr. Evans opened a tub of lanolin cream, scooped some out, and massaged it into his hands and forearms.

"That makes sense." Ronnie raised her head. "His family and friends in Moorcroft insist he was a nice, normal guy. The man Patrick and I saw in his final moments had left his marbles out on the playground."

"I think Dr. Farham can attest to that, too." Abraham's stint covering for Dr. John had ended and he'd returned to his practice on the Wind River Reservation. Patrick would miss his friend. He pulled at his lips. "The things he said and did were completely around the bend. Yet, hearing him talking to himself and my dog, it was clear he believed his actions were rational. Logical. Justified."

Dr. Evans put the lid back on the lanolin cream and set the tub on a metal shelf by the sink. "It doesn't sound like he knew about his condition, then. I wondered. Very sad. Even sadder that so many people died at his hands, of course."

"And he almost killed my dog, too," Patrick added.

"But to answer the question of whether the knife to the temple—"

"A lucky throw. Or unlucky, depending on your perspective."

"—or the bullet to the chest caused his death, it was a race to the finish. Both would have been fatal, in my opinion. And they occurred simultaneously. I wish I could give you a definitive answer. But I'm going to have to call it a dead heat. Pardon the pun."

Patrick and Ronnie exchanged a glance. Dr. Evans raised the body bag and began zipping it over the corpse that had been Bull Folske's living body only a few days before.

"I told you to stay in the back and just be a witness," she said. "Do you always have trouble following instructions?"

"The complaint has been raised to me a few times in my life." Patrick grinned at her. "But what will this mean for you and me?"

"Nothing, really. The sheriff is declining to press charges. Though, if you want to get technical, justifiable homicide in defense of a dog is iffy. But he had killed five people, and we had reason to fear for our lives, too."

"Me especially. He was pointing that gun at Ferdie, and Ferdie was running for me."

"Well, if the county attorney changes his mind and comes after us, there's our defense." She raised a hand at Patrick's worried expression. "But don't worry. He won't."

The county attorney, Max Alexandrov, had a long-distance romance going with Patrick's sister. Patrick hoped Ronnie was right.

Dr. Evans pushed Bull's table back to the cooler. He opened the door and cold air rushed into the room. As he slid the foot of the table in, the legs folded underneath it. When the table was fully enclosed, he shut and latched the door. "For what it's worth, Mr. Folske would have probably begged you to do it if he had had the chance. He had to be in tremendous pain, physical and psychic. If I'm ever in his condition, I hope I'm not forced to endure it to the bitter end."

Patrick and Ronnie both shook hands with Dr. Evans, thanked him, and walked out to the parking lot and their adjacent vehicles.

"I need to hustle," Patrick said. "The Sibleys and the Flints are meeting to discuss Ben. The investigator called with news."

Ronnie winced. "I wish I'd known that Ben hadn't told Trish he was in town before I opened my big mouth to her. I hurt her, and I'm so sorry."

"You didn't do anything wrong. The Sibleys picked up the phone after he left and called us anyway." They had also asked the Flints not to tell Ben they'd gone back on their word to him, if the issue ever arose. "She was going to find out no matter what."

"I'm glad she went through with cheerleading tryouts. She asked me if I cheered in high school, you know."

"When?"

"After school on Tuesday. She came by the station."

"Well, did you?"

"I did, actually. And it seemed to make a difference to her. She wanted to be sure she could still be a serious adult if she did something she had always associated with frivolity. I told her even serious people are allowed to have fun. I hope she makes it. It's hard to be a morose cheerleader, and I'm afraid this Ben situation isn't going to get easier any time fast."

Patrick was afraid she was right. "Tryouts and voting were this morning. By now, she knows."

"Well, then, good luck, Dad. And just so you know, the uniforms and trips to games and competitions get pretty spendy."

Patrick groaned and opened his truck door. Earlier in the week, the coach had sent home an itemization of the expenses associated with cheerleading. Patrick had been shocked speechless. Susanne had signed the acknowledgement form and passed it to him. He'd said, "I never dreamed how much this honor would cost us. Are we sure she really, really wants to do this?" Susanne had handed him the pen and glared at him. *It is what it is.*

Waving a final goodbye to Ronnie, he backed out and headed toward Main Street. At least Susanne and he had finally worked out an equitable division of labor. He'd made a blood oath to carry a share of the kid and home life duty reliably as well as to prioritize her dreams equally with his own. Honestly, he felt like a bootheel that he hadn't realized he wasn't. And Susanne had promised to report Professor Renwick's behavior to the college, both toward her and the student who had saved him by bringing him to the Buffalo ER. Which she had done, with Patrick by her side. He hated to throw his weight around, but he'd witnessed the man's behavior first hand, and he wanted to be absolutely certain the college took the issue seriously. The department head had taken statements from Wes and Kathy on Wednesday. On Thursday, Susanne learned that her complaint had started a string of female students coming forward on the condition of anonymity, reporting that he forced them to have sex with him in return for better grades. Patrick was proud of her for giving the others the courage to speak up. Meanwhile, the family was living in the Occidental Hotel while George Nichols and a crew worked on the extensive repairs at their home and Ferdinand enjoyed a visit with Aunt Ronnie and Uncle Jeff. Their next-door neighbors at the hotel were the Sibleys, who'd also suffered frozen pipes in the storm. Luckily, they'd escaped with their lives, thanks to Ben. What was a little water damage compared to that?

Patrick parallel parked his truck beside Susanne's Suburban outside the Silver Spur Cafe. He saw the Sibleys' truck a few spaces over. He hoped they hadn't been waiting for him long. He trotted to the door, took a deep breath, and walked in.

The group was seated at a table near the door to the kitchen, closest to the smell of bacon and hash browns, served all day every day.

Patrick greeted them, "Hello, everyone."

Henry half stood, and they shook hands. Then he slid into a straight-backed chair beside Susanne.

"Hi, Patrick," Vangie said.

Baby Hank waved from a highchair at the end of the table.

"I just ordered you a coffee," Susanne said.

"Thanks." He pressed a kiss on her cheek.

She smiled at him. A genuine smile. His breath caught. *Still.*

Twenty years later, she still took his breath away. He smiled back, wider even than hers, still grateful to be forgiven.

A waitress sashayed up with a tray of cinnamon rolls. Patrick's stomach rumbled. He wasn't that late to their lunch, but he was ravenous. She set down three of them.

"No cinnamon roll for me?" he asked.

His wife batted her eyelashes. "You're in training. You made me promise not to sabotage your superman diet."

Patrick groaned and asked the waitress to bring him a sandwich as the others laughed. He sipped coffee as the others took their first bites and made sounds of bliss.

After a minute, Henry put his fork down. "I guess we should get down to brass tacks. The investigator called last night. He gave us addresses for where Ben lives and works."

Susanne squeezed Patrick's knee.

"I don't suppose that matters much since you guys are back in touch with him," Patrick said.

"Sort of," Vangie said. "He said he was going to give us his phone number and address, but he forgot to do it before he left. He did promise to write and to let us visit this fall. It was wonderful to see him. He was very loving. But he was a little bit cagey."

"Part of me doesn't want to tell Trish we know where he is. Does that make me a bad mother?" Susanne said.

Henry and Vangie shared a look. He nodded at Vangie to go ahead.

Vangie licked her lips. "Ben said he's found someone else. I don't know the details, but that's what he told us."

"That's odd," Susanne said, her face tensed in thought. "When Ronnie saw him, he was coming from Buffalo in the south, not from the north. And Bull Folske told Patrick that a young man whose description and truck matched Ben's was outside our house about an hour before that, although who knows if we can believe him. Trish does, though, and she's convinced Ben saw another boy over at our house. That he drove away because he thought *she* had a new boyfriend."

Just hearing about Wyatt made Patrick's blood boil. Trish wasn't the only Flint offspring with a broken heart this week. Kelsey and Wyatt were the new "it" couple of the teenage set. Patrick couldn't believe the older boy had stolen Perry's girlfriend right out from under his nose. And managed to do it in the middle of a horrible storm with a serial killer rampaging around them and through the hospital. For that matter, the thought of Kelsey didn't fill him with warm fuzzies either. It takes two to tango, and she was the one who'd owed Perry kindness, and instead treated him poorly.

Vangie shrugged and gave a sad smile. "It's not impossible. We do know he can occasionally make rash decisions on very little information."

Henry pushed a piece of paper across the table. "Here's the address. Do with it what you will."

"Thanks." Patrick folded the paper and slipped it into his wallet.

"Enough of the hard topics. I have news," Susanne said.

"Spill," Vangie said. "I hope it's good. I could use good."

Susanne took a deep breath, paused, then smiled. "Trish was elected to the cheerleading squad today."

"Oh, that's fantastic! A perfect distraction for her."

Patrick felt relief, a little happiness for his daughter, and a little sadness that she was moving away from being his adventuring buddy into interests that didn't include him. But wasn't that the essence of growing up? Trying on new things like shoes in a store, seeing which ones fit best. He just hoped this Trish could still be the little girl of his heart sometimes. The one who couldn't be more like him except when she looked in the mirror.

Baby Hank dropped the spoon he'd been banging and screeched.

Vangie picked it up. "I think that's our signal that it's time to leave."

Henry dropped a twenty on the table. "Coffee and cinnamon rolls are on us. You guys take your time."

Patrick and Henry pushed the twenty back and forth between them a few times until Susanne settled the issue. "Our treat next time."

The Sibleys were packed and gone in a short minute. Susanne put her head on Patrick's shoulder.

"We have to tell her, you know," Patrick said.

He felt her nod. "Maybe she'll be satisfied with just writing to him."

Patrick mentally added the cost of a trip to Alaska to next year's cheerleading expenses. "Maybe," he said.

"I wouldn't have given up on you."

"I hope you never do. Even when I'm thickheaded and unhelpful."

Susanne scooted her plate in front of Patrick, then put a bite of cinnamon roll on a fork and held it up for him. He opened his mouth and she slipped it in. *Glory hallelujah.* It was every bit as good as it looked.

"You're stuck with me, Patrick. We'll figure out how to balance things. We always do."

He swallowed his bite and swiped his mouth with the back of his hand. "I promise I'm going to do better."

"And I promise I'm going to hold you to it. For the rest of our lives." She pulled the cinnamon roll plate back. "But I'm not sharing the rest of my cinnamon roll with you. Consider it your penance."

Patrick smiled and drank his coffee. He knew he was getting off easy.

EPILOGUE: DECIDE

Patrick

Patrick tapped the steering wheel in time to the music on the radio. No one else in the car was paying attention to the radio. It was a tune from the band that was fast becoming his favorite, the Eagles. "Life in the Fast Lane." Not that it described their situation now. They had been slowly ferrying through Alaska's Inside Passage and onward to Ketchikan. After more than three hours, they were still waiting to disembark.

The rest of their trip north hadn't been very fast either. They'd passed through forests, mountains, rocks, and snow. Lots of snow. A family vacation to Ketchikan, Alaska, in what still passed for winter hadn't been on Patrick's wish list. But here they were, kids out of school but completing assignments on the road. Susanne out of class and off work with permission from the professor filling in until a replacement for Renwick could be hired. Because Renwick had "resigned" at the end of the investigation into his actions. Besides the similarity of the stories told by his female students, his department secretary had overheard him conditioning grades on sex with two of them. Corroboration. He'd finally admitted it, sort of, at least that he'd had sex with the young women and that they'd received good marks in his courses. But he'd characterized each of the students as oversexualized and fixated on him. *And I don't feel sorry for that pig, not a single bit.* Susanne with a mountain of textbooks, reading and notetaking on the drive up. Patrick taking two weeks of rare vacation days. They'd used five days of it on the drive up, but every mile was worth it. It was gorgeous. Banff, Lake Geneva, Jasper, and now the islands off the coast. Just today they'd seen a black bear, bald eagles, seals, sea lions, and early-season killer whales trolling for the first few king salmon returning to the spawning rivers. Maybe he'd bring the family back some day when they had more time. And when there wasn't snow on the ground.

Sightseeing in the Suburban had been good decompression time for them, too, after their ordeal with Folske a few weeks before. The impact of the trauma didn't seem to be lingering, thankfully, and they were able to focus on other things. As a family, they discussed how social temptations were flying in the face of family rules, and how the kids could handle the pressures. Patrick and Perry talked football. Perry had been invited to practice with the varsity football team, where Wyatt was a starter and had been elected captain. Patrick was proud and excited for him. Perry said he was still undecided about whether to do it, however. *That's the heartbreak and humiliation talking.* Patrick hoped that after some time to recover, the boy wouldn't let the negative outweigh the positive.

Although she wasn't morose, Trish stared out the window for most of the trip and spoke very little. Cheerleading practice would start when she returned, but she hadn't mentioned it or the phone that had been ringing off the hook since the cheerleaders had been announced. She'd never been part of the popular crowd, but it looked like that was going to change. Patrick hoped she didn't leave Marcy behind. As apathetic as Trish was about making the squad, Marcy was crushed not to.

It seemed that all his daughter cared about, still, was this boy. Ben. The one they were *all* going to see. He and Susanne had thought long and hard about whether to make this trip, finally deciding it would give Trish closure one way or the other. It certainly wasn't one they could risk her making alone if they said no.

He snuck a glance at Susanne. Teenage love. He remembered well how it felt. The desperate longing. The inability to see past the here and now into other possibilities. For him, it had turned out okay. A smile lifted his lips. Better than okay. He just hoped it would for his daughter, too.

Slowly the vehicles began exiting the ferry. Ahead, a giant sign loomed over the road, framed by snow-topped mountains. WELCOME TO ALASKA'S 1ST CITY. KETCHIKAN. THE SALMON CAPITAL OF THE WORLD.

"We're here," he said, turning off the radio.

"Whoa." Perry yawned, stretched, and leaned over the back of the seat between his parents. "Cool."

Trish didn't say a word. He glanced in the rearview mirror. Her eyes were open and taking it all in.

Susanne reached for his hand. "Why don't we check into our hotel and get settled first? I'm sure some of us would like showers."

"Not me," Perry said.

Trish's voice was steely. "Take me straight to Ben's. Please."

Patrick swallowed. Their whole return trip could crater in the next five minutes. He looked at his wife. She gave the tiniest of shrugs.

He said, "We could drive by, I guess. Invite him to dinner if he's there."

"Thank you," Trish said.

Susanne opened the map and assumed the role of navigator, calling out the turns as they went. They'd marked the route to Ben's home and workplace on it before they ever left Buffalo. Ketchikan was a quaint town, with as many fishing boats as cars and homage to the salmon everywhere. It was also a small town, and in only five minutes, they'd found the boarding house that the investigator said was Ben's home, a three-story wooden house in a peeling egg-shell blue. The whole structure seemed to list slightly toward the water and the legions of fishing boats crowded up to docks across the road from it.

Patrick pulled over in front of it. He put his arm on the seat and turned to look at Trish. "Ready?"

"I want to go alone," she said.

Susanne shook her head violently.

"I'll come with you," Patrick said. "You're a teenage girl. This is a place grown men live."

"Fine." Trish opened the door and got out. She walked toward the house without waiting for him.

"Can I come, too?" Perry said.

"No," Patrick and Susanne said at the same time.

He smiled at his wife. "Wish us luck. We'll be back soon."

Her face was pale. Drawn. Her love for and worry about Trish wrenched at his heart. "Good luck. I love you both."

He trotted after his daughter, catching up to her as she reached the front door. He held it open for her. "Do you want to do the talking or do you want me to?"

"What do you mean?" With her hair in a high ponytail, she looked impossibly young. Too young to be in love.

"We aren't going to be able to just walk to his room." He gestured at a front desk. "It's a little bit like a hotel."

"Oh. Okay. You talk then."

He stepped up to the desk and rang a bell.

Moments later, a man with a curly gray beard appeared wearing a bloody apron. A tweed flat cap covered an otherwise bald head. "What can I do for you this fine afternoon?" He winked. "A room? A charter?"

"Good afternoon to you. Actually, we've driven all the way up from Wyoming to see a friend who lives here."

The man wiped his hands on a clean spot on his apron. "Oh? And would that be young, strapping Ben Jones you're looking for? I seem to recall he hails from somewhere in the land of geysers and buffaloes."

Trish stepped up to the desk. "Yes. Ben Jones. Please."

The man's face fell. "Oh, how I'd love to help you, lass, but Ben's moved on."

Patrick put a hand on Trish's shoulder.

"Moved on where?"

"I don't know, and he didn't say. Packed up and left weeks ago. Told me to rent his room."

"Maybe he just got a different room somewhere else?"

He puckered his lips, which made his beard and mustache waggle. "It's possible." He smiled, showing crooked teeth, with one broken in half. "But I know who could tell you. Cap."

"Cap?"

"The feller Ben worked for. He docks his boat right across the way." He took off his cap and mopped his scalp with the sleeve of his shirt, then used both hands to reposition the hat just so.

Patrick smiled. It was impossible not to like this guy. "How do we find Cap and his boat?" They had the address of the marina, but not a slip number.

"You can't miss it. He calls it the Fishy Business. The names painted right on the tail. Quite literally. The back is painted like a fish tail."

Trish pivoted on a heel and headed for the door.

Patrick reached out his hand. "Thank you, sir."

They shook, with Patrick only remembering the bloody apron after he'd made the gesture.

The man lowered his voice. "If it's any consolation to the young missy, Ben was a good boy. No liquor or women or shenanigans with him."

"It is. Thanks."

Patrick left, chasing after his daughter. She was moving quickly. He raised a finger to say "one minute" to Susanne as they passed the car. "Trish, stop."

She didn't. His daughter was already on the other side of the road. He had to wait for traffic before he could cross it. Then he jogged down the dock. The wooden structure bounced gently in the water with each of his steps.

By the time he caught up to Trish, she'd found the Fishy Business. Three men were topside. One was applying a fresh coat of paint, its odor nearly as overpowering as the fishy smell. Another looked to be repairing fishing net. The third was toting a toolbox. He seemed to have a whole quart of engine oil splashed over his body.

"Cap?" Trish called. "Is one of you Cap?"

Two of the men looked at the man with the toolbox.

He raised a hand in greeting. "Depends on who's asking. And seeing as it's a pretty young thing, I'm Captain Harley. Folks call me Cap."

Patrick was out of breath. He stopped beside his daughter. The men seemed okay, and Cap was friendly. "I'm Patrick Flint. This is my daughter, Trish. We're looking for Ben."

Cap set down his toolbox and walked over to them. "So, you're Trish."

Trish stood tall, her chin up. "I am. He's mentioned me?"

"He has. Seems when he ran away from home, he forgot his heart there. And you've come to see him?"

"Yes. It took us months to find him. His family and my parents hired an investigator. Ben thought he was in trouble with the police, but that's not true. And we had no way to tell him."

"He'll be relieved to learn that. But, Miss Trish, he's not here."

Patrick heard Trish swallow, but she didn't cry.

"Where is he?"

"He said he was going to fix things back home. I saw the last of him weeks ago."

"Fix things?"

"That's all he said. Ben wasn't much of a talker."

She laughed, but Patrick heard a catch in her voice. The sob threatening to come out. He felt his body deflate, like all the energy had seeped out. *We've come so far. She's come so far.* "No, he isn't. Well, if he comes back, could you tell him I came to find him?"

The crusty fisherman's voice was soft and gentle. "It will be the first thing I tell him."

"And that I wish he'd just come home."

He and Trish nodded at each other, holding eye contact.

Then she said, "Thank you."

Instead of walking back to the car, Trish headed for the end of the pier. Patrick stayed a stride behind her, giving her space. Sea birds were diving for the scraps fishermen were throwing into the water. Their caws and cries were shrill. Piercing. Patrick didn't know what to say. Her pain was palpable. Her hopes had been so high and fragile. If his heart felt like it was splitting in two, what did hers feel like?

She stood facing the water. The wind lifted her ponytail. If she was cold, she didn't show it. "That's it then." Her voice was strong and flat.

Patrick wished she was still a little girl. He could have lifted her in his arms, kissed her tears, and made her laugh until she forgot her troubles. Instead, he put an arm around her shoulders and squeezed her tight. "We've done all we can do."

"Maybe he's on his way home."

"Maybe so."

"Wherever he is, whatever he's doing, this was it, Dad. He'll either come back or he won't. I'm not waiting around anymore."

Why did Patrick have to still a tremble in his lips? "I think you're doing the right thing. You've got a bright future ahead of you. You have to live it."

She nodded, once, briskly. "All right then. I guess we should get going. Check into our hotel. Eat some fish."

Patrick swallowed. "That's my girl."

"One thing, though. Could we take the long way home? Through Seattle? And eat at that needle restaurant that turns around?"

"We can put it up for a family vote. But it sounds fun."

As if of one mind, they turned and strolled back to the car. Halfway there, she reached for his hand. He held it the rest of the way. *My girl.* He opened the back door for her, smiling at her as she climbed in, then shutting the door firmly. He took one last look around. He frowned. A tall, dark-headed young man with a duffel bag over his shoulder was walking down the same dock he and Trish had just left.

Ben? But it couldn't be. Cap and the man in the boarding house had both said Ben was gone. He squinted, staring after the man a moment longer. This man had long hair and a lankier physique than Ben. Most importantly, his gait was different, steps shorter. His posture more rounded. *Nah.* Not Ben.

Inside the car, he heard Trish explaining what had happened.

He took a deep breath. The mood in the car felt somber. "I was thinking Italian food for dinner. Anything but salmon."

"DAD," Perry said, and everyone laughed. Even Trish.

***

Continue with Flint family adventures in *Skin & Bones* (*Patrick Flint #8*) where **Yellowstone meets INTO THIN AIR.**

Or try something new in *BIG HORN* (*Jenn Herrington #1*): When an investment guru turns up dead in the septic tank behind her husband's new Wyoming lodge, Jennifer must put the campaign that could make her the youngest ever female district attorney in Houston on hold to defend the well-lubricated lodge caretaker, or he'll go down for a murder she's convinced he didn't commit. Read more Patrick Flint and family in the Jenn Herrington books, starting with murder mystery/legal thriller *BIG HORN*.

Before you do, don't forget to snag a free Pamela Fagan Hutchins ebook starter library by joining her mailing list at https://pamela-fagan-hutchins.myshopify.com/pages/the-next-chapter-with-pamela-fagan-hutchins, which includes Patrick Flint story *SPARK* and much more.

***

For Eric, who wears himself out taking care of everyone else, and grudgingly lets me take care of him . . . sometimes.

ACKNOWLEDGMENTS

When I got the call from my father that he had metastatic prostate cancer spread into his bones in nine locations, I was with a houseful of retreat guests in Wyoming while my parents (who normally summer in Wyoming) were in Texas. The guests were so kind and comforting to me, as was Eric, but there was only one place I wanted to be, and that was home. Not home where I grew up, because I lived in twelve places by the time I was twelve, and many thereafter. No, home is truly where the heart is. And that meant home for Eric and me would be with my parents.

I was in the middle of writing two novels at the time: *Blue Streak*, the first Laura mystery in the What Doesn't Kill You series, and *Polarity*, a series spin-off contemporary romance based on my love story with Eric. I put them both down. I needed to write, but not those books. They could wait. I needed to write through my emotions —because that's what writers do—with books spelling out the ending we were seeking for my dad's story. Allegorically and biographically, while fictionally.

So that is what I did, and Dr. Patrick Flint (aka Dr. Peter Fagan— my pops—in real life) and family were hatched, using actual stories from our lives in late 1970s Buffalo, Wyoming as the depth and back-drop to a new series of mysteries, starting with *Switchback* and moving on to *Snake Oil*, *Sawbones*, *Scapegoat*, *Snaggle Tooth*, *Stag Party*, and *Sitting Duck*. With *Sitting Duck*, I had a desire to focus on thrills/suspense and this book is my homage to *The Shining*. As always, it starts with a real life Patrick/Peter story that has made the family laugh over the years.

I hope the real life versions of Patrick, Susanne, and Perry will forgive me for taking liberties in creating their fictional alter egos. I took care to make Trish the most annoying character since she's based on me, to soften the blow for the others. I am so hopeful that my loyal readers will enjoy them, too, even though in some ways the novels are a departure from my usual stories. But in many ways they are the same. Character-driven, edge-of-your-seat mysteries steeped in setting/culture, with a strong nod to the everyday magic around us, and filled with complex, authentic characters (including some AWESOME females).

I had a wonderful time writing these books, and it kept me going when it was tempting to fold in on myself and let stress eat me alive. For more stories behind the actual stories, visit my blog on my website: http://pamelafaganhutchins.com. And let me know if you liked the novels.

Thanks to my dad for advice on all things medical, wilderness, hunting, 1970s, and animal. I hope you had fun using your medical knowledge for murder!

Thanks to my mom for printing the manuscript (over and over, in its entirety) as she and dad followed along daily on the progress.

Thanks to my brother Paul for the vivid memories that have made Perry such an amazing fictional kid.

Thanks to my husband, Eric, for brainstorming with and encouraging me and beta reading the *Patrick Flint* stories despite his busy work, travel, and workout schedule. And for moving in to my parents's barn apartment with me so I could be closer to them during this time.

Thanks to our five offspring. I love you guys more than anything, and each time I write a parent/child (birth, adopted, foster, or step), I channel you. I am so touched by how supportive you have been with Poppy, Gigi, Eric, and me.

To each and every blessed reader, I appreciate you more than I can say. It is the readers who move mountains for me, and for other authors, and I humbly ask for the honor of your honest reviews and recommendations.

Thanks mucho to Bobbye for the fantastic *Patrick Flint* covers.

Sitting Duck editing credits go to Karen Goodwin. You rock. A big thank you as well to my proofreading and advance review team.

SkipJack Publishing now includes fantastic books by a cherry-picked bushel basket of mystery/thriller/suspense writers. If you write in this genre, visit http://SkipJackPublishing.com for submission guidelines. To check out our other authors and snag a bargain at the same time, download *Murder, They Wrote: Four SkipJack Mysteries*.

BOOKS BY THE AUTHOR

Fiction from SkipJack Publishing

THE *PATRICK FLINT* SERIES OF WYOMING MYSTERIES:

Switchback (Patrick Flint #1)

Snake Oil (Patrick Flint #2)

Sawbones (Patrick Flint #3)

Scapegoat (Patrick Flint #4)

Snaggle Tooth (Patrick Flint #5)

Stag Party (Patrick Flint #6)

Sitting Duck (Patrick Flint #7)

Skin & Bones (Patrick Flint #8)

Spark (Patrick Flint 1.5): Exclusive to subscribers

THE *JENN HERRINGTON* WYOMING MYSTERIES:

BIG HORN (Jenn Herrington #1)

WALKER PRAIRIE (Jenn Herrington #2)

THE *WHAT DOESN'T KILL YOU* SUPER SERIES:

Wasted in Waco (WDKY Ensemble Prequel Novella): Exclusive to Subscribers

The Essential Guide to the What Doesn't Kill You Series

Katie Connell Caribbean Mysteries:

Saving Grace (Katie Connell #1)

Leaving Annalise (Katie Connell #2)

HER Silent BONES (*Detective Delaney Pace Series Book 1*)

HER Hidden GRAVE (*Detective Delaney Pace Series Book 2*)

HER Last CRY (*Detective Delaney Pace Series Book 3*)

Juvenile from SkipJack Publishing

Poppy Needs a Puppy (*Poppy & Petey #1*)

Nonfiction from SkipJack Publishing

The Clark Kent Chronicles

Hot Flashes and Half Ironmans

How to Screw Up Your Kids

How to Screw Up Your Marriage

Puppalicious and Beyond

What Kind of Loser Indie Publishes,

and How Can I Be One, Too?

Audio, e-book, large print, hardcover, and paperback versions of most titles available.

BOOKS FROM SKIPJACK PUBLISHING

FICTION:
Marcy McKay

Pennies from Burger Heaven, by Marcy McKay

Stars Among the Dead, by Marcy McKay

The Moon Rises at Dawn, by Marcy McKay

Bones and Lies Between Us, by Marcy McKay

When Life Feels Like a House Fire, by Marcy McKay

R.L. Nolen

Deadly Thyme, by R. L. Nolen

The Dry, by Rebecca Nolen

Ken Oder

The Closing, by Ken Oder

Old Wounds to the Heart, by Ken Oder

The Judas Murders, by Ken Oder

The Princess of Sugar Valley, by Ken Oder

Gay Yellen

The Body Business, by Gay Yellen

The Body Next Door, by Gay Yellen

The Body in the News, by Gay Yellen

MULTI-AUTHOR:

Murder, They Wrote: Four SkipJack Mysteries,
by Ken Oder, R.L. Nolen, Marcy McKay, and Gay Yellen

Tides of Possibility, edited by K.J. Russell

Tides of Impossibility, edited by K.J. Russell and C. Stuart Hardwick

NONFICTION:

Helen Colin

My Dream of Freedom: From Holocaust to My Beloved America,
by Helen Colin

Ken Oder

Keeping the Promise, by Ken Oder

ABOUT THE AUTHOR

Pamela Fagan Hutchins is a *USA Today* best selling author. She writes award-winning mystery/thriller/suspense from way up in the frozen north of Snowheresville, Wyoming, where she lives with her husband in an off-the-grid cabin on the face of the Bighorn Mountains, and Mooselookville, Maine, in a rustic lake cabin. She is passionate about their large brood of kids, step kids, inherited kids, and grandkids, riding their gigantic horses, and about hiking/snow shoeing/cross country skiing/ski-joring/bike-joring/dog sledding with their Alaskan Malamutes.

If you'd like Pamela to speak to your book club, women's club, class, or writers group by streaming video or in person, shoot her an email. She's very likely to say yes.

You can connect with Pamela via her website
(https://bit.ly/PamelaFaganHutchins)
or email (pamela@pamelafaganhutchins.com).

PRAISE FOR PAMELA FAGAN HUTCHINS

2018 USA Today Best Seller
2017 Silver Falchion Award, Best Mystery
2016 USA Best Book Award, Cross-Genre Fiction
2015 USA Best Book Award, Cross-Genre Fiction
2014 Amazon Breakthrough Novel Award Quarter-finalist,
Romance

The Patrick Flint Mysteries

"Best book I've read in a long time!" — Kiersten Marquet, author of *Reluctant Promises*

"*Switchback* transports the reader deep into the mountains of Wyoming for a thriller that has it all--wild animals, criminals, and one family willing to do whatever is necessary to protect its own. Pamela Fagan Hutchins writes with the authority of a woman who knows this world. She weaves the story with both nail-biting suspense and a healthy dose of humor. You won't want to miss *Switchback*." -- Danielle Girard, *Wall Street Journal*-bestselling author of White Out.

"*Switchback* by Pamela Fagan Hutchins has as many twists and turns as a high-country trail. Every parent's nightmare is the loss or injury of a child, and this powerful novel taps into that primal fear." -- Reavis Z. Wortham, two time winner of The Spur and author of *Hawke's Prey*

"*Switchback* starts at a gallop and had me holding on with both hands until the riveting finish. This book is highly atmospheric and nearly crackling with suspense. Highly recommend!" -- Libby Kirsch, Emmy awardwinning reporter and author of the *Janet Black Mystery Series*

"A Bob Ross painting with Alfred Hitchcock hidden among the trees."
"Edge-of-your seat nail biter."
"Unexpected twists!"
"Wow! Wow! Highly entertaining!"
"A very exciting book (um... actually a nail-biter), soooo beautifully descriptive, with an underlying story of human connection and family. It's full of action. I was so scared and so mad and so relieved... sometimes all at once!"
"Well drawn characters, great scenery, and a kept-me-on-the-edge-of-my-seat story!"
"Absolutely unputdownable wonder of a story."
"Must read!"
"Gripping story. Looking for book two!"
"Intense!"
"Amazing and well-written read."
"Read it in one fell swoop. I could not put it down."

What Doesn't Kill You: Katie Connell Romantic Mysteries

"An exciting tale . . . twisting investigative and legal subplots . . . a character seeking redemption . . . an exhilarating mystery with a touch of voodoo." — *Midwest Book Review Bookwatch*
"A lively romantic mystery." — *Kirkus Reviews*
"A riveting drama . . . exciting read, highly recommended." — *Small Press Bookwatch*
"Katie is the first character I have absolutely fallen in love with since Stephanie Plum!" — *Stephanie Swindell, Bookstore Owner*
"Engaging storyline . . . taut suspense." — *MBR Bookwatch*

What Doesn't Kill You: Emily Bernal Romantic Mysteries

"Fair warning: clear your calendar before you pick it up because you won't be able to put it down." — *Ken Oder, author of* Old Wounds to the Heart

"Full of heart, humor, vivid characters, and suspense. Hutchins has done it again!" — *Gay Yellen, author of* The Body Business

"Hutchins is a master of tension." — *R.L. Nolen, author of* Deadly Thyme

"Intriguing mystery . . . captivating romance." — *Patricia Flaherty Pagan, author of* Trail Ways Pilgrims

"Everything about it shines: the plot, the characters and the writing. Readers are in for a real treat with this story." — *Marcy McKay, author of* Pennies from Burger Heaven

What Doesn't Kill You: Michele Lopez Hanson Romantic Mysteries

"Immediately hooked." — *Terry Sykes-Bradshaw, author of* Sibling Revelry

"Spellbinding." — *Jo Bryan, Dry Creek Book Club*

"Fast-paced mystery." — *Deb Krenzer, Book Reviewer*

"Can't put it down." — *Cathy Bader, Reader*

What Doesn't Kill You: Ava Butler Romantic Mysteries

"Just when I think I couldn't love another Pamela Fagan Hutchins novel more, along comes Ava." — *Marcy McKay, author of* Stars Among the Dead

"Ava personifies bombshell in every sense of word. — *Tara Scheyer, Grammy-nominated musician, Long-Distance Sisters Book Club*

"Entertaining, complex, and thought-provoking." — *Ginger Copeland, power reader*

What Doesn't Kill You: Maggie Killian Romantic Mysteries

"Maggie's gonna break your heart–one way or another." *Tara Scheyer, Grammy-nominated musician, Long-Distance Sisters Book Club*

"Pamela Fagan Hutchins nails that Wyoming scenery and captures the atmosphere of the people there." — *Ken Oder, author of* Old Wounds to the Heart

"I thought I had it all figured out a time or two, but she kept me wondering right to the end." — *Ginger Copeland, power reader*

Made in the USA
Middletown, DE
06 February 2024

49117110R00168